1919 - Misfortune's End

Paula Phelan

ZapMedia • New York

ZAPmedia
New York, NY
info@zapmedia.com

1919 - Misfortune's End

ZAPmedia is a registered trademark of ZAPmedia.

Cover designs by Sandy Frye
Cover photography © ZAPimages

Manufactured in the United States

Publisher's Cataloging-In-Publication Data

Phelan, Paula A.
  1919 : misfortune's end / Paula Phelan.

    p. ; cm.

  ISBN-13: 978-0-9778192-0-1
  ISBN-10: 0-9778192-0-5

1. Nineteen nineteen, A.D.--Fiction. 2. United States--History--1913-1921--
Fiction. 3. Irish Americans--Massachusetts--Boston--1913-1921--Fiction. 4.
African Americans--Washington (D.C.)--1913-1921--Fiction. 5. Historical fic-
tion. I. Title. II. Title: Nineteen nineteen

PS3616.H45 N56 2006
813/.6

To Molly & Izzy

TABLE OF CONTENTS

FORWARD

As an amateur history buff I find myself constantly surprised by events and people I had previously been unaware of, in time periods I thought I knew well.

What I have discovered is that history, like the news from which it is derived, is synthesized. Not as part of a grand scheme to obscure the truth, but rather, to condense, summarize and highlight key events. Writing this work as a novel, I have endeavored to offer some new perspectives about an important turning point in American history.

The idea for 1919 Misfortune's End was first sparked by learning of the strange and tragic Molasses Disaster in Boston and separately, the more unbelievable and horrifying treatment of African American soldiers, then arriving home from the First World War.

My research of that year uncovered numerous surprises, amidst the emergence of familiar characters that I would never have associated with 1919. These included Helen Keller, Duke Ellington, J. Edgar Hoover, and Margaret Sanger – figures that we carry in our memories with a certain iconic aura. As individuals, they had many facets to their personalities, so I turned the light onto the contours that history chose not to reflect. Just as important, in my view, were the individuals who changed our lives forever and whose names have been lost in the chronicling of history - Beulah Henry, James Weldon Johnson, Walter White, Mitchell Palmer - and key events such as the deportation of Emma Goldman, lynchings in American cities, the beginning of the end of legal segregation and the real reason why WWI ground to a halt.

In this book we meet two fictional families that live in Boston and Washington, DC and experience first hand, the events of those times. These families are a composite of real people who lived and died during that year.

When I research a piece of history, I like to retrace the steps of the everyday people of that era. I chose to write this book as historical fiction so that I might be able to inject the past with the feelings and lesser known realities of the time.

"No harm's done to history by making it something someone would want to read."
David McCullough

List of Characters

The Kelly Family - Boston

Patrick Sr. ~ police officer of 28 years; lives in Charlestown, MA
Harriet ~ wife of Patrick Sr.; temperance advocate
Thomas ~ eldest son; lawyer
Patricia ~ eldest daughter; suffragette
Patrick Jr. ~ son, maimed in war; fireman
Rosie ~ wife of Patrick Jr.
Liam ~ son of Patrick Jr. and Rosie; four years old

Kelly children deceased

Erin ~ daughter, died from influenza, October 1918
James ~ son, died from influenza, October 1918
Timothy ~ son, died in war, July of 1918

The Johnson Family - Washington DC

Benjamin ~ works as secretary and aide to
President Woodrow Wilson
Claire ~ wife of Benjamin; manages domestic staff
and events for art collector Duncan Phillips
June ~ eldest daughter; nurse
Emmet ~ eldest son; just returning from war
Louvenia ~ middle daughter; inventor
Kay ~ youngest daughter; singer and actress

Johnson children deceased

Roy ~ son, died in war; September 1918

Winter 1919

BOSTON

Patrick Jr.

With the whine of the first bullets Patrick Jr. pulled his wife to the firehouse floor. After two years in French fox holes, he knew how to stay alive. But this was the North End of Boston. And the world was at peace.

"Who the hell's firing a machine gun?" he shouted. Rosie, crouched beside him, pregnant with their second child, shivered with fear. He drew her close.

"Don't worry darling. Probably some soldier has gone off his bean. The police will put him to rest." He held her tightly, as he worried that his own Da might be the one called out to put the man down.

The gunfire ceased and was replaced by a loud hiss. Patrick didn't recognize the sound. He crawled to the door to look out. Lapping over the doorsill was a light brown liquid. He got to his knees, peered out and saw that the street was covered by six inches of brown sludge. The air smelled sickeningly sweet. Patrick put his finger into the muck and discovered it was hot, almost boiling. He sniffed, then tasted it. Molasses.

He glanced up at the massive tank that stood fifty-feet high, beside the firehouse. A thirty-foot geyser of steaming molasses rose from the tank, arching into the cloudless blue sky. The sound of gunfire had been rivets tearing from metal seams. The tank was about to explode.

"Rosie get up. Now!"

He yanked Rosie to her feet, glancing at her lace-up shoes. He knew they'd be no match for the glue-like substance beyond the door. He'd have to carry her. Patrick ran to his locker and pulled on his fire boots. Then, without breaking stride, he leaned over, placed his shoulder into Rosie's abdomen and lifted her off her feet. His mission: to reach high ground with his bride before the tank blew.

As Patrick stepped into the freely flowing, now ten-inch deep, flood of molasses, he was deafened by the scream of rending steel.

He yelled to Rosie above the din, "If we can get across Commercial Street and up to Copps Hill, we should be safe." In the war Patrick had survived bombs, grenades, mustard gas and snipers suffering only the loss of his left hand. Yet somehow he knew he would not escape this disaster. Patrick Jr. understood today was his day. He'd go down fighting.

In the street the sugar mixture was rising at a surprising rate. With each step he curled his toes, struggling to keep his boots on as the sugary muck tried to pull them off. He began to sweat. The liquid was cooking his feet. With another footfall, he'd no longer be able to keep on his boots. Patrick braced himself to step barefoot into the near-boiling goo.

With a screech from hell the tank blew apart. One of its panels flew off, severing a steel post, which supported the elevated train track sixty feet away. The tracks crashed to the ground. Rosie let out a muffled cry. Patrick turned to see the train and its passengers on the verge of falling to their deaths. Only the conductor's quick reflexes stopped the train, inches from the track's termination.

Patrick thought he glimpsed his sister Patricia on board. But before he could speak, his bare leg sank into the now knee-high molasses and he screamed out in pain. With fierce determination he slogged on through the black swirls.

Half way across Commercial Street he heard the final panels of the tower give way and millions of gallons of molasses rushed toward them.

"Patrick," Rosie shouted over the chaos.

"Just another few yards."

"Patrick – I love you."

Rosie was saying goodbye. He turned to see an eight-foot tidal wave coming toward them. He swung her off his shoulder and crouched with her in his arms.

They were kissing as the wall of sweetness washed them away.

Patricia's view

Patricia Kelly's plan was to surprise her brother Pat and sister-in-law and take them to lunch on this magnificent day.

She'd gotten on the El at Park Street, after listening to speeches on the Boston Common. For the past two weeks the temperature had hovered near zero, but today it was in the forties. People on the sidewalk had unbuttoned their winter coats and were enjoying the spring-like weather.

Patricia wanted to share this happiness with her brother. She'd missed Pat intensely while he'd been in Europe. She realized, after he had shipped out, that Pat was the one who kept her cynicism and drive in check. He was her touchstone to life's grace. He didn't come home unscathed, having lost his hand to a grenade. But he did make it home, which was more than many of the young men in their neighborhood, and she was grateful to have him back.

As the train turned the corner onto Commercial Street the first thing Patricia saw was an enormous geyser shooting out of the molasses holding tank. Steam rose from the flood of brown fluid that covered the street.

A cloying, sweet smell reached her nose, reminding Patricia of her mother's baked beans, a staple in the Kelly home. The brown river that was forming beneath the train was molasses, the substance for making brown bread, ginger snap cookies and rum.

The train slowed to a crawl, inching its way up Commercial Street. The sound of gun fire made the driver nervous. The passengers watched in horror as the panels from the huge tank peeled off and flew in every direction, as if a giant child was throwing a tantrum. The screech of metal split the air.

As a panel flew towards the train, Patricia instinctively ducked. The steel sheet embedded itself in the supporting structure of the El, just below her feet. Like a puppet who's strings had been cut, the tracks dropped into the stream of brown syrup. Then, with a thunderous roar, the tank let loose the rest of its contents.

At that moment, Patricia saw her brother, only a few hundred feet away, carrying his wife over his shoulder. Rosie seemed to stare straight at Patricia, as the horrible brown wave rolled down the street.

Patricia watched helplessly as the swell consumed a cart, a horse and a little boy who was trying desperately to reach his mother. She witnessed her brother's fire station shudder, then buckle and finally collapse from the force of the molasses. The surge devoured everything in its path. Houses and stables groaned, resisting the tide's demands, but ultimately everything acquiesced including Patricia's family.

Some passengers in the train panicked, screaming to get out. Others sat trembling and crying. Patricia remained silent, paralyzed. But her mind was racing. Despite the imminent danger her thoughts were somewhere else. She knew this news would kill her mother. Harriet had just begun to emerge from the deep depression brought on by the loss of her children, Erin and James, to the plague a few months earlier. Patrick Jr.'s return from France had brought back Harriet's smile.

Charlestown: Harriet and Liam Kelly

"Liam sweetie, how about we 'ave some cocoa?"

The little boy's eyes sparkled at the mention of the treat. His smile warmed Harriet. Her stern face softened for a moment. Liam alone could unlock the door to forgotten memories, letting in a fresh breeze so welcome after a long hard New England winter.

"Nana, can I help you make it?" His expression revealed that the joy of preparation would be as great as the drinking.

"You may, child."

Harriet set aside her tatting and rose from the table. Liam put away his picture book.

As she pulled the milk from the icebox the local firehouse alarm wailed. Startled, Harriet dropped the bottle. Then the alarm in the North End sounded off, followed by sirens of other townships. She crossed herself and said a prayer.

"Liam, let's clean up this mess Nana made and go out for our treat. Get your things boy."

"Yes ma'am," he said, flushed with the excitement; then a look of adult worry passed over his small brow.

"Nana is there a fire?" And before she could answer he asked, "And is Da and Granda there?"

She kept her eyes fixed upon him and never turned away.

"I dinna kin. Hurry and put on your coat and shoes and we will go and find out."

Harriet had no doubt that her son Pat, just home from the war, was at the fire since it was within a mile of his station. What's more, a four-alarm fire would bring out all the local police. Her husband Patrick would be in command. She felt a pull to be with them.

Patrick on duty

Patrick Kelly and the boys at the Charlestown police station were playing a friendly game of Whist when the alarms went off. His first thought was for his son, Pat. Patrick Sr. had called in every favor collected in his thirty years on the force, to get his son a position at the naval yard firehouse. Jobs were scarce and with his war injury it would have been nearly impossible for Pat to get the job on his own. Patrick was proud of his son, an honest, hard working young man with a growing family.

Now as the alarm rang out Patrick feared he'd made a mistake. What if something were to happen to his son? What then of Pat's pregnant wife Rosie and their son Liam?

Patrick jumped to his feet and yelled to the dispatcher.

"Charlie, what is it?" Before Charlie could respond, two more alarms went off in the distance.

"It's a bad one Patrick, and your boy's in the middle of it," answered Charlie with the phone receiver still held to his ear.

"What happened?" asked another policeman.

"Seems there was an attack on the pier, some kind of explosion. A lot of people are dead and injured. Everyone's been called out."

Patrick ran towards the truck shouting as he ran, "Charlie, I'll take the boys with me in Number Five."

Number Five was a Tin Lizzie fire truck. The three-year-old Model T Ford had taken such a pounding, it was surprising that the doors still hung from their hinges.

Patrick was in command of four men. They were family men, in their thirties, past their hard-drinking years. They were dependable, but in situations like this, he wouldn't mind having a few daredevil young bucks, men who would throw caution to the wind. But those boys were gone.

Between the flu epidemic and the war there were no young men to be found. Those who had returned from the war, like his own son Pat, were missing limbs or worse, missing their spirit.

As the garage door of the station house swung open, the sweet smell of molasses poured over them. The men turned to one another, confused. Trevor, one of Patrick's crew, was working the siren in the front seat. They rode in suspenseful silence toward the disaster site.

Thomas Kelly at court

Thomas was arguing a case at the federal courthouse, a labor dispute between a South Boston textile manufacturer and his workers. He represented the manufacturer. The majority of workers were women, lead by a fierce suffragette whom Thomas assumed was a friend of his sister, Patricia. What's more, he suspected that his sister had given the woman, a key witness for the prosecution, tips on how to best him. But his sister couldn't beat him in court. While she could argue him into the ground at home, he was a different man in the courtroom, especially today with his hair slicked back and wearing his lucky yellow bow tie.

Thomas always wondered why Patricia hadn't become a lawyer, with her natural talent for argument. Instead, she set out to win the vote for women. She stumped, spoke and was one of the most respected and feared women on the Boston political scene. Thomas secretly took pride in her bluntness, but at home he always gave her hard time.

When the sirens sounded, all eyes rose to the high windows, anticipating smoke. Seconds later a boy ran in, carrying a note for the judge.

The jury box was empty, since this was a hearing, and the gallery held but a few law students and die-hard courtroom followers. As the judge read the note his expression became grave.

"There has been an accident, an explosion. We must evacuate immediately. There's the possibility of a bomb in the building. The room broke into chaos. The judge raised his voice. "Please do not panic, collect your things and leave directly. Check with my clerk tomorrow to determine when we'll reschedule this hearing."

As he packed up his papers, Thomas began to wonder. A number of terrorist pipe bombs had been mailed to prominent businessmen over the last few months. Some of these attacks had seemed suspicious to Thomas. Could they have been staged to cast blame on the immigrant population?

Thomas shook off the 'dandy' persona that he wore in the courtroom and adopted his father's calming authoritarian demeanor in order to help empty the courtroom. Once outside in the spring-like weather he wasn't concerned about the reason for the unexpected recess. He would enjoy having a few hours to relax. He decided to pay a visit to Miss Parker, a recent flirtation of his, on Beacon Hill. Then the odor assailed him, an overpowering sweet smell that coated the air.

Thomas found himself drawn to it. He walked towards the Haymarket searching for the vats of baked beans that he knew must be cooking.

Patrick Sr. mourns

They laid Rosie and Patrick Jr. to rest a week after the accident. All the men in both the police and fire departments turned out. The wake lasted for three days. Prohibition was not yet signed into law and Patrick Sr. tied one on. He didn't go home, unwilling to let the depth of his sadness follow him there. Instead he passed out in the back room of O'Malley's pub. Harriet didn't complain. She sent Thomas over nightly to make sure his Da was all right.

Even before the tragedy, Patrick Sr. had been spending most of his nights in the pub. Since prohibition would soon shut the bar down, he and his pals had vowed to visit O'Malley's every night until a padlock sealed the door.

A week after Rosie and Patrick Jr. were laid to rest, Patrick Sr. sat in the pub beside John O'Neill, a tall man of fifty, wiry and practically toothless.

Patrick's words slurred as he spoke, "John, I tell you, the boy never minded his hand bein' missin', he never complained." Patrick swayed on his stool. He placed an elbow on the bar to steady himself. "T'was only Pat's body that was damaged. His spirit was untouched by the war. How many young men can ye be sayin' that about? Much less maimed soldiers? What say ye to that, Mr. O'Neill?"

"Pat Jr. was a fine lad, the best among us," O'Neill stood and raised his drink to the rest of the men in the bar, "To Patrick Jr., may he find St. Peter in good spirits."

The men responded in kind, holding their glasses in the air and downing their drinks quickly.

Patrick Sr. responded with a half-smile at the salute, but a worried frown returned to his timeworn face. He reached and grabbed O'Neill by the collar, drawing the man's ear close to his lips and whispered, "But John, what do I say? How do I explain this? My strong brave boy comin' to such an undignified end. Who dies by molasses? It ain't a fit death. What do I say to the relatives in New York, much less the old country?"

Patrick wanted his son remembered as a hero. He wouldn't allow Pat's death to become a joke.

"The answer is simple," O'Neill offered, "Pat died at war or in the line of duty as a fireman." He thought for a second, "No, you dare not say he died a fireman's death. People will ask questions. Everyone likes to hear about the heroic deeds of fireman, but no one ever wants to hear details about the war. Let's leave it at that. Pat died in the war."

O'Neill pulled away from Patrick and ordered another round of whiskey. With glass in hand, he raised his drink to the assembled crowd of men in another toast. "To Pat Kelly Jr. a war hero who died in the trenches of France. A beloved son and husband. We'll miss him terrible."

"Here, here to Pat Kelly, Jr.," the men responded. Some were sober enough to understand the subtlety of the pledge. Others were drunk enough to believe what they heard. From that day forward, in Charlestown, Pat Kelly Jr. died a decorated war hero. No one ever associated his name and molasses again.

Harriet's dilemma

Peeling potatoes in her kitchen, Harriet sat with her friend and next door neighbor, Stella Vaughn. Harriet could not hide the tumultuous storm brewing within her. Stella was quiet, wary of Harriet's famous temper.

"It's somethin' awful Stella, so many questions, so many people interested. I mean, no one asked after Erin and James when they died. Erin was her father's favorite daughter you know, not Patricia, his namesake. And my handsome James, home on leave, we'd been hopin', with the war almost over he wouldn't be shippin' out again." For a moment, Harriet's face softened with his memory, even as her eyes shone with disappointment, "But then he come down to breakfast one mornin' lookin' peaked and by that eve he was gone. Erin followed the next day."

"Ye had a terrible bad year, Harriet. What with losing Timothy to the war as well. God must have good things in store for ye, giving ye such a heavy burden. It's all part of a plan."

Harriet spoke again, as if she had not heard Stella. Timothy's death was a different story, one she was unwilling to discuss. "It's a queer thing," she said. "Patrick was stationed at the Charlestown armory, where they brought the dead, during the epidemic. They took in 50,000 bodies there before it was over. He never wanted to talk about it. I never saw a word written about the deaths in the paper. I searched, day after day, to find Erin and James' obituaries, but they never appeared. Finally I realized, none of the influenza victims' names appeared. We were lied to Stella." Stella nodded wondering where Harriet's train of thought would take her.

"Thomas is my son you know?" Harriet watched Stella's eyes for signs of comprehension.

"Aye Harriet, good lookin' and smart too."

"Nay Stella. What I'm meanin' to say is, Thomas is not Patrick's son. Patrick married me when Thomas was three. I brought him from Ireland after his Da died fightin' the English." Stella was shocked. She had never known this secret. No one knew this in all of Charlestown. Everyone assumed Thomas to be Patrick's son.

Harriet went on. "My parents were both gone and my brother was here in the States. He got me a job at the mill. Patrick and I met when wee Thomas had gotten into a little mischief and lifted some penny candy. Patrick was called to the store and when he saw me and my boy - well...."

"I remember, Harriet... twenty five years ago you were quite the stunner," said Stella.

"Nonsense. Anyway we couldn't take our eyes off of each other and Patrick was bold. He claimed that Thomas just needed the guidance of a father. I told him he had a lot of cheek to say it, but one thing led to another..."

She paused. "Would ye like some tea, Stella?"

"Aye."

Harriet began the familiar comforting task of making tea. She filled the kettle with water and set it on the stove. Stella picked up Harriet's knife and began peeling the potatoes. She asked, "But how are ye going to explain Pat's death? I mean, it'll sound like a joke to most."

She did not see the rod of anger that made Harriet go rigid. Harriet didn't turn to face Stella, but in a deceptively even voice she said, "Never you mind..."

Still unaware that she had struck a nerve, Stella interjected, "But ya can't say it was..."

"Damn you to Hades!" roared Harriet. Stella, startled, dropped the paring knife. Harriet continued to shout, the blue veins vivid in her pale face. "It's not enough I've lost three sons and two daughters, but that you have to remind me of it?"

Stella rose, blinking at Harriet, "I was only sayin'…"

"Blazing saints, I know what ye were sayin' woman. Everyone knows my son died peculiar. I think you should leave now Mrs. Vaughn."

Stella grabbed her sweater and scurried to the door. She didn't care to witness any more of Harriet's temper. As Stella stepped through portal, Harriet spoke, through clenched teeth, "Good life to you, Mrs. Vaughn." Over her shoulder Stella replied, "And to ye as well Mrs. Kelly. To ye as well."

Thomas and Liam

"I have a gift for you, young man." Thomas held out a package wrapped in shiny paper. Liam grabbed it and tore it open.

"What is it, Uncle Thomas?"

"A book. What do you mean 'what is it?' Open the cover. It has pictures."

"Oh boy," said Liam and he sat down, right where he had been standing, holding the book in his lap.

"It's a book called Aesop's Fables, written by a Greek slave almost 2,000 years ago. Aesop was given his freedom because he wrote such beautiful stories."

"Did he paint these pictures too?"

Thomas chuckled, "No, Liam, they were done by a popular artist who is alive today. His name is Milo Winter." Thomas squatted beside the boy, and noted that the illustrations seemed to leap from the page.

"Read me a story, Uncle, read me this story about a mouse." Liam pointed his finger at one of the illustrations.

"Perhaps after dinner. Your Nana has made a nice meal and Granda will be home soon. So let's you and I go wash up and I'll read to you the minute we're finished eating."

With that, Liam scampered up the stairs to the washbasin at the end of the hall. Thomas followed, pleased he could bring a smile to the little boy's face. He wished there was a magical gift he could bring home to his own Ma and Da that would do the same.

Patricia and God

Several weeks after Pat and Rosie's death, Harriet and Patricia sat quietly over tea in the kitchen.

"Do you believe in God, Ma?" asked Patricia.

"What's this about? I lose a few children and I should be givin' up on the Almighty?"

"No, Ma, I was just wondering how you keep your faith. You've experienced such hardships. Don't you ever consider telling the Lord to take a flying leap?"

"Blasphemy from the mouth of my own daughter. As soon as we finish our tea, you must run down to Father Joseph for confession," said Harriet. When Patricia looked contrite, Harriet continued, "Child, the Lord has his ways and they're mysterious. What could I, a know-nothin' from Galway, understand of his greater plan?"

"And yet you toss salt over your shoulder and cross the street to avoid walking under a ladder."

"That's just common sense. What's gotten into you? Are you missing your sisters and brothers?"

Patricia's face crumbled. Her lower lip quivered as tears welled up in her large blue eyes. "I miss them awful Ma. I miss Patrick and Rosie and all the others. How do you bear it?"

Harriet went to her, resting her hand on her daughter's shoulder. Patricia almost flinched at the touch – her mother had never been one to show physical affection. Patricia couldn't remember the last time her mother had touched her. Maybe at her confirmation when Harriet had righted a misplaced hair that had fallen into Patricia's face.

"There you go, lass." And the words, the words were the same both now and then.

"Ma, why don't you hug?"

Harriet's hand pulled away from her daughter. She turned back towards her work at the stove. "What nonsense. If you're done cursin' God and feelin' sorry for yourself why don't you help me with dinner."

"You heard me. Why don't you touch any of us?"

"What craziness are you talkin'? Did you not just see me put Liam to bed?"

"Yes, Ma, you touch us when we're small, but never after we can remember."

"Nonsense. Focus on your own business."

"You're my Ma."

"Just as God intended."

Harriet's touch

None of her children had ever called her on it before. Harriet loved her children, but she couldn't bring herself to touch them. She didn't know why, she couldn't explain it, but she was certain that it had something to do with him, Colin, her first husband. He had touched her too much. In the beginning it had been with pleasure. She and Colin couldn't get enough of each other. But then when the drink got into him, he felt the need to get into her no matter what her condition. When he didn't get what he wanted he got mean. After the first baby that lived, his touch was always mean.

Harriet had built a wall around herself, as protection from him, but after she left him, she couldn't pull it down. Not even for her own children. A chill passed through her at the thought of the man who had frozen her heart. She cinched her black wool shawl tighter.

Thomas and Helen

Thomas worked for an old established law firm in Boston. The cases they handled were usually political in nature, which Thomas found intriguing. Today he had a meeting at a research firm hired by his managing partner to review surrender treaties from previous wars. Their offices were in Watertown several blocks from the famous Perkins School for the Blind. Perkins was a renowned institute that trained sightless people to live within society. Thomas thought the school's aim was commendable, but it gave him the willies to be around so many blind people at once.

To Thomas, many of these poor sightless wretches hadn't yet

learned the basics, so they were apt to step out into traffic or walk into a fire hydrant. He couldn't bear watching them stumble about. He usually sent his assistant to pick up the research, but today Thomas had questions to ask and so he needed to come himself. Naturally it was one of the coldest days of the year.

Hungry, and not wishing to tempt pneumonia, Thomas ducked into a sandwich shop before fulfilling his mission. Inside it was warm and full of delicious smells. He spied a seat in the corner and made his way toward it, passing several tables filled with Perkins students.

'Amazing they can eat without incident', thought Thomas, just as a glass of water crashed to the floor, splashing his pant leg.

"How dreadfully clumsy of me, sir. Did I get any on you?"

The woman before him wore tinted glasses and a concerned expression. She held out a fresh napkin to Thomas. When he failed to respond she drew back her hand.

"Would you let me buy you lunch?"

"No thank you. But thank you anyway." Thomas squeezed over to the table in the corner. He rooted around in his briefcase for something to read.

His eyes kept returning to the companion of the woman who had spilled the water. Despite her age she was quite striking. Thomas liked his women older, and married. He had found that married women were both grateful and unavailable, a perfect combination of attributes. But, Thomas sensed that, this woman was different. She exuded a powerful, ethereal quality. Then he recognized her. He had recently attended a series of vaudeville performances at the Orpheum Theater. Miss Helen Keller and Mrs. Annie Sullivan Macy were one of the acts.

Thomas stood and walked over to their table. The first woman, Mrs. Macy, placed her fingers in Helen's palm and began tapping out a code.

"Excuse me, but I've changed my mind. May I join you?" asked Thomas.

"It would be our pleasure, sir." Mrs. Macy palmed to Helen that a handsome man had just joined them and was interested in Helen.

Helen turned her unflinching eyes upon Thomas and began to speak. The garbled words sounded like they were coming down a rain barrel, but she spoke with deliberation, "How do you do sir?"

Thomas blushed. The statue of Venus had spoken to him. "Fine I'm sure. How do you do?"

Mrs. Macy spelled out his words into Helen's palm and Helen began to nod. "Lovely" she said. "Although I wish it were warmer."

For some reason this seemed funny. Thomas laughed and Helen smiled as Annie's non-stop messages traveled from Helen's palm into her brain. Thomas turned to Annie.

"Miss Sullivan I presume?"

"It'd be Mrs. Macy, thank ye. And this is none other than Miss Helen Keller herself."

"Your charge."

"I should say not. Miss Keller is my companion and friend. We have a symbiotic relationship. I'm her eyes and ears while she's my voice and wit." Helen continued to smile and then spoke again in that otherworldly voice.

"And you sir? Do you have a name?"

"How rude of me. I am Thomas Kelly. I'm a lawyer, which I hope you won't hold against me. My offices are in Boston I am here on business. Are you both teachers at the Perkins school?"

"No, not for many years," said Annie. "We had a falling out some time back. Helen has been good enough to accompany me here to visit some of my old friends at the school."

"Amazing." Escaped from his lips. Annie meanwhile spelled out to Helen that she had made another conquest, a young man in his thirties, serious, with black hair and pale blue eyes. A clothes horse, like Helen, but despite that Annie added he probably possessed a good heart.

Helen spoke and Thomas strained to understand her. "Mr. Kelly, are you free to take lunch with me tomorrow in Boston? I have a performance at two p.m., but then not another until seven. It would be a pleasure to see you again and spend more time together."

Thomas blushed, both at her forwardness and her suggesting they would 'see' each other. He was accustomed to women being much more coy.

"I should warn you Mr. Kelly, she can be quite forward. But I'm not responsible for her bad manners." In anticipation of Helen's response, Annie pulled back her arm, leaving Helen to slap the air.

"I'm flattered. May I treat you two ladies to tea tomorrow at the Ritz?"

"We'd enjoy that," said Mrs. Macy and Helen nodded in agreement. "Until then, sir" said Annie holding out her hand for him to shake. He was surprised when Helen did the same, but with her hand, something came over him and he kissed it instead.

The two women left and his lunch arrived, but he was no longer hungry, mesmerized by the exotic creature he had just met. The best part was he'd be with her again tomorrow.

The Kelly women rally

Harriet yelled up the stairs, "Patricia, 'ave you seen Liam's jacket?" She continued to paw through the family's winter wraps, which hung on hooks on the wall.

"No Ma. Perhaps it's in his room. Thomas and he went out yesterday. I'll look."

Liam's room was a pigsty. Toys, books and bedclothes lay sprawled everywhere. The mess was shocking. Patricia recalled her own childhood and her mother's need to keep everything in its place. This was a new Harriet, one more focused on her activities outside the house than the tidiness within. Patricia spied the coat peeking out from beneath the bed.

"I found it, Ma. I'll bring it down." Patricia wondered, why hadn't her mother been as involved in the community when Patricia was child? Was it because she was busy with her children or had her sense of purpose evolved after her children were grown? She would ask her mother someday over a cup of tea, but not now, they were both late.

"Here you go, Ma," said Patricia holding out the coat as she came down the narrow set of stairs.

"Thanks, love." Harriet began bundling up Liam. He was a good boy and stood quietly, tolerating his Nana's rough treatment.

18

"Patricia, I need you to watch Liam today."

Patricia froze where she stood and stopped pulling on her gloves.

"Ma, what are you saying? You know I have a rally today."

"Take Liam with you. The fresh air will do 'im good."

"Do you really believe a suffragette rally is the place for a four-year old boy?"

Harriet turned to face her daughter, "Are you suggesting that a prohibition meeting is a better place?"

The seriousness with which she said it made Patricia laugh and Harriet's granite face broke into a thousand lines of mirth. The two women recognized, for a moment, how similar they were. Fighting, stubborn, Irish women, and woe be to the man who stood against them.

St. Patrick's day

Nothing was finer than dressing up in his best black uniform. His brass buttons were polished so bright that he could see his own reflection. Patrick always felt this day of celebration was in his honor. He wished he could visit Chicago and see them dye the river green. At least that's what O'Malley had told him they did.

Patrick placed his cap rakishly over his brow and grinned in the mirror.

"What a handsome devil you are Patrick Callahan Kelly." He noticed that he needed a shave and a haircut, but there was no time for that now.

"Woman, where did you get to? It's time to leave." Patrick waited, but there was no response from upstairs.

"Harriet Josephine Kelly get your bloody backside down here or I'll come get it myself."

"Hold your horses you big blowhard. You'd think the Pope himself made you the patron saint." Harriet came down wearing her favorite dress. She had added so many layers of lace and embroidery to cover the worn spots, it was hard to tell what of the original dress remained. 'Aye she's a thrifty one, that wife o' mine,' thought Patrick, in a rare moment of sentiment.

"And after the parade Mr. Kelly, just where are you plannin' on goin' in all that finery? Seems to me with prohibition in effect there ain't goin' to be any drinkin' to be had. You can just come back home after the parade and fix the plumbin' in the water closet."

All of the charming thoughts he was having about Harriet evaporated with her reminder that this St. Patrick's Day would be dry. Except for that nasty 3.2 beer. In all of Patrick's 57 years he had never experienced a St. Patrick's Day without at least a sip of Guinness. Family legend had it that even as an infant his mother fed it to him from her finger.

He knew that Clancy and Murphy had a store of confiscated bottles of beer, and policeman or not, Patrick Kelly was first and foremost an Irishman. Harriet would be furious.

"Now who's dawdlin'?" asked Harriet. "Time's a wastin'. We need to get down to the station and get you fitted for your harness. Isn't the standard yours this year?"

"Aye and proud I am to carry it."

"Yes Da – it's your day. Let's go."

WASHINGTON DC

Patricia Kelly in DC

Several weeks later Patricia found herself stamping her feet on the sidewalk to fend off the cold. "It's freezing," complained Patricia.

"I know dear," said Alice Paul, "but it's an honor to be here, to stand vigil in a relay of hundreds of women.

Earlier that day the nation's capitol had been filled with women, from every state in the union, carrying banners and shouting slogans. Each woman infused with a sense of purpose and hope, after hearing a rumor that the House of Representatives was poised to bring the Nineteenth Amendment closer to reality. This was the fruition of Susan B. Anthony's dream.

"The urns are lovely don't you think?" said Alice trying to take their minds off the cold.

The National Woman's Party had donated the urns with the proviso that they would burn twenty-four hours a day until the Nineteenth Amendment became law. The Parks Department had allowed them to set up the urns in Lafayette Park, directly across from the White House.

"It'd be better if he was actually there," said Patricia sourly, as she nodded towards the executive mansion.

"Naturally dear. But he's not. He's probably feasting on quail tonight in some fancy Parisian restaurant, but he has to come home eventually and we'll be here to greet him when he does," said Alice Paul.

This thought warmed Patricia. She wanted to be standing right here when the motorcade pulled up and President Wilson glanced over to see who was protesting. He would learn that these hardy women had been standing in the park every minute of every day since January 1, 1919. In truth she doubted it would make a difference. Wilson seemed to be more concerned with world affairs than with what was going on, literally, in his own front yard.

"Posh, it doesn't matter," said Alice, "not everyone is overseas. Congress will be back in session next week. And they'll see. They'll feel a sense of shame." Patricia was honored to be on duty with Alice. Alice Paul was the President of the National Woman's Party. Alice was responsible for taking the suffrage campaign to the federal level, insisting upon a constitutional amendment.

"When does our relief team show up?" asked Alice.

"Ten minutes," said Patricia, who was in charge of the vigil schedule. "Right now the shifts are two hours, but we may change them to three hours if the weather is good. Nights when it's raining or sleeting, maybe less. No one should be exposed to the elements for too long."

"Hey you!" yelled a man from across the street. "What are you protesting?"

"Emancipation!" Alice yelled back.

"You don't deserve it." He began to cross the street.

The women were prepared for a fight. Both had been jailed numerous times. They could manage one brute.

"Did you hear me?" he growled. "You didn't fight in the trenches, you didn't watch as your friends were blown to bits. I did, and I tell you I don't want to come home and have some woman tell me what to do and when to do it."

The women knew to let it be. They did not engage him. He'd been drinking. They stood together beside one of the urns.

"Are you listening to me?" He asked, becoming more agitated.

"Do you hear what I'm saying? You're wasting your time. I'll never allow you to get the vote nor will my brother or my father or any of my friends. Why don't you just go home, where you belong?"

"If you're saying...," Alice began. Patricia pinched Alice's arm to get her to stop. But the beast within the man was already ignited.

He strode over to Alice until he stood so close, that as he yelled, the hair around her face moved from the force of his breath.

"You rotten bitch. How dare you speak to me? To me, a hero, a soldier."

Before he could continue, the relief team arrived and two new women flanked their sisters. At first unconcerned about being out-numbered, the man then became aware that there were police in the park, perhaps paid to protect the women.

"I'll be damned if you'll use my park to light your way."

With that he shoved the women aside and went to the urn, taller than himself, and pushed it to the ground. The urn smashed into hundreds of pieces. The explosive crash made the women jump. Sparks rose up in the sky and a small pool of fire rolled out into the street as the embers were set free. The man, pleased with his destruc-tion, ran to the other urn, toppling it into the street with the same effect.

Patricia was simultaneously furious and exhausted. 'Won't it ever get any easier?' she thought. 'And where were the police she had hired to protect them?' Taking charge, Patricia spoke in a calm voice, "Alice, please go find a policeman."

Just as she spoke, two policemen came running over and forced the man to the ground.

"What are you doing? You could have killed one of these women or yourself. Are you crazy?" asked the older patrolman.

"I'm not looney. This just isn't what I was fighting for," answered the young veteran.

"Yeah, yeah. Tell it to the judge." The younger policeman cuffed the man's hands and then hauled him to his feet. The elder officer turned to the women.

"My name is Donnelly. I'm sorry for the mess and the incident. Are you all right?"

Each woman gave a hesitant nod, except Patricia. She was livid.

"Where were you?" She shouted at Donnelly. "Is this the protection I paid for? We had an agreement. My father's a Boston policeman. I know how this works."

"Good." Was Donnelly's unsympathetic response. The officer examined the pile of rubble around their feet. "I guess you'll have to call it a night. You and your friends can start up again in the morning."

"No thank you, sir. We'll stay right here. We'll not be intimidated," said Patricia.

Her response surprised him and his face filled with concern, "I don't recommend it, Miss, there could be others," he paused for effect, "others more determined."

"Consider your suggestion taken under advisement," said Patricia, "but we've survived much worse and mostly at the hands of police officers like yourself. Instead sir, I'd appreciate it if you'd call for backup."

Donnelly realized these women wouldn't be budged. He felt relief that they weren't his sisters or daughters.

The Congresswoman from Montana

A month later, Patricia was still standing duty when she heard a woman's voice come from the shadows of Lafayette Park. "You should go home," it said.

"I beg your pardon?" replied Patricia.

"You heard me. It's one thing to give everything to the cause. It's another to lose yourself in it." Jeannette Rankin emerged from the darkness, wearing a cowboy hat and a long western duster.

She stood in front of Patricia Kelly and demanded, "How many days have you been standin' here?"

"Three days," replied a defiant Patricia.

"How long were you supposed to stand here?"

"Two hours."

"That's what I'm talking about, two hours versus seventy-two defines a fanatic. No one will follow a fanatic. Can't trust 'em. Fanatics aren't like regular people. The problem isn't in being a fanatic, but if you are one you've got to at least appear normal." The

Congresswoman from Montana pulled a rope of tobacco from her pocket and offered it to Patricia. "Would you like a slug?"

"No Ma'am." Patricia had never actually met Congresswoman Rankin, but she certainly knew of her. She was a legend. Rankin had been elected to Congress from the state of Montana, even though women didn't have the right to vote. What's more, she was no shrinking violet. Only a few hours after being sworn in, she stood alone in voting against Wilson's request to go to war. Her unwavering commitment to pacifism was equaled only by her determination to win emancipation.

"You know who I am?" asked Rankin.

"Yes Ma'am."

"Good, then you know I mean what I say. I got into Congress not because I pulled stunts like you. I got there 'cause I appealed to mens' good sense. I could talk like a man, reason like a man, and yes, drink like a man." She spit into the gutter and laughed. "I guess it's a damn good thing I fit in the drinkin' part under the wire."

"I'm committed. That's why I stay at my post," said Patricia.

"You mean someone should have you committed. Remember, after this is all over and we've got the right to vote, you'll need to get a life. I suggest you start corralling one now, so that you don't wake up and find yourself fifty-five years old with nothin' to show for it. Except maybe a scrapbook of leaflets and newspaper clippin's."

The easy smile slid from Rankin's face. "It's time to grow up and realize that true success is in the blending of life with passion. Hell, my constituents kicked me out after my first term because I opposed the war, but so what. I have a life. And if I had to do it again I'd vote the same way. They can take away my political ambitions, but they can't take away my life. It's mine." She cocked her head at Patricia, "Are you gettin' my drift?"

Patricia didn't really understand, but she could admit that her back ached. She was cold through and through and willing to pass the torch on to one of the many women who had volunteered for the vigil.

Rankin saw the younger woman relax.

"That's the girl. Why don't you stop by the Willard Hotel before you leave town and I'll show you around? I'll also give you some pointers on life and what's next on your agenda. "

"Thank you, Miss Rankin. I shall."

"My pleasure. Us girls got to stick together." She winked and melted back into the morning fog.

FRANCE

The unseen war

As the train passed through the French countryside, Woodrow Wilson sat alone at his desk, the weak light of winter filtering through the windows. The bitter cold and perpetual twilight of Europe made him cranky. There were plenty of external events to blame: the devastation of the French landscape, the dismal economy at home, the loss of his integrity. He had become the most loathsome of liars.

Wilson ran for his second term pledging to keep the U.S. out of the war. Less than a year after he was re-elected, he conscripted young men into uniform.

He had convinced the German people to surrender to him, and he had said it would be with dignity. In a moment of inspiration Wilson wrote the Fourteen Point-Plan, giving Germany a way to surrender and pay retribution without making the populace destitute. The plan, shredded by the Allies, made the German defeat complete, at an economic, emotional and spiritual level. How would history remember him?

'And now this', he thought, as he sat with the satchel before him, its contents untouched.

Edith appeared in the doorway. Seeing her in the shadows, Wilson imagined her to be Ellen, his first wife. At the thought of her, he was overwhelmed with regret. He sat motionless at his desk. He felt the pressure of a giant elephant's foot holding him down, the pain so intense he wondered if he was having a heart attack.

From the doorway, Edith watched the emotions pass over her husband's face. She went to him and spoke in a low voice, so the servants could not hear. "Dearest, what's wrong?" She crouched beside his chair in order to scrutinize his face, taking one of his hands in her own. She repeated, "What is it, Woodrow? Are you all right? Should I call Dr. Grayson?"

Tears filled his eyes. After Ellen's death, he had never expected to love again, never to be vulnerable to another. Yet here was Edith Galt, so different, so direct, his intellectual peer. Ellen had listened as she knitted, but rarely spoke. She had supplied a release valve for his pent up anxiety. But Edith was different. With Edith he could discuss matters of politics.

Edith would listen to his arguments and evaluate what was valid and what was ego. She distilled complex problems to their essence, and admonished him for his pedantic opinions. He and Edith were a fine match and he thanked God for his good fortune.

"Edith," he paused, wanting to express his love for her, but instead, revealed what troubled his mind. "Edith, I've failed the American people. I've let them down."

"Are you speaking of the war?"

"How did I let the industrialists talk me into it? How could I have been so gullible?"

"Woodrow, you were neither gullible nor wrong. You were in and out of the war in less than two years. In so doing, you placed the U.S. in the catbird seat. We're destined to become the supreme power of the world, ending Britain's 300-year tyranny and imperialistic expansion." She looked into his eyes that were partially concealed behind his smudged pincer glasses. Edith gently reached up and removed his spectacles to clean them with her silk handkerchief.

Standing, she continued, "Besides, you have a chance to make it right, to create a legacy by which future generations will revere you as a visionary."

"You mean the League of Nations?"

"Yes. How are the revisions coming?"

"Slowly."

"May I help you?"

"Would you listen?"

She nodded.

"But first I must share with you a report I received this morning. Dearest, please prepare yourself."

He reached into the satchel and removed a green leather folder stamped "Confidential" in gold letters across its cover. Before she opened it she caught sight of her reflection and reached up to reposition an errant hair. Wilson admired this about her. Everything in its' place.

This was always how she approached a problem. For large issues she would first define logical containers in which to keep each part of a problem. The she would break down the containers into components and put them away, solving the most perplexing riddles. But this issue would not be put away easily.

As she read the memo, her knees began to buckle. Like a shot, Wilson was out of his chair and helped her to the small divan in their compartment. She covered her mouth with her handkerchief. Then, dry-eyed, she studied him.

"Woodrow is it true?"

"Yes, it appears to be."

"But, how?"

"How what? How is it we didn't know? How did this stay a secret? How did the war continue as long as it did considering almost all the young men were dead? Which part startles you the most?"

"How is it that 50 million or more people died without riots in the street? How is it possible that people speak of anything else? I haven't heard the flu discussed in weeks. Yet here you hand me a dossier, which states that our best scientists believe, by the time it has run its course, it will have killed 70 million people." He watched her as she did the math in her head.

"Woodrow, that's more people dead than in all the wars of history added together."

"Yes darling. And now, we discover that almost a million of those deaths were on our soil. But on the front lines, in other countries, the totals were staggering. The truth is, although the war ended after America joined in, our guns didn't finish the conflict. It was the plague we brought with us. The war ended because both sides ran out of boys to put on the front lines."

"But a million people in the U.S.! What did we do with the bodies? Why aren't there expose's about this in the paper?" She paused, arriving at the same question he had. "Why aren't they blaming you?"

"That, my dear, is what I was sitting here contemplating. How could something so monstrous have escaped the attention of my antagonists? To hell with the war, a total of nine million people died over the last six years. And who knows how many of those were actually flu victims. Here we have a worldwide crime and I have not been accused of it. Why?"

"Why indeed." Edith continued to read the report. It acknowledged that approximately one billion people had been infected with the flu, over half of the earth's population. What's more, those who survived were afflicted with a lingering, severe depression. Doctors were uncertain how this depression would manifest itself over the years. For now, there had not been a dramatic rise in suicides, however, there had been an increase in violent crimes. No one knew if there was a connection.

Edith's eyes reflected her disbelief. Then she considered Wilson.

"Woodrow, you're just recovering from the flu. How's your mental state?"

He laughed at the directness of her question.

"Dearest, only you would know for sure." And he kissed her passionately as he had during their courtship. Close to her ear he whispered, "As long as I have you, I can face any black day."

Benjamin in France

Benjamin Johnson hated being away from his home and family. But he had had no choice. At the White House, he was the President's personal assistant. On the road Wilson's valet filled the role, but the valet had died from the flu while in England. Wilson sent for Benjamin, not wanting to break in a new man during the sensitive negotiations at Versailles. Benjamin, Wilson had promised, could go home as soon as he had hired and trained a man-servant that could anticipate the President's needs and whims.

Benjamin found a splendid chap in London. Born to service, John Williams had been a valet for his entire life, as was his father and his father's father. Williams learned fast and Benjamin found that Wilson now called on Williams more than Benjamin himself. After pointing this out to the President, Wilson agreed that Benjamin could take the first ship back to the States, after the entourage arrived in Paris.

Benjamin had missed Christmas at home, but he hoped the English gifts he had bought for the women in his life would appease them. As the train pulled into the station, Benjamin held back, as Wilson emerged into the adulation of the French crowd. "Viva Wilson, Viva Wilson" all of Paris seemed to shout with one thunderous voice. The Parisian police strained to hold back the thankful crowds. Premier Georges Clemenceau greeted the President warmly. The cameras were rolling and both statesmen were aware of their presence.

"Monsieur Johnson?" asked a man in uniform. He was shorter than Benjamin and wore a small mustache. Benjamin assumed he was going to ask about some matter concerning Wilson's logistics.

"Yes, I'm Benjamin Johnson. How may I assist you?"

"No Monsieur, it is I who wish to assist you." Benjamin gave the man a puzzled look.

"Monsieur, if you could come with me for a moment." Benjamin hesitated and glanced towards the President, who was receiving an official greeting from the mayor of Paris.

"Please do not concern yourself. We will take care of President Wilson's needs. Besides, he will be here for several hours, if I know our mayor." The man smiled and beckoned Benjamin to follow.

They entered a large government building. Inside the door stood half a dozen officials, along with a hundred French men and women of all ages. A distinguished, gray-haired gentleman stepped forward and removed his stovepipe hat to bow deeply to Benjamin.

"Mr. Johnson it is an honor to meet you. I am the regent of Metz, France." Again the man bowed.

Benjamin was confused, "I'm sorry, but you must have mistaken me for someone else. I am here as valet for President Wilson. I'm no one of importance."

"Ah, but you are wrong, sir. To us, to the people of France you are very important." The people in the room nodded and smiled. "We are aware, sir, that two of your sons, Emmet and Roy Johnson, served with the Hell Fighters, in the 369th infantry. It is to these brave men of America we owe the greatest debt of gratitude." The politician spoke to Benjamin and the crowd.

"More than any other regiment, French or American, your sons' division fought in the most dangerous engagements, winning the hearts and most sincere appreciation of the French people." The crowd erupted with applause. The man held up his hand for silence.

"It is most unfortunate that because of their skin color your country has chosen not to acknowledge these brave young men with the medals they so richly deserve. So we have set out to rectify this... oversight."

"Your first son, Emmet Johnson, left France three days ago wearing our medals. To us he is a soldier of honor and courage. You should be proud." The dignitary continued speaking as he pulled a velvet box from his coat. "This is France's highest Medal of Honor, the Croix de Guerre, for your son Roy Johnson, who gave his life for our freedom. He and his men went forward when others pulled back. Roy Johnson fought to ensure democracy in our country. Sir, today we wish to pay homage to you. We want to thank you for your sacrifice and acknowledge the courage with which your son fought. Please accept this medal and our deepest gratitude. It will not take the place of your son Roy, but may it remind you that he and Emmet have earned our respect and will live forever in our hearts."

The official shook Benjamin's hand and backed away with a bow. The room exploded with applause and cheers.

"Viva la Hell Fighters, Viva Monsieur Johnson, Viva la Hell Fighters." Benjamin fought back tears and said, "Merci."

On board - heading home

The transport ship was filled to capacity. Every square inch had been put to use to bring home another fighting man. The mishap of the Titanic a few years earlier crossed Emmet's mind. 'Too many people, not enough lifeboats.' But the soldiers didn't care - they were going home. The overall mood on the ship was buoyant. Or at least it started out that way. When the soldiers left France their joy was almost palpable. One of Emmet's bunkmates broke into song every few minutes at the thrill of going home. They all shared the feeling, combined with regret for friends that had not survived the grim ordeal.

This was the first chance any of them had had to look ahead, to live beyond the moment, beyond the trenches. Emmet's quarters were with the other colored men. A few white men had hitched a ride on the predominantly black transport ship to get home a few days early. The blacks didn't begrudge them the space.

The mood on the ship began to change after their third day at sea. The chaplain's sermon on Sunday got the men thinking. The preacher had talked about the sweethearts, and parents that had missed them. How their hometowns were grateful for their sacrifice.

The little, bespectacled, bald man, with the white skin and weak hands, didn't say anything specific, but he cast a shadow of doubt over those who heard him. And that doubt traveled with the speed of the Spanish Influenza throughout ship. The men went from enthusiastic back slapping soldiers to subdued veterans, each facing the uncertainty of their own return.

Would the girlfriend be waiting? Was his job still there for him? Were his parents fit and hale? He hadn't written enough. What was in that last letter from home? Something about Aunt Sadie and cancer? And what of all those who had died in the great epidemic? Would there be more loss at home than on the battlefield? Who might not be there anymore? What sad news had been kept from him? There were rumors of skyrocketing prices and plummeting salaries.

A cloud of cynicism engulfed the men when they were one day from the U.S. coastline. Tired of waiting in line for food, the bathroom, or a shower they began to snipe at each other. Soldiers wondered aloud whose idea it had been to cram so many onto this boat. Was it their own or the Army's? If they were discharged upon arrival where would their next paycheck come from? How much was the family depending on it? What would they live on until they found a job?

These were the thoughts that were swirling in the minds of the returning troops when the first fight broke out. A colored soldier had used a bar of soap in the third deck lavatory. The third deck housed a small band of white soldiers from the south. The ignorant among them acted like being colored was a disease you could catch.

Emmet knew how to deal with blatant racism. But he began to wonder what he would face back home in Washington. He had not experienced Jim Crow laws for two years. He had lived with white men openly and freely. He had not thought about what it would be like to return to a segregated south. For DC was the south, a little patch of land cut out of two slave states. Robert E. Lee himself had lived in Arlington, VA a mere two miles from Emmet's door.

Somehow Emmet had forgotten how ugly it all was, how unfair. He had assumed, mistakenly, that like the war, it was over. But on this ship, a floating microcosm of America, racism had raised its loathsome head and reminded the soldiers of what lay ahead.

NEW YORK

Arrival in NY harbor

All of the American fighting men cheered as the Statue of Liberty came into sight. But Emmet and the other black soldiers did not shout with the same enthusiasm. The Hell Fighters understood that they were not returning to the land of the free, but rather, to the remnants of slavery. Some questioned how it could be that they had risked their lives on another continent to save others from tyranny, only to return home and be treated as second class citizens?

Emmet thought about his father. He wondered what Benjamin would say. His father was the smartest man Emmet had ever known. His intelligence was exhibited through his analytical mind and cool demeanor. Benjamin never jumped to conclusions, but weighed out the pros and cons of every situation and moved forward with a clear purpose and agenda. Emmet anticipated with pleasure the long discussions he would have with his Dad when he reached home.

As they passed near the base of the Statue of Liberty, her arm raised in greeting, Emmet felt a wave of hope wash over the ship. The men, including himself, began to recall sweethearts and family they had not seen in months or years. They began to appreciate the miracle of being alive. Each man, without exception, was eager to get off the ship and return to a life that did not include death and war.

Emmet Johnson in New York

"Emmet, let's go up to Harlem and get drunk." said Billy Ray. He and Emmet had become good friends during the voyage. Billy was from Boston and had been to NYC before. He talked of the bars and dance halls.

"You're on Billy Ray, but what about prohibition? Aren't the bars closed?"

"Emmet Johnson, where there's a will, there's a way," Billy flashed a smile and surreptitiously let Emmet peek at the ten dollar bill that he had stuffed into his shirt pocket.

"Let's go," said Emmet ready for adventure.

The soldiers weren't 'officially' discharged, so they came ashore in full uniform. They would remain in uniform until they reached their original enlistment office. For Emmet that would be D.C., for Billy it was Boston. The 56,000 men that disembarked in New York harbor appeared to be invading. They were intent on soaking up all the fun there was to be had in the metropolis. And New York City was ready for them. There were parades and honors bestowed on individuals and divisions. Emmet's regiment, while not having received the highest medals of honor, had nonetheless, won more medals than any other division in the war.

And Billy, true to his word, was able to get all the alcohol that he and Emmet could consume. They paid a premium, but the bar owners had set aside plenty of liquor for the returning soldiers. The soldiers were drunk on being alive and single malt scotch.

Emmet stayed in New York at one of the Black Star Hotels for three weeks. He knew that his frenetic partying and the satisfying of his anxious needs had to happen before he would be fit company for his family. New York was just the place for Emmet the soldier to perform the exorcism of his demons in order to convert back into Emmet, brother and son. He exhausted all of his back pay and replaced the better part of his somber mood with one of gratitude for being alive. But there was still a darker emotion beneath the surface of Emmet's easy smile, one of regret and unanswered questions.

Emmet packed up his duffel bag and took the A train to Grand

Central Station where he would board the Federal Express for the last leg of his journey. He carried with him two books, W.E.B. Dubois's Black Souls and Lenin's book, Imperialism.

Emmet was ready to begin a new chapter in his life.

Benjamin Johnson coming home

Benjamin stood on the deck of the ocean liner George Washington, with France behind him, looking towards America. The winter seas were rough and he was thankful for the scarf and mittens Claire and Kay had knitted for him. But it was Louvenia's new invention that kept him warm. The hand warmers looked like pliable gray clay. When placed near the fire they absorbed warmth, and stayed warm for almost twenty minutes. The trick was not burning the outer coating. The invention was destined to improve the lives of fishermen and seafarers. Louvenia wrote that she was working on creating larger pieces that could withstand the weight of a man so that they could be placed inside boots as well. Benjamin wished her God's speed in her endeavor.

Despite his near frozen toes, Benjamin couldn't bear returning to the steerage compartment. He'd been housed with the many immigrants fleeing Europe. Their fear and anxiety were palpable.

Upon seeing Benjamin many had tried to give him gifts or offer a portion of their meager rations to honor the colored men who had fought in their villages, and saved them from German soldiers. He was again moved by what a significant difference the negro soldiers had made. He couldn't be prouder of his sons Roy and Emmet. And despite not wanting to make this journey he was now grateful for it, having learned that his son Roy had not died in vain.

When he had first heard that Roy was to be sent to Siberia to fight the Red Russian Army under the flag of the White Russian Army, Benjamin had almost asked the President for help to have his son brought home. But before he made the request a telegram had arrived, informing them that Roy had died of influenza in a French hospital. At the time, Roy's death had seemed pointless. But now, having looked into the eyes of the French citizens, Benjamin felt differently. He couldn't wait to tell Claire.

"You hoping to see land sir?" asked a young sailor.

"No, just had to get out from below."

"Can't blame you, all those garlic eaters are too much for me. But hey, another day or two and you'll be showered with ticker tape." The sailor seemed slightly jealous of the adulation Benjamin was to receive.

"What are you talking about?"

"Don't you know? When we land in New York they've got a big ticker tape parade lined up for the troops."

Benjamin hadn't heard, but he was thrilled. It meant Emmet might be in New York and would return home soon.

"Do you know if the transport for the Hell Fighters of the 369th infantry has arrived yet?"

"Yes sir, I heard they pulled into port a couple of days ago. I don't know how the captains of those ships think they're going to round those boys up again, now that they've been unleashed on the town. I know if it was me I'd make a bee line...." The sailor stopped and blushed.

"Yes son, I know," said Benjamin. He realized that his own son was no different and that to try and find him in the tumult of tens of thousands of people would be impossible. Instead, he'd go home on the first train and wait for Emmet there.

"I better get back, I'm on duty," said the young man. "I'm responsible for making sure that all of the Wilson's luggage gets on shore at the same time.

"No small task," acknowledged Benjamin.

"You ain't whistling Dixie on that one, sir. Those two travel with their house on their backs. They almost need a ship just to cart them around." He hesitated, "I don't mean no disrespect mind you."

"None taken. I know what you mean; I've been traveling with them these past few weeks. But you've got to understand, son, they need a lot of clothes. They change for every meal and then there are special events. What's more, are you aware they carry all their own food?"

"Why's that?" asked the young sailor.

"They don't want to change their eating habits so they carry their own."

"I see," said the sailor, pondering the implications. "But then they miss out on a lot of good food don't they? I mean, I never had snails until I went to France, and what about that goose liver? What do they call it? Patty? Seems a shame to miss all the food that France has to offer." The sailor made a face, as if recalling a nasty taste. "They didn't miss anything in England though, dreadful food. I wouldn't feed it to my dog. Well I'll be seeing you, sir." He tipped his hat to Benjamin and was off.

Benjamin pulled his coat tighter. Even the hand warmers were cold now.

He considered going to W.E.B. Dubois's stateroom. The great philosopher/writer was returning to the states to take the top position at the NAACP in New York. Dubois and Benjamin had shared many philosophical discussions during the voyage. But tonight, Benjamin headed for his own quarters to cherish the thoughts of his family at home and his son Emmet.

WASHINGTON DC

The Johnson women at home

It seemed incredible to Claire that all her daughters were home for dinner at the same time. With Benjamin away, they seemed to have found reasons not to come together for meals. But tonight June, Kay, and Louvenia all sat with their mother, saying prayers over a proper supper.

Dinner with the girls was a noisy affair, each speaking over the other's sentences.

"I tell you I saw Edward Ellington," said Kay.

"The Duke? Where? When?" asked June.

"Last night outside of the Howard Theater. He was standing there just as big as life and twice as handsome."

"Is the Howard open again?" asked Claire innocently. All three girls stared at her, incredulous. "What?" Claire asked defensively.

"Mother," Louvenia responded using her lecturer's voice. "The Howard Theater reopened last month." Lou said it in the same voice she would use to explain a scientific truth to a small child. The Howard was the black theater that attracted the best talent on the Orpheum Vaudeville circuit. Between Vaudeville acts they showed films by new black film-makers like Oscar Micheaux. Claire had often attended these, her favorites being the comedies of Harold Lloyd. All of her children considered the Howard Theater their second home.

"I'm sorry, I didn't know. June, does that mean that the epidemic is abating?"

Putting down a forkful of meatloaf and mashed potatoes, June responded. "Yes mother, we're down to less than 200 deaths a week." June paused as she thought of the tens of thousands of people she had watched die over the last few months. Then she visibly shook off the thought and picked up her fork, returning to the present. "We finally have enough beds to accommodate the sick, but I'm afraid most of the care givers have taken ill in the process. We haven't enough people to attend to even the dozen patients that wander in daily."

"Kay, why don't you volunteer?" asked Claire. "It would be the Christian thing to do. You could help your sister."

Kay broke off the conversation she was having with Louvenia about a new play. Kay stared at her mother to determine if she was serious and then looked to her older sister June for help.

"Mother, I'd be no good at nursing. June here, she's practically a saint. I'm the bad seed, the black sheep, how many times have you told me so? What good would I be nursing sick people?"

They all began to giggle, recalling times when Kay had been a less than helpful nurse. Lou began, "Mother, do you remember when you sent Kay down to my lab to 'help me' clean up? She began mixing chemicals and almost burned down the house." June chimed in, "and the time when I took sick and you sent Kay to 'tend me'. Rather than bringing me a cool cloth for my head she boiled a towel and attempted to wrap me in it. Had it not been for you discovering what she was up to, I might not have survived."

Even Claire couldn't resist. "I remember when Kay thought she would be nice to your father and cut his toenails. She took out a pair of scissors and cut off the top of your father's big toe. The poor man walked with a limp for weeks." With each story the women succumbed to laughter.

Between tears and laughter, Claire acquiesced. "All right, Kay. It's true, you'd probably have those poor patients begging for mercy. I take back my suggestion."

Lou was the first to break the spell of the Girl's Night. "I'm in the middle of an important experiment. I'm afraid I need to get back to work."

Kay asked, jokingly, "Will you be burning down the house?"

Louvenia, Claire's studious middle daughter, responded, with a serious expression, "I'm not planning on it, Kay, but it's always a good idea to be prepared." And with that she walked off to the basement. The three remaining women looked at each other and roared with laughter.

The Howard Theater

"And now for the amateur portion of our show," the barker announced. "We have a pretty young lady who is going to sing for you, Miss Kay Johnson."

The audience afforded Kay a polite applause. Many were leaving to go to the lobby for a Pepsi Cola or Cracker Jacks. Kay tentatively began the Layton and Creamer song.

> *"Now won't you list-en*
> *dear-ie while I say*
> *How could you tell me*
> *that you're going a-way?"*

The sound of her voice was so sweet, so refreshing, that audience members stopped in the aisle and turned back to listen. She had a trill in her throat they had never heard before. The song was familiar, but her arrangement was unique. Women began to shush men and soon everyone who had been standing took their seats. When Kay finished, she gave a dainty bow. The theater was silent for a moment and then broke out in applause. Kay beamed with pleasure.

The manager of the Howard rushed backstage to greet her.

"Hey there little lady, who taught you to sing like that?"

"A friend of mine. You may know him, Edward Ellington." When the manager remained puzzled, she added, "Duke Ellington."

Winter 1919

The manager grinned broadly and winked at Kay. "Duke's quite the man about town. You two going together?" Every theater owner tried to sign Duke up to play.

Kay felt her relationship with Duke was none of the man's business and proceeded to change the subject. "Did you like my act, Mr. Steed?"

"Why sure I did. Didn't you hear that applause? Say, could you come back next week? Let's plan on having you compete in a few more amateur shows and see if you can reproduce your success here tonight. If you can, you never know, there might be a spot on the roster for you." He tipped his hat and raced back to the curtain to watch the next act.

Kay was so happy she wanted to kiss someone.

Kay volunteers

Kay dreaded entering the makeshift hospital at the Armory. She couldn't believe she'd been roped into it last Sunday at church. The Reverend asked for volunteers to help comfort the latest influenza victims. The next thing Kay knew, her mother had volunteered her. It wasn't fair. Kay had so little time as it was. She was in school full-time and worked four hours a day as prop mistress at the Howard Theater. Her precious free time was needed for singing lessons and auditioning. Instead, here she was about to make a fool of herself by attempting to help dying people. Her sister Saint June had offered some comfort, suggesting that there might be a blues song for Kay to write from the experience.

Kay opened the large Armory door with the expectation of being overwhelmed by the reek of death and disinfectant. Instead, the building smelled of balsam incense, infusing the room with a pleasant soothing odor. Once her olfactory senses had adjusted, she walked over to the admitting nurse, a large older woman, wearing a crisp white uniform and a starched hat. Her jaw set, as if ready to say no to any request brought through the door.

"Excuse me, but my church signed me to help out today. My name is Kay Johnson." The nurse frowned, as she searched the list of names on a clipboard in front of her. Kay hoped that maybe she wasn't needed.

"Ah yes, here you are, Ruth Johnson. Are you June's sister?" asked the nurse almost smiling. 'Another June admirer', thought Kay.

"Yes and no. My name's Kay Johnson. My middle name is Ruth." The nurse looked nonplussed. "And yes, my sister is June. Saint June," she said it as a joke but the nurse only stared taking stock of Kay. After a long pause she said, "Why don't you go inside and get to work?"

"And do what?"

"Comfort the dying."

She said it so matter-of-factly that Kay thought she was kidding.

"Comfort them how, exactly? With a song, a dance?"

"Whatever they want. They're the ones dying." Kay was at a loss. The nurse took pity on her. "It's not so bad. In fact, it's a lot better. During the worst of it we took over all of the Convention Hall Market. At the height of the epidemic we had to put the overflow into church halls around town. We're down to fifteen to twenty victims a day. Be thankful you weren't here when we were losing hundreds, sometimes thousands in a single day. But then, I'm sure June told you what it was like."

Kay suspected the nurse was lying. She'd never heard of numbers like that. She knew that scores of people had died. Friends of her's. "Fifteen to twenty a day you say?"

"We can handle it and to be honest with you, most of us that are still standing have gone numb. We've had a war right here in the U.S. that's taken far more lives than anything overseas, but people want an enemy they can see, so the flu was ignored." She stopped and pulled out a surgical mask from her desk and handed it to Kay. "Do you know why they call it the Spanish flu?"

"Because it came from Spain?" answered Kay tentatively.

"The reason they called it the Spanish flu was because only Spain was reporting on it openly. All the other countries including the United States were hiding the size of the epidemic. The politicians didn't want a panic. And I'm not sure it wasn't the right thing to do, since there's no cure." She softened for minute. "Did you lose anyone in your family?"

"Yeah, my brother, Roy. He died from the flu in France."

"I'm sorry, you must miss him. The truth is that once people con-tract the disease they go fast, a couple of hours, maybe a day." She gave Kay a smile. "I'm sorry, I didn't mean to be flip with you before. Volunteers tend to help by writing letters or people's wills. Some folks even want to be read to. Anything you do will be appre-ciated."

The nurse stood up and brought Kay a smock. "Here, you should wear this and the face mask, also make a point not to touch anyone. If you must, make sure to wash your hands in disinfectant right away. That's why the incense, to hide the smell of the disinfectant, which we use rather liberally."

Kay added, "and it hides the smell of death." She immediately regretted her words.

The nurse stiffened, "That's right," she said, and her icy façade returned. "Let me know if you need anything." And she went back to her desk.

Through the double doors lay a large room of cots and in each one a body. The space was full of sound, a dull buzzing made up of snoring, whispers and whimpering. Kay wasn't sure where to start or how she would convince her feet to move forward into the room until a teenage boy saw her and asked, "Are you an angel?"

She laughed, "No, just a prop mistress."

"Would you sing to me. Just a little song please?"

Kay didn't know why it came to her, she didn't like the song much, but the next thing she knew she was singing in a soft voice, "Amazing grace, how sweet the sound..."

Swiftly she was accompanied by humming from the beds around her and she wondered, for just a moment, if this might be heaven.

Hoover submits findings

"Special Assistant Hoover, please sit down," requested Attorney General Palmer. "So tell me, what has your research turned up?"

Hoover sat forward in his chair, his blue eyes wide, "It's bigger and more menacing than we'd realized sir," he stammered. Palmer hid a smile at the twenty-four-year-old's solemn pronouncement.

"Really, how so?"

"It's all here in the brief, sir." Hoover placed a thick sheaf of papers on the desk and pushed them towards Palmer. Palmer did not reach for the tome; instead he leaned back in his chair.

"Why don't you summarize it for me, Mr. Hoover."

"Well sir, my research on the Communist Party is far from exhaustive. However, in the report I describe how it began, its leadership and the different philosophies put forth under the name of Communism. I've created a dossier on everyone with influence that I suspect to be a Communist, or to be influenced by Communism."

"And how many people is that, Mr. Hoover?"

"I didn't bring the dossiers sir," said Hoover anxiously. "The documents fill the better part of a filing cabinet. However, I've included a list of people I'm tracking at present." Hoover paused and pointed to the report. "May I, sir?"

Palmer realized Hoover was asking to have his papers back to procure the list. "Certainly." As Hoover came nearer, Palmer felt an unsettling energy about the boy. Something akin to a fighting dog who doesn't know when it's best to let go. An animal bred to kill and die in the ring. Palmer recognized Hoover as a significant asset, if he could control him. If Palmer followed through on his desire to run for office, he could aim Hoover at his opponents and have him search for lapses in their moral character.

Hoover pulled out several sheets and handed them to Palmer, who accepted them reluctantly, not really wanting to be bothered with the details.

"Based on my research sir, I believe the United States is in peril, grave peril, from the Communists. Given free reign they'll destroy the very fabric of our society, endangering the rights of individuals and dissolving the peace we have come to know and cherish. Communism means anarchy and the death of democracy." Hoover sat back, satisfied with his speech, but uncertain of its impact on his boss.

Palmer reviewed the list of alleged Communists. He had expected it would be full of the unpronounceable names of immigrants, but instead it included senators, congressmen, business leaders and prominent citizens.

Palmer leaned forward across the desk, still holding the list. He struggled to keep the excitement out of his voice.

"Can you back all this up, Mr. Hoover?"

"Yes, sir."

Palmer considered the list of names for a moment and lit a cigarette. After a time he turned his gaze to Hoover and studied him. Hoover did not flinch. Palmer was drunk with the power Hoover had placed in his hands. "Mr. Hoover, you have a new job. I'd like you to expand your files. Why don't you take a couple of agents and begin identifying the most radical immigrants living within our borders. Also give me your personal list of the ten most notorious citizens you believe to be Communists."

"Yes, sir. When shall I report back?"

"Let's say two weeks from this Friday."

"Yes sir."

Watching him leave, Palmer wondered how Hoover had gotten around the height requirement for the new Bureau of Investigation, but it didn't matter. This ambitious fellow would become Palmer's secret weapon to ensure his place as the next President of the United States.

Wilson and Palmer's weapon

The well dressed, slightly effeminate young man sat calmly on a bench in the hall, exhibiting poise beyond his years. His boss, a tall gentleman of substantial bulk strode up and down the corridor in an attempt to abate his nervousness before meeting with the President of the United States.

In truth, Attorney General Mitchell Palmer was not afraid of Wilson. What Palmer feared was that time was running out. He believed himself to be on a mission from God, to destroy the anarchist sentiment in the country, before it rotted the minds of the weaker citizens. Palmer hated the dirty, illiterate, foreign-speaking rabble that washed up on America's shores. He acknowledged that the foreigners were stalwart, able to withstand hardship and deprivation.

Palmer likened them to cockroaches – all but indestructible. He saw himself as their exterminator.

Benjamin Johnson opened the door to the Oval office and addressed the two men. "The President will see you now."

Palmer and the younger man entered without acknowledging Benjamin. Palmer's hand was extended, as he reached the President's desk in two quick strides.

"Mr. President, what a pleasure. Thank you for taking time out of your busy schedule. Let me introduce you to our newest, brightest star in the Bureau, Mr. J. Edgar Hoover."

Wilson eyed Hoover, unimpressed with his modest stature.

"Mr. Hoover," said the President as he reached out to shake Hoover's hand. Hoover's handshake was, as Wilson had suspected, cold, damp and soft. Wilson motioned for the men to sit in the chairs before his desk.

"Keep a close eye on this young man, Mr. President," said Palmer. "He's destined to go places. First in his class at college, a diligent worker and the greatest analytical mind in the Bureau. He'll outlast us all, sir."

Wilson was unswayed, "Where did you go to school, Mr. Hoover?" Wilson believed the quality of a man lay in his education.

"I had wanted to go to the University of Virginia sir, but due to financial constraints I attended George Washington law school at night, while clerking at the Justice Department," Hoover spoke rapidly, regretting his lack of control over the modulation in his responses. Wilson, however, admired a man who could speak his mind without the circuitous route of most politicians.

"GW is a good school and Palmer here says you did well?"

"I graduated with honors sir."

Finished with Hoover, Wilson turned to Palmer. "So where are we at? I can tell you the Congress is challenging me about your activities as well as the very creation of a Bureau of Investigation. They say it's unconstitutional and I'm not sure that I disagree with them."

Palmer's face began to color, a fine pink glow started at his neck and rose towards his hairline. "That's what they say now," responded Palmer, "but wait until they receive a bomb in the mail. Then

49

they'll change their tune." He held himself in check, so as not to lose his temper in front of the President.

"Now don't go getting any ideas Mr. Palmer. I don't want to hear that any of these explosives are attributable to you." Wilson's thin lips formed a grim smile. Hoover observed that Wilson appeared to be part reptile, cold and capable of striking out at anyone without provocation. "Tell me, Mr. Palmer, what have you discovered of our Red friends?"

"Sir, they're here and in great numbers. We've started arresting dozens of the leaders. Mr. Hoover is already tracking over 100,000 people. He's using the same categorization system he learned at the Library of Congress."

"Is that so?" said Wilson.

"Actually sir," broke in Hoover. "I'm now tracking approximately 200,000 individuals with ties to the Communist or Socialist parties. I have detailed dossiers on 10,000 individuals who are under various forms of surveillance."

Wilson perked up at this.

"Are these dossiers on American citizens Mr. Hoover?"

"Yes sir, some of them, although the vast majority are aliens."

"Use caution, Mr. Hoover. You realize that your current activities are in violation of Articles One, Four and Fourteen of the Constitution which forbid the government to keep files on its citizens. You'd best destroy these files when you're done with them."

"Yes sir."

"Mr. Palmer, Mr. Hoover here appears to be quite a find. But I've got to tell you, Congress is all over me like a hair shirt to disband your organization. They insist that you focus your investigations on solving actual crimes, rather than monitoring the actions of U.S. citizens."

Palmer winked at Wilson, certain that they had an understanding. He assumed Wilson was asking him to make the Bureau more invisible, more stealth-like. Meanwhile, Wilson was seriously considering abolishing the newly formed organization. He didn't trust Palmer or Hoover.

Wilson stood up from the couch and walked behind his desk. In those few steps he decided to let Hoover finish his cataloguing of undesirables, work Wilson could later use to crush his political enemies. Once it was completed and his agenda fulfilled, Wilson would close down the whole damn agency, an 'unconstitutional' organization if ever there was one. Meanwhile critical international matters needed to be addressed. In a few days he'd return to Europe. He resented spending time on the domestic agenda. Why couldn't the country take care of itself while he cared for the world?

Benjamin stood in the corner, at his post, watching and listening. He believed Palmer to be a dangerous idiot; a greedy egomaniac who would not be able to control his appetite and would eventually be consumed by the same ball of flames that had brought him into office. Hoover, on the other hand, was vermin. Nothing would exterminate him. Hoover was slippery and fully capable of hiding behind the seal of the President in order to fulfill his own destiny. Benjamin made a mental note to keep an eye on this man's career because, he suspected, once Hoover was done with the Reds he would find another minority to watch. Benjamin suspected the negro community would soon find its way onto Hoover's short list.

Red scare

"Claire?"

"Yes dear?" She was lying beside Benjamin unable to sleep.

"Claire, something's happening at work." He paused, considering his words, "Something I don't understand. I'd like to talk it over with you."

"Do you want to go downstairs? I'll make us a cup of tea or warm milk."

"Yes, let's." But before they left the bedroom he turned to her and said in a low voice, "It's important Claire."

He needn't have told her. In their 31 years of marriage he had never asked her to get out of bed to discuss a problem, no matter how perplexing.

The house was quiet, the girls sound asleep. Claire prepared mugs of chamomile tea and put shortbread cookies on a plate.

"Claire, do you remember your philosophy courses at Howard?"

51

"Vaguely. It was long time ago Ben."

"Yes, I know, but do you recall the creation of ruling systems, tyranny, democracy, communism and the like?"

"In truth, no Ben, but tell me what's on your mind."

"I'm certain I'm not breaching any oath of office. And I've got to discuss my concerns with someone. If I don't, they just keep circling around and around in my head."

"Go on Ben."

"The rulers of this country have an almost phobic opinion of Communism and now Socialism. They don't recognize these ideologies as simply alternative forms of emphasis, but rather align them with worshiping the devil." He glanced up at her, with revelation in his face. "That's it, somehow they've mixed it up with religion."

"Dear, this country has always done a pretty good job of mixing government with religion."

"No, no it's more than that. This country runs on democratic principles, but when it comes to capitalism, religion falls to the wayside. Our government supports the capitalist mantra to such an extent it's blind to alternatives. It will kill, maim and cheat anyone who gets in its way."

"Hasn't it always been like that? The strong feed on the weak."

"No Claire, not like this. They've developed secret organizations to foil independent parties. These are legitimate parties, who want to improve the life of the individual rather than the wealth of the corporation. At times, when I'm listening to these men of industry, I feel like I'm watching Nathaniel Hawthorne's play The Crucible. It's a witch hunt and they're after blameless people whose main fault is that they do not idolize money." He paused to eat a cookie.

"Claire, they're like the Klan, indiscriminately lynching people. They don't care who they hang, whether the victim is guilty or not. They have the taste of blood in their mouths. Innocents will swing."

"Ben, what's happened? What's made it so much worse?" In twenty years of working at the White House Claire had never seen Ben so distraught.

"The terrorist pipe bombs didn't help. Assuming they were sent by terrorists."

"What are you saying Ben? That a government organization may have planted the bombs?"

"It's possible. This administration is desperately afraid of power resting in the hands of the people. Certain men have convinced Wilson that the average citizen is not smart enough to make up his own mind. And this has played into Wilson's arrogance. He has allowed the powerful few to rule this country, with senators in their pockets. Special interests govern America. Haven't you noticed how Washington DC has grown, practically overnight? People with corporate agendas are arriving with open checkbooks and requests for their business or state. The government is for sale and anyone who stands up and complains is locked away as a Red." He raised his cup and breathed in the comforting aroma of the chamomile.

"I'm sorry to be ranting like this Claire. It's just that I'm shocked by the depths of our government's fear and greed."

"Benjamin," she said taking his hand, "do you remember when June used to sneak out at night and you put restrictions on her, which, to her, were excessive. Why did you do that?"

"Because I was afraid. Afraid of what might happen to her."

"I think that's your answer, my dear. Fear. The government views us as children, unable to decide for ourselves. They're unwilling to give us the freedom to make up our own minds. Worse, they're certain, that given a choice, we would pick the wrong path."

"What is happening to America, the land of freedom?" said Benjamin.

"Now Ben, you're not that naive. We live in a Republic. We elect officials to make our laws and decide what is and isn't best for us. Dear, we don't live in a democracy. In truth, communism is closer to a democracy than our current form of government. Nevertheless..."

Ben slumped in his chair, his head hung down. "Claire, I'm about to tell you something you must never repeat."

"Perhaps you shouldn't tell me."

"I have to. Claire, we're sending our boys to Russia. Now that the Great War is over, were going to wrest control from the revolutionaries. Once we were revolutionaries. Why can't Wilson understand that? Instead, we want to dismantle a government that stands for freedom, a freedom won by Russian revolutionaries with their own blood."

Claire said nothing, but continued to hold his hand. Ben had worked for several presidents: Cleveland, McKinley and the beloved Teddy Roosevelt, but never had he suffered so much angst. A sinister secretiveness blanketed this administration. She wanted Ben to quit. She'd been suggesting it for months, but Ben was waiting. He didn't believe Wilson would win a third term despite the populist polls. He would leave the White House with Wilson. In any case, it wouldn't be sorted out tonight.

"Ben, let's go to bed."

"Yes dear."

And they returned to the small room where they had spent thousands of nights taking comfort in each other's arms.

Emmet travels home

The train was packed, standing room only. Soldiers filled the seats, doorways, aisles, even luggage racks. But no one complained, because they were going home. They had fought in an ugly, despicable war, where friends were killed. By the time the influenza had arrived and ravaged the troops, it was almost a relief. Men were beginning to question why they were there and who they were liberating. It was the 'war to end all wars', that concluded with a sneeze instead of mortar fire.

Emmet didn't mind the cattle car treatment. Whites and blacks stood shoulder to shoulder, filled with anticipation. Returning home felt surprisingly similar to leaving for war. Emmet knew things would have changed at home and even if they hadn't, he knew he had changed.

Emmet turned to the young white soldier standing beside him. He couldn't have been more than twenty-two. In a low voice Emmet asked, "How do you feel about going home?"

The private eyed him with astonishment. "What do you mean, mister?" he replied with a southern drawl. But he didn't hesitate to answer. The boy was wound up and ready to talk. "Do you mean am I glad to be seeing my family, ready to eat real meals, be clean, warm

54

and dry for days? Boy, am I. But if you're askin' me if I'm worried –
worried that this entire train of bubbas, like the one before it, and the
one behind it, are all wanting the same job that I am – then yeah, I'm
worried. My family's been going without for the last two years, supportin' the war effort and now with prices going through the roof
they can't afford milk for the children. I'm worried." He reached into
his shirt pocket for a cigarette. He had one and offered to break it in
half to share with Emmet. Emmet shook his head and the soldier
shrugged and lit up. What about you? What are you expectin' after
the hugs and homecomin' dinner?"

"I don't know," said Emmet, "I'm concerned. A lot of the old boys
on this transport are going home to Jim Crow country. They won't be
happy with the freedoms colored men like myself are expecting from
now on."

"You got that right. I'm one of those old boys. I'm headin' for
Mississippi. Don't get me wrong, I thought you colored boys were
incredible soldiers. Fought with a bravery that down right frightened
me. How come you never brought it against us big mouth crackers?"
He paused and blew a smoke ring. "Not for nothing, but from here
on out I bet you're not goin' to take it lying down. You're a soldier
boy now." He smiled and held out his hand to Emmet. "Bobby Joe
Watts, infantry. Served in France."

"Emmet Johnson with the 369th. Were you in the Argonne Forest
campaign?"

"You bet, quite a mess, huh? Did you lose many friends there? I
lost half my unit."

"Eighty percent of my unit was killed. Just about broke me. I
watched 'em die." Neither man spoke for a minute reliving the awful
reality of the war. The train whistle blew, interrupting their thoughts.

"Trenton next stop. Next stop, Trenton," shouted the conductor
from the front of the car. He didn't even attempt to pass through the
mass of men.

"Emmet, I got a question for you, if you don't mind me askin'.
What's this Marcus Garvey fellow about? He seems kind of crazy to
me, but then he ain't talkin' to me, so maybe I jus' don't understand."

Emmet mused, "He is kind of crazy, but he's also dynamic. He's a great speaker. He can move men's imaginations. He's saying 'to hell with it'. Don't bother being a second-class citizen. Let's go back to our homelands in Africa. Let's take the knowledge that we've gained in America and build our own countries in the motherland. Despite the fact that none of us has ever been to Africa." Emmet shifted his position so that he could lean against the train seat. Bobby Joe did the same.

"I went and heard him speak in NY while we were there," said Emmet. "He's preaching pure separatism. He even supports the Klan because of their separatist stand. You can imagine that drives the NAACP folks crazy. But I liked what he said about us finding our own heroes and developing our own economic base. Unlike a lot of politicians, he's taken action. He started the Negro Factories Corporation and the Black Star Line. I don't know how many colored he's found jobs for, but it must be thousands. I stayed in one of his hotels, ate in one of his restaurants, even got my uniform cleaned at one of his dry cleaners."

Emmet continued, "I asked the people who owned these businesses what it was like to work with Garvey's organization. They said it was great. He franchised all these little businesses in order to help colored folks get started and then turned them over to the individuals to run them. I've got to say there's a lot of good sense in his actions." Emmet raised his eyebrows in apology.

"But heck, why does he have to wear that ridiculous uniform?" asked Bobby Joe.

Emmet laughed, "I have no idea. The costume destroys his credibility. But at one point I was ready to sign up and head for Africa, then I remembered that's what the war was about. The European ruling class bickering over who owned what colonies in Africa," he paused, thinking that he may have said too much. "Sorry, I'm afraid the war has made me a little cynical."

"Tell me about it," said Bobby Joe. "I'm so cynical I doubt my family will recognize me. But go on, tell me more about Garvey."

"I've got to assume the government's watching him pretty closely. I mean he's talking about things that have got to make the establishment worried. If nothing else, he's taking money out of the pockets of the industrialists and that's the quickest way I know to be put in jail or die in America."

"Ain't he nominated himself the president of Africa? How can he do that?"

"Face it, it's never going to happen," said Emmet. "You were in Europe. By the end, we all knew the real purpose of the war was to help England and France steal the German territories in Africa. German lands rich in oil. Now that everyone has a car they're all going to need gas. Who's to say how long the oil fields in Pennsylvania will hold out."

Bobby Joe interrupted, "I heard they found some more oil in Ohio."

"I suspect Garvey is underestimating European interest in Africa. He's not ready to take on the English, nor, I dare say, the United States government. We've cut our own deals on the dark continent."

"Yeah," said Bobby Joe with a smile. "It's too bad, I know a lot of crackers in Mississippi that would have supported Mr. Garvey's plan," Bobby Joe winked.

The conductor squeezed into the cabin shouting, "Philadelphia next. Philadelphia station. Change trains here for Pittsburgh, Detroit, Ohio, Chicago and points west."

Emmet held out his hand to Bobby Joe. "I've enjoyed talking to you."

Bobby Joe shook it without hesitation, "Same here. I wish you luck at home."

"And I you. I'm going to get off here," said Emmet. "I'll hitch the rest of the way. I'm not all sorted out yet. I'd like to be a little more settled before I see my family. Know what I mean?"

"I do, but I've got another day or two before I get home, so I'm hoping it comes back to me – who I was before I left."

"Good luck, Bobby Joe."

"Same to you, Emmet."

Emmet pressed through the men, holding his duffel bag in the air over his head, in preparation for the next stop.

Winter 1919

Scientific American

Louvenia's Scientific American had arrived. With its appearance her spirits lightened and she skipped to the icebox to get some lemonade before she sat down with her prize.

Claire, witnessing her daughter's good mood, couldn't help but comment, "You act like a beau sent you flowers." Claire said it good-naturedly as she rolled out a piecrust for the Phillips family.

"Momma, there might be an article in here on non-corroding metals."

As she flipped through the pages she saw a patent had been submitted for a pop-up toaster, a notion that had never occurred to Lou. Also, two British scientists claimed to have proven Einstein's theory of relativity.

"Imagine," said Louvenia out loud.

"Imagine what dear?" said her mother as she crimped the edges of her pie shell.

"What a wonderful time to be alive," said Lou. "We're on the brink of so many new discoveries. Mother, our world is about to change and things will never be the same again." Claire wiped her hands clean on her apron and sat down to listen to her child's visions.

"How so, darling?"

"First of all, the world will begin to shrink. Trains and telephones started the transformation, but now we have airplanes. In just a few days, nonstop flights are scheduled to cross both the Atlantic and the Pacific."

Claire smiled at her daughter's enthusiasm, but doubted her credibility.

"And roads, Momma, miles and miles of roads that will enable every family to move out of the city and into the country to enjoy green grass and clean air."

"But I thought you said everyone just moved into the cities. Isn't that what you told me?"

"Why yes, now that the war is over young people don't want to work on the farms, but what I'm describing is different. Now you'll be able to live in the country and work in the city. The car will take you there. And you'll drive on black ribbons of highway made of something called asphalt. Asphalt will make roads smooth and consistent and a lot less expensive to build and maintain than concrete."

Louvenia took a gulp of lemonade, "But it's mass communication that will change everything, Momma. Remember how different things were once Poppa brought the phonograph home?"

"Yes. You all stopped playing the piano," Claire said with a frown.

"Exactly, before we had only ourselves to make music and now we have everyone from Caruso to Bert Williams. Something new has been invented Momma, and it'll be bigger than the phonograph. It's called the radio. It will send music and voices through the airwaves. Each family will have a radio box in their home that runs on electric power. You won't have to get up and wind it. The radio will be available all day as a source of music and information, all you'll have to do is turn it on." Louvenia saw her mother's brow furrow with doubt.

"Momma, just think! You'll have choices! Sure, starting out there'll be one or two 'air stations' to listen to, but in the next ten years I believe we'll have dozens. There'll be political stations, comedy, music, and who knows, maybe cooking. They'll put on plays."

"What good will it be if you can't see anything?"

"It's like a phonograph that's always on and has six records playing simultaneously. You just turn to the disc you want to hear."

"But how will I know when to listen?"

"They will list programs in the newspaper telling you when to listen during the day."

Claire stood up, shaking her head, "I've had my fill. Your future sounds noisy and I'm not sure I'm going to like it." She went over to her daughter and kissed her cheek. "But I know you'll keep me informed, so that I won't look like a ninny, once all these things become commonplace."

As Claire turned back to her apple pie she asked, "Louvenia, why didn't you take the job Madame Walker offered you? She'd have been very generous and you could have had your own lab."

"Momma, it isn't the type of science I want to practice. I want to change people's lives not the texture of their hair."

Winter 1919

Claire raised her hands in acquiescence, "All right, just asking. It seems you are going to need resources behind you to invent the future." With that, Claire left. Louvenia knew her mother was right, and this was why she had devised a plan.

June's letter

June awoke in the night and went to the bathroom to look at her face in the mirror. She wasn't surprised when she saw her reflection tinged with blue. The illness had crept up on her. For all her knowledge of the disease it still took her by surprise. She returned to her room and dressed quietly so as not to awaken Kay.

She put on her coat and slipped out the front door, heading up the street towards the Howard University infirmary. She felt fortunate that a cab appeared almost instantly. Sitting in the back seat she had time to evaluate her symptoms, pressure behind her eyes, an inflammation of the upper gums, exhaustion and a headache. She diagnosed herself as having the flu with a fifty-fifty chance of survival.

As a member of the staff, June knew what to ask for from the night orderly. She was grateful that there was an empty bed near the window that allowed for a cool breeze. While still lucid she decided to put her affairs in order and began to write a letter to her family. When she grew too weak to continue, she called to a volunteer to help her finish the hand-written the letter.

> *Dear Mother and Father,*
>
> *I am writing this to you, as I am certain I have contracted the flu. I'm so sorry. I know how hard it was for you losing Roy just a few months ago. And I can hear you warning me not to contract the disease. Unfortunately, this is one of those times you were right, mother.*
>
> *Yet it wouldn't have mattered, because this is my destiny. I would have tended to the sick as my life's vocation, with or without a plague at my doorstep. Just as you have both worked so hard; to provide each of your children with a good education, set a high moral standard and instill in each of us*

a deep respect for our race.

I hope I am wrong or rather, that I'll survive the epidemic. At this moment, my joints ache and a fierce headache has grabbed hold of my head. If I do not survive this trial I want you both to know that I love you very much. That my life up until now has been wonderful and there was nothing more I could have asked for.

Take care of Louvenia. Make sure she doesn't blow herself up. I wish I could see Emmet's face when he returns. Give him a hug and kiss for me and go easy on Kay. She's not like the rest of us Johnsons. She's special. She has a gift, which you may not understand, but that she must explore. Free her and she will make you proud.

I must rest now. May God bless you both and if God sees fit to take me, I'll make a home in heaven where we all can live.

> *Your devoted daughter,*
>
> *June*

The next day the flu attacked with a force that left June panting. Her chest filled with phlegm, coughs racked her body. Her joints were so sore it hurt to move or to stay still. Her mind no longer functioned linearly. Faces, events and colors popped in and out without her bidding. Her throat was on fire. She asked for water again and again, yet it did not sooth, only irritated her stomach. In twenty-four hours her skin had gone from smooth and supple to sallow and dry. Her elbows, lips and hands felt like sandpaper. The disease was sucking away her vitality.

When the fever came, June was ready to go, unwilling to tolerate the intruder any longer. Without a whimper she left this world to find her brother Roy and to wait for the others.

Claire at the Phillips

Duncan Phillips was a handsome man, kind and enthusiastic. His house was always full of interesting people, mostly artists. He was called, 'a collector', which meant he didn't work. His father had been among the richest men in America, surpassed only by Andrew

Winter 1919

Carnegie and J.P. Morgan.

Claire worked for the Phillips family doing office work, household management, or whatever needed to be done. There were several full-time maids. Claire was often asked to manage the lavish parties the family threw. Occasionally she would be put in charge of training a new girl. The wealth and splendor of the Phillips' did not awe Claire. She was, after all, the niece of Madame Walker, the first black woman millionaire in the U.S. Claire could have worked at any one of Madame Walker's beauty schools, but she hated the smell of the chemicals and many of the products caused her to break out in a rash.

Madame Walker complained that Claire was wasting her business degree on the Phillips'. But Claire felt uncomfortable about nepotism, and she also didn't want the press to connect the dots between Madame Walker and herself, and then to Benjamin and the President. She knew it was silly, but she'd seen greater nonsense occur. No, the Phillips' were a wonderful family. They treated her with respect and showed appreciation for her efforts. They had also allowed her a flexible schedule, which made it easier to take care of her family.

"Claire, could you come in here for a minute?" called Mr. Phillips. "I just purchased this new piece. I'd like to know what you think of it." It was a large canvas of a tree budding in the spring with the branches outlined in white.

"I like it. The outlining gives it a cooling effect. You can almost sense the dampness and chill in the air of spring. It's a Van Gough?"

"Very good Claire. Yes indeed, I got a good deal. You'd be surprised how his work has caught on in the last ten years. I wish Bonnard had experienced such a bump." Despite his comment, Claire knew that Duncan Phillips did not buy art for its resale value, but because he loved the pieces and wanted them in his home, which was now nearly covered in canvas.

The Phillips had actually bought the property next door, to store paintings not currently on display. "Claire, have I mentioned our plan to turn the house next door into a museum, open to the public?"

"I heard you mention it a few months ago. When would it happen?"

"The accountants came up with a way to create a non-profit entity that would be responsible for the preservation and maintenance of the art. That's a great relief to me, since I won't live forever." He laughed.

"Mr. Phillips, you've a long way to go before then."

"Thank you Claire, I hope you're right."

"I need to get back to work Mr. Phillips. We have guests coming this evening and I want to speak to your new girl about the table presentation."

"Claire, thank you for your comments."

"My pleasure," said Claire heading for the kitchen.

Kay and the Duke

Kay watched with excitement as Edward 'Duke' Ellington and his friends finished their set at the Willard Hotel. She felt like every cell of her being was alive, even her fingernails. Duke joined her at the empty table. They had met socially, but this was the first time they had a few private moments together.

"I don't know how to explain it," she said. "I feel like I'm vibrating when I'm near a performance. My whole body is in tune with the frequency, not just my ears." She blushed, realizing that she had blurted out her feelings to the most sought-after bachelor in town. "Don't mind me, I'm talking nonsense."

"No you're not." Duke paused to select his words. "You're alive from the inside right? Not just mixing with people and things, but it's like life is trying to spring out of you. That you're part of the creation and…."

"I've got it," Kay interrupted, forgetting her embarrassment. "It's like stepping into the river of creation. The river of creative ideas – the source of all new things, songs, poems, painting, books, babies." Their eyes met.

Duke nodded in agreement, "Exactly. In the source." The rush of enthusiasm between them was replaced by a sense of kinship between souls. They sat back, in comfortable silence and watched the party attendees mingle.

"Do you think that's what is meant by, 'He brought me to the banqueting house,' in the Song of Solomon?" mused Duke.

"Maybe," said Kay. "But I have to tell you I want to feel like that all my life. My father insists that I get a college education. He's determined that I become a doctor or a lawyer or something, but that's not who I am. I want to be alive, not buried beneath a ton of books and other people's ideas. I want to create, I want to perform."

"Then do it. Nothing's stopping you. You're of age. Make your own life." As Duke said it, he resonated with Kay's struggle. He too had parents with great expectations. "Kay, I know it's not that easy. My parents want me to become an accountant. True, I'm good with math, but somehow they've got it in their heads that I'm responsible for elevating the stature of the race."

Surprised, she turned to him. "Mine too. My father believes I'm supposed to show all young negro women what a good education will mean to them. Don't get me wrong, I appreciate the opportunities a good education offers." She bit her lower lip. "I guess what I'm saying is I want to be free to make up my own mind."

Duke drew in a deep breath and exhaled. He seemed to be preparing for a feat that required exertion. "Kay, have you thought of leaving, of going north to New York? The river's always flowing there, people like us are making a go of it in Harlem. Writers, musicians, painters, you name it, everyone is showing up in Harlem." He considered her for a long moment. "It's a secret, but I'll let you know. You're the first person I've told. I'm going, Kay. Going to New York. I'm going to be a musician and if I fail, so be it. There'll always be accounting jobs. But I'll never be satisfied unless I try."

Kay's disappointment at losing her new-found friend could be heard in her whispered question, "When are you leaving?"

"September, after summer school is over. I should have enough credits to graduate. That way my family won't shoot me for leaving before I receive my degree."

Kay nodded. She felt trapped. She had two years left on her sentence. Duke read her thoughts.

"Kay, when you're ready, I'll be there. Join me. By then I'll have NY at my feet. Besides," he added, with a twinkle in his eye, "Once you arrive, who will be able to resist you, Miss Kay Johnson?"

Louvenia and the Smithsonian

"Momma, Momma." Louvenia dashed into the house, banging doors and shouting like her hair was on fire. "Momma, come quick."

"What is it?" asked Claire emerging from the kitchen her hands, wet from washing string beans for dinner.

"Momma, I got a job."

Claire smiled with relief. All this over a job. "How wonderful dear, what is it?" She hadn't seen Louvenia this happy since she'd won first prize in the science fair when she was eleven.

"At the Smithsonian. The Smithsonian. I'm a researcher at the Museum of Science. "Louvenia was overcome. She had never been so happy. She dropped into a chair at the table. She picked up a string bean from the bowl and pointed it towards her mother. "Momma, do you realize what this means?"

"Actually dear, I don't. What does it mean?"

Louvenia leapt from the chair. "It means, I'll be categorizing and working with all of the inventions ever created here in this country and many from other countries as well. That I'll touch and catalog every modern convenience that has ever come into existence. I'll be the docent that explains how men and women of inspiration brought an original idea into the world." Louvenia sat back and noted her mother's face. She still wasn't reaching her mother with the significance of her words.

"Momma, objects have energy. They have memory. Spending time with those objects one could start to understand the source of their inspiration." She wasn't sure she had explained herself clearly. "Momma, this means that my own experiments will improve. That I'll be around the very objects that will inspire me to new levels."

"That's nice dear, but is it better than the job cousin Walker offered you?" It was an innocent enough question, but Louvenia responded with a grimace and Claire watched her daughter depart into another realm, although she was still sitting only a few feet away.

Louvenia whispered, "Momma, don't you know me?" She stood up and left the room. Her joy had evaporated, leaving behind a chill, in spite of the warm, spring-like day.

Winter 1919

Emmet comes home

"He's here! He's here!" shouted Kay from the third floor. "Emmet's walking up the street. Emmet's home!"

Louvenia raced up from the basement. Benjamin rose from the couch where he was taking his Sunday afternoon nap. Claire ran from the kitchen pulling off her apron. She went to the hall mirror to check her hair. She turned and saw Lou, covered with dust and a dirty face.

"Louvenia, is that any way to greet your brother?"

"Emmet won't mind, he's seen far worse where he's been."

Claire didn't want to consider what her son had experienced, not yet. She was so thankful he was home.

Benjamin opened the front door expecting to greet Emmet. Then Kay yelled from the upstairs window.

"Emmet, Emmet you're home!"

Benjamin heard her feet pounding down the three flights of stairs. Without pausing at the doorway Kay, not fully dressed, pushed past her father, her loose hair flying.

"Kay Johnson, you get back here this minute," shouted her father.

She paid no attention. Kay ran into the street and launched herself into the arms of her brother. Benjamin willed himself to keep from running after her. He ached to join his daughter, to weep and wail and thank God for his son's safe return. Memories of Roy and June blurred his vision. Benjamin had lived with the assumption that he'd never see Emmet again. But here he was, walking up the street with one arm around Kay and the other toting a duffel bag. Tears formed in Benjamin's eyes as he stepped back into the house to compose himself.

Claire, standing beside Benjamin, understood as her husband turned away. She remained rooted in the doorway, but Lou could wait no longer. Covered in soot, Lou bolted and tackled her brother and Kay on the sidewalk, causing the three to land in a heap. Lou joyously kissed her brother's face. As they stood, Emmet picked up a sister in each arm and carried them up the porch stairs. He set them down in front of his mother. The girls ducked out from under his arms.

Emmet fell to his knees at the sight of his mother, unable to maintain the manly composure he had hoped to display. He grabbed her around the legs and held her.

"Momma."

Claire removed her son's cap and stroked his head as she had done a hundred times when he was young. "It's all right son, you're home." Reluctantly Emmet stood, afraid he would be overcome with tears. He kissed her cheek and asked, "Where's Poppa?"

"In the parlor. He's waiting for you."

Emmet walked into the front room and saw his father staring out the window.

"Sir?"

Benjamin turned to face him. "Emmet. Welcome home, son." Emotion filled his words. Benjamin tried to remain stately, but as he reached out to shake his son's hand, he suddenly grabbed the boy by the shoulder and pulled him into a bear hug. He was so relieved at Emmet's return, he thought he might never be able to let him go.

Kay and Emmet

Two days later Kay still couldn't be happier that her brother was home. Of all her siblings, they were the closest. Kay had a sense of adventure, an appetite for life that Emmet found contagious.

As he went upstairs to his room he paused at her bedroom doorway to find her painting her fingernails. She looked up and smiled, "Emmet darling, so many glorious things have happened while you were away." She finished her nails and began to blow on them. Do you know about radio?"

He entered the pink room and sat on the edge of the bed. "You mean short wave radio for sending telegrams?"

"No silly, for playing music. There's a new company called Radio Corporation of America or RCA for short. They have these big boxes that transmit music. You just flip a switch and music plays all day long."

"And this is good, why?" asked Emmet wanting to get a rise out of his little sister.

"Why? Are you crazy? Now you don't have to get up and change the record after every song." She took on a mock grown-up face for a moment. "There's nothing more disruptive when spooning than to have to get up and change the record." She laughed, her mirth brightening the room.

"So what else have I missed, little sister?"

"Where should I begin?" She glanced around the room for clues. "You must've noticed EVERYONE has a car. We're the only family around without one, but now that you're home, I bet Dad will buy a beauty. The Pierce Arrow is a favorite, but I'm partial to Apperson 8. For the owner who considers his car something more than a mere conveyance, a car that reflects patrician taste." She giggled after reciting the ad. While considering, her freshly polished fingernails she added, "Once we get a car, I'm going to take a class at the YWCA on how to fix it. Then I can get a driver's license and not worry about getting a flat."

Emmet laughed. "I'd like to see you change a tire! I can't imagine you messing up those pretty nails." He took hold of her hand to evaluate the job. "Since when did you start painting your fingers and how did you convince the parents it was all right?"

Kay pouted. "Don't you like the color? I guess you're right, makeup and such personal adornments were forbidden before you left. But with Aunt Walker sending over samples all the time, trying to get Momma and Lou to come work with her, I guess the parental resolve weakened." She didn't mention the correlation between their parents' rules relaxing and the deaths of Roy and June. Lou and Kay knew that they could ask for just about anything now, but did not take advantage of their parents sorrow. Rather than explain, she asked Emmet sincerely, "What are you going to do now that you're home? You know there aren't any jobs."

"Let's not talk about me yet. What else have you been up to?"

He stretched out on the bed, propping up his head on his hand, but careful to keep his shoes off the satin bedspread.

Kay followed suit and returned to her bubbly self. "Well, I've been sort of dating this delicious gentleman. He's from the District and…" her voice dropped to that of a conspirator. She even peeked over her shoulder. "…he's a musician."

"You don't say?"

She nodded in assent. "Yep, he plays the piano, and well, lots of instruments, but he's going to be a great bandleader. That's his goal."

"What type of music does he play?"

Kay stared at Emmet with incredulity.

"Jazz, silly. Where have you been?" As soon as she said it she knew how ridiculous she sounded and they both laughed.

"What's this Mozart's name?"

"Edward Ellington, but everyone calls him Duke. You'll meet him tomorrow night. We're going out to the Washington Hotel. I'm expecting you to be there so I can show you off to my friends."

"Well I…"

"There's no 'Well I….' You're home and need some educatin' as to the ways of the youth in DC."

"Yes ma'am, I'll be there."

"You better be."

"Kay? Emmet? Are you up there? Dinner's ready," called Claire.

"She still cooks for you? You're old enough to cook for yourself."

"She likes it or she's used to it. Whatever, I know not to look a gift horse in the mouth." Kay lunged at Emmet and tickled him, and then leapt from the bed, straightened her stockings and garters and bounded down the stairs for dinner.

Spring 1919

BOSTON

Chinatown

Patrick was standing near the phone when the call came in.

"12th precinct, Sergeant Kelly here."

"Patrick it's you. That's grand. Patrick, it's Gerald Murphy. I've good news." Gerald's words were slurred and Patrick suspected he'd been drinking.

"Gerald, does the news have anythin' to do with the fact that you're not goin' to be here in twelve minutes when your shift starts?"

"As a matter of fact, Patrick, my wife had twins."

"Blessin's to God. Congratulations, Gerald. I hope they aren't as ugly as you."

"Thank the Lord no, they're little cherubs, a boy and a girl." Patrick heard Gerald take another swig from a bottle. "Patrick, I need to ask a favor."

"Be out with it."

"My wife had a hard time. The doctors say I should stick around. Could you take my shift, Patrick? I'm sorry to be askin' so last minute."

Patrick didn't hesitate, even though he'd just finished a sixteen-hour shift of his own.

Spring 1919

"Consider it done, Gerald, and give my love to Donna. Let her know our prayers are with her."

"Thank you Patrick." And the phone clicked off. Patrick realized he wasn't sure what Gerald's beat was these days. The department was in chaos, as everyone tried to attend all the necessary meetings in preparation for the new union. Men filled in for each other all over the city. Patrick went to the roster and was surprised to discover Gerald was scheduled to work in Chinatown in order to cover for Bill Mayo. Chinatown was a tough beat. Prostitution, slavery, drugs, gambling and sweatshops. An officer needed his wits about him to work Chinatown.

"McIntyre, is the coffee fresh?" Patrick called out to the desk sergeant. He would need a cup or two before heading downtown.

Warlords

Murphy's assignment was a straight beat walk. Patrick was to patrol the sidewalks of a ten-block area and make sure there wasn't any trouble brewing. He began the shift at midnight and over the next eight hours he would test the doors of retail establishments to ensure they were locked. He'd worked the district, years ago, and was grateful he hadn't since.

The weather was with him, being cool and dry. He could never get used to the smells that assailed him in Chinatown. They were pungent, full of unidentifiable spices. Patrick was old-fashioned, or so his kids told him. He didn't like to eat anything he couldn't name. So he never indulged in the food at the Lucky Pearl or Little Dragon.

Two hours into the shift Patrick heard something. The noise might have been two cats fighting over scraps, but he had learned to trust his instincts. As he walked along Kneeland Street he heard a scuffling of shoes. The sound came from the alley between a restaurant and a cleaners. Most of the buildings were three or four story walkups. The upper floors contained sweatshops of illegal aliens working off their passage to America. But at this time of night, the shops were usually closed.

Patrick stopped and listened carefully. He heard the faint sound of chimes, or maybe music. He inched toward the sound. It was com-

74

ing from a basement. He suspected it was an opium den and knew he should call for backup. But he didn't want to be wrong, so he ventured forward to see.

He crept down the metal stairs that led to the basement door. Now the sound of a phonograph playing oriental music was clear. He heard a muffled cry. Patrick's adrenaline kicked in and every muscle in his body tensed up. Someone was in trouble. He was sure of it. He drew his gun and kicked open the door.

The opium crib contained a series of bunk beds with half a dozen stoned patrons, completely unaware of his presence. In the middle of the room stood two young men in traditional silk pajamas. They were slim and muscular. Between them they held a beautiful young Chinese girl of perhaps sixteen.

The men spoke to each other in Mandarin.

"I don't know what you're sayin', but put your hands up." Patrick motioned toward the ceiling with his gun.

The men attempted to argue in Chinese.

"I don't care what you be tellin' me. Let her go." Patrick pointed the gun at the man with the deepest scowl and reached for the girl. The second man released and raised his hands like he'd seen in the movies. But the fierce one locked eyes with Patrick and said in perfect English, "I'll get you for this."

Patrick pulled the girl toward him. She was trembling. Still holding her, he backed out the door and slammed it behind them. The girl wore only a slip, but Patrick couldn't concern himself with that now. He knew that in order to survive he'd need to reach the police call box on the edge of Chinatown. At fifty-seven he hadn't much call to run, but he ran tonight and the lithe sprite beside him ran even faster. By the time he reached the call box she'd run down an alley and disappeared. Patrick was relieved she was gone. He suspected she was an illegal and she'd been through plenty tonight without being put in a detention cell and then deported.

"Boston 23rd? This is Patrick Kelly in Chinatown. I've an opium den and slave traders at Kneeland and Tremont. Send over a paddy wagon and four or five men with a photographer." Patrick suspected the perpetrators would be gone by the time the wagon got there, but he was sure some society elite would still be lounging in the bunks and the police force needed to cultivate all the friends it could these days.

The Bunker Hill Monument

Thomas was sitting on a bench at the base of Bunker Hill Monument as Annie Macy and Helen Keller approached. He would often look out at this very spot from his boarding house window. Never for a moment had he considered the thrill he might experience at the appearance of the enchanting Helen.

"Mrs. Macy, Miss Keller, good day to you ladies." Thomas stood and removed his hat. There was a chill in the air, but he was grateful for it, as he felt himself flush.

"Good morrow to you Mr. Kelly. What a fine obelisk you have here." Annie Sullivan Macy leaned back to take in the top of the Bunker Hill monument. "Tall too."

"Yes, we in America don't like to do anything on a small scale."

"I'd say," responded Annie. As she spoke Helen tapped her hand. "Miss Keller would like to know why you've brought us here."

"With Miss Keller's permission I'd like to take her to the top."

Annie dutifully communicated the request to Helen, but then spoke directly to Thomas. "Sir, you'll not be getting' me up there. Even if there's an elevator."

"Mrs. Macy, it's perfectly safe and I thought it'd be something Miss Keller and I could experience alone." Helen was nodding, but Annie was not convinced.

Thomas went on, "It's not about the view, which is excellent, but rather about the experience of climbing the two hundred and ninety stairs."

"Mr. Kelly," Annie began.

Helen stopped Annie mid-sentence, "I'll do it," she said.

Annie shrugged and said, "I don't know why she's doin' this, but she be askin' you to know what's this about?"

"Mrs. Macy, is there some way I could communicate with Miss Keller directly?"

"Aye, Miss Keller has made the same request. Let's all sit on the bench and I'll teach you the basics."

Helen sat between her teacher and Thomas.

"First, Helen should get use to your face and voice. She'll explore both with her left hand while she holds out her right to receive messages." Once Helen's hands were in place Annie spoke to Thomas, "Say my name and then Miss Keller's. Our names are the foundation from which we work."

Thomas did as he was told.

"Now start telling us about this set of stairs to the sky," said Annie.

"It's a monument or rather, as you said Mrs. Macy, an obelisk that was built on the site of an important battle of the Revolutionary War. The structure was erected in 1842 and is two hundred and twenty one feet tall, half the height of the Washington Monument in D.C."

"If you could speak a little slower Mr. Kelly," said Annie. "Miss Keller would like to know which was built first, this monument, or the one in D.C.?"

"The Bunker Hill Monument. The one in D.C. didn't even begin construction until 1848 and was not completed until 1885, thirty seven years later." Thomas's heart was pounding. He hoped Helen couldn't sense it.

"Mr. Kelly, let's teach you a few words." Annie opened his hand and began spelling out words. "This means 'Stop'. In case she needs to catch her breath. Here is 'Let's go back'. In case she realizes what a fool's notion this is midway up. Here's 'Continue,' because she's a stubborn mule." Helen had placed her fingers on Annie's lips and now slapped her companion's arm at being called a mule.

"I got it," said Thomas. He stood and bowed to the ladies. Helen reached out for his arm.

Her hand upon his forearm felt like a precious bird perched ready to take flight.

Thomas started for the monument and turned back, "Mrs. Macy, this may take a while. Shall we plan to meet you here at half past the hour?"

"You needn't worry. I'll be here Mr. Kelly. You just take good care of her." As she watched Helen leave with Thomas she felt a pang of jealousy, for what she could see needed no sight. Lightening had struck Helen and Thomas and they were a couple. Annie felt the mixed emotions of loss and happiness. She stood up and went inside the small museum, adjacent to the monument, so that she could answer Helen's questions about the famous battle later.

Patricia for office

"Can you believe it?" said Patricia, setting aside the paper and pulling off her reading gloves in agitation. "Can you believe that English and French women get the right to vote before us? America, the great example of democracy."

Her brother quipped back, "What more do you want? The Sullivan Act is repealed. Women can smoke in public now."

Across their parents' modest parlor Patricia glared at Thomas.

"Emma Goldman and Margaret Sanger were arrested again this week for speaking about birth control. What are you fancy lawyers doing about that?" As Patricia spoke she felt her blood reddening her face in agitation.

"Don't turn all strawberry on me, you're right. Ours is a backward, provincial, patriarchal society."

Patricia waited for his amused comeback that she would once again shout down.

Instead Thomas leaned forward and asked, "Pat how old are you 25, 26? You're not going to marry so why not fight us? Get a law degree and take us to court. Don't leave your future in the hands of men. Think of Lady Astor. She's going to be elected into British parliament. She'll be the first woman ever, and the kicker is, she's American. Come on Pat, you can do it."

She thought he was still teasing her, but wasn't sure. "You mean lie and cheat and be a general scoundrel like the rest of you politicians?" she grinned, waiting. Then it became evident he was serious.

"I mean it Pat. You'd be a great senator. Women make up fifty-two percent of the population in this country. You're a smart girl, a fighter. Go make a difference." He leaned over and picked up the paper she had just set down. She offered him the gloves to protect his hands from the printer's ink, but he waved them off.

She asked, "You're serious? Ma and Da would throw a fit."

From behind the paper he said, "And when has that ever stopped you?"

"But where? What school would take me?"

He lowered the paper to answer her. "Who wouldn't take you? There are several women's colleges in Boston and Cambridge or you could become a cause célèbre and storm into a men's school if you wanted. Hell, make a stink and go to Harvard or Boston College. Some notoriety would help you land a prestigious job after you graduated. If I were you, that's what I would do." He lifted the paper and returned to the headlines.

It was true she had no intention of marrying. She liked public speaking and motivating large crowds, but she didn't see how that translated into politics. She said aloud, "But if I were a politician wouldn't it all be about compromise? I wouldn't be any good at that. I suppose I might be able to motivate and mobilize people, but I don't have the patience to sit down and make deals about issues that are important to me."

"What?" Thomas was reading the paper and had lost track of the conversation. "What are you going on about?"

"I'm not sure I'd make a good politician. I haven't the temperament to compromise."

"You admit it! I've been telling you that for years." He slapped his knee ready to laugh, but held back. Both sister and brother recognized this was the first serious and real conversation they'd ever had with one another.

"Sorry." He sat back in the chair, set aside the paper and steepled his fingers on his chest. "You're right. The fine art of negotiation is not in your blood. You're more the bomb throwing type." She started to argue. "I don't mean it in bad way. I don't mean you'd hurt anyone, but that you're determined to make people reconsider the beliefs they hold dear."

He paused and considered for a moment. "So how are your skills best applied to move the masses in order to reach the politicians that enact the laws?"

Patricia stared at him, stunned they were having this conversation. For a moment she believed she was dreaming.

"I've got it." Thomas erupted and jumped up from his chair. He knelt down before her. "Patricia, you should run for president." He gently placed his finger to her lips to prevent her from arguing.

"Think about it. What better forum from which to gain national visibility without having to pay the price of politics? You could reach millions with your message."

She said tentatively, "You do realize it's been done before?"

Thomas responded without hesitation, "Virginia Woodruff, 1867. She would have won if she'd been as good a public speaker as you are. She had the money, but not the looks or the fire."

"Thank you brother, but Miss Woodruff was gorgeous."

"Poppycock. Besides your greater beauty will be revealed as you speak. I'll ask around and determine what party is considering an unusual candidate that'll promote their plank. You should consider law school and meanwhile, take some classes."

"In what?"

"Elocution, public speaking, dress, hair, etc. All the things people notice when someone stands in front of them."

"I don't care about being pretty."

"It doesn't matter what you care about, but what the audience will focus on and it will not be your message at first, but how you look, then how you sound. A fraction of what you say will seep into their awareness. That's why politicians repeat themselves, ad nauseam, because it takes six or seven times before their message finds purchase in the minds of the audience."

"You talk about all of this as if it were a science."

"Don't be naïve, dear sister. Public speaking is a science. Orators have been presenting since the beginning of time. Critics meanwhile have sat on the sidelines determining what works and what doesn't and then writing about it."

"It never occurred to me."

"Get thee to a library little sister, get thee to a library. Meanwhile I'll work on where and when you should run."

He stood and patted her shoulder. Then he went upstairs for a nap before Sunday dinner.

Thomas, Patrick and the law

"That was a fine Sunday dinner," said Thomas, feeling content and full. Noting that he and his father had the parlor to themselves he ventured, "Da, could I chat with you about something?"

Patrick Sr. stopped reading the sports page, surprised that Thomas still wanted his opinion about anything.

"I'm all ears son, what is it?"

"I have a difficult decision to make about my career."

"I'm happy to hear you out, but I doubt I'll be of much…"

Thomas cut him off, "Da I need your common sense. You're the most practical man I know."

"I'm all yours." Patrick set aside his paper and turned to give Thomas his full attention.

"You know that I've studied international law and have found it agreeable. My current firm has invited me to work on the Versailles Treaty, which is a great honor. And I've been asked to go to Europe next month to participate in the negotiations." Thomas paused, still uncertain how to describe his feelings. Patrick waited patiently.

"I don't want it." Thomas's face flushed with embarrassment. "It's not that I couldn't do it, nor that I wouldn't find it interesting. What's more, it would establish my position in international law, but it's just not where my interests lie. I want to pursue labor law."

Patrick nodded. He sensed there was more and now was not the time to interrupt.

"With the reception that Wilson received in France, the treaty is a fait accompli. Besides, now it's no longer about the law, but politics. And I have very little interest in that."

Patrick smiled. He couldn't imagine an Irish lad, much less an Irish lawyer, not interested in politics. He reminded himself the boy was still young.

Patrick asked, "Labor law? Meanin' what exactly?"

"You know there's so much unrest everywhere, the Carmen strike, the firemen, the barrel makers, steel, coal, you name it. Everyone's going on strike. I suspect it's only a matter of time before the police are out on the picket lines."

"Nonsense son, we can't strike, we're civil servants. If we strike who'd keep the peace?"

"Nevertheless. I think I'd be more useful helping to interpret the needs of the working men, the industrialists and the captains of industry."

"Captains are they now?" Patrick chuckled and reached for his pipe.

"It's a figure of speech Da," said Thomas not wanting to be distracted. "I believe I'd be of more use staying here in Boston."

Patrick noted all of Thomas's pent up energy, waiting to spill out and convince someone of something. Patrick was proud of his son, Harriet's son. Thomas was a good man.

"Thomas, I have two questions for ye. Are you ready lad?"

Thomas's face filled with anticipation, like a cocker spaniel eager to please. "Yes Da."

"The first question's about the law. Do ye love the work? Does it bring you to your feet in the mornin' and is it the last thing you think about at night?"

"No Da, international law doesn't engage me any more. But the complexities of labor law enthrall me."

"So you 'ave your answer. Labor law it is."

Thomas nodded, satisfied. He would give his notice the following week so that they could find a replacement quickly. "What was the second question Da?"

"Ah, the second question is closer to my heart. What's her name?"

Thomas was taken aback.

"Who?"

"The girl, the girl you've fallen in love with and don't want to leave?"

Thomas sputtered and shook his head, certain he had misheard his father.

"Thomas Daniel Kelly, don't forget I was a young man myself once. I know love when it's lookin' me in the eye. Who is she and is she beautiful?"

"Da, how can you bring that up when I'm being so serious about my career?"

"And you think love isn't a serious matter? Just wait until she

82

breaks your heart and then tell me it ain't serious. Come on son. I've watched you fallin' for this girl. Who is she? Why haven't you brought her 'round? Why keep her a secret? Do you suppose we won't approve? Is she a Protestant?"

Thomas hesitated, but then caved in. "You're right Da. As usual. You should've been a detective."

"You needn't be a detective to know when your boy falls in love. All you need is eyes. Now tell me about her."

"She's not like other girls…" Patrick smiled. Thomas continued, "No Da, she really isn't, she's blind and deaf." Sensing a shift in his father's mood Thomas hurried on, "but once you meet her you'll realize she's the most remarkable woman. She's capable of great thoughts, perceives my moods without ever seeing my face. She beholds the world through her fingertips and brings a fresh perspective that seeing people never notice. In short, Da, she's extraordinary."

In a soft voice Patrick asked "And ye want to marry her?"

Thomas's head snapped to attention. He had never seriously considered marriage before, but as his father said it, he realized that was exactly what he wanted. He wanted Helen with him always.

"Yes Da, I guess I do," Thomas responded, in awe of his father.

"Was she blind at birth or did it happen later?"

"Later, she had an illness."

"Good, that means your babies will have sight and be at the same risk as any other child bein' born." Patrick's thoughts reached for his other children now gone, but he refused to follow their memories. He wanted to stay focused on Thomas. "Does she love ye?"

Thomas sat back from the edge of his chair and considered the question. After a moment he leaned forward, "I couldn't say. I know she's taken with me, but in love? I don't know. She has a lot of beaus."

"What's that you say? A deaf and blind girl with suitors? She must be somethin' special."

"She is."

"So when are we goin' to meet her?"

Thomas' face looked like he was five years old.

"I don't know how Ma will take it. She's sort of…" He paused and came up with, "set in her ways."

"That she is, but all she's ever wanted is your happiness. She'll love your girl as much as you do, once she realizes how important she is to you. By the way, what's this Madonna's name?"

"Helen, Da."

"Our very own Helen of Troy." Thomas beamed and Patrick thought to himself. 'The face that launched a thousand ships and a mother's disdain.' Patrick anticipated rough seas ahead, but knew his family could weather them.

The threat

"Nana, Nana a man gave me a note." Liam ran into the house breathless and unaware of the mud he tracked across the floor.

"Liam Harry," Harriet responded when she saw her clean floor muddied. "You go back outside and wipe your feet. Look at the work you've caused me. I've a mind to have you clean up this mess." Grabbing his arm at the elbow and almost lifting Liam off his feet she forced the boy to go back outside and right his wrong.

"There now. Here be a doormat. And what do ye do with it?"

With a sullen expression Liam said, "Wipe my feet Ma'am."

"That's right. I want you to do it so much it becomes second nature, like crossing yourself when you enter church."

"Yes Ma'am." Harriet loved this child more than life itself, to see him sad broke her heart. He had been so happy when he came looking for her.

"Let's go sit in the parlor and you can deliver your message like a grown up."

Liam perked up at the thought of 'visiting' in the parlor.

"Yes Ma'am'" He raced to his favorite chair and waited until his Nana sat in hers.

"Now, what is it Liam?"

"A man came up to me in the street."

"What man?"

"I don't know, he was big and wore nice new clothes. He wore one of those funny round hats."

"A bowler?' she asked tentatively.

"Yes, that's it, a bowling ... he gave this to me to give to you. What does it say?'

Harriet took the paper from Liam's hand. He didn't sit back down, but stood beside her chair. The note was written on quality paper, but bore no address or clue as to the sender. Upon its single sheet were words written in perfect penmanship.

Harriet Kelly
Stop your work with the Anti Saloon League
or harm will come to your boy.

That was all of it. Harriet assumed it meant Liam, but then there was also Thomas. Who would send such madness? Who could be threatened by her activities now that her battle was won. She went to the phone and called the police station.

Harriet tried to hide her fear as she spoke to Liam. "Bring me your favorite book child and I'll read to ye."

"Yes Ma'am," he said with a grin as he ran upstairs. Harriet stepped into the parlor and picked up the phone. The operator answered and connected her to Patrick's precinct.

"Hello, is Patrick Callahan Kelly there please?"

A moment later Patrick's calming voice was on the phone.

Harriet tried to suppress the hysteria she felt. "Patrick, you must come home right now. Something has happened."

"For the love of God, what woman!" Patrick knew he couldn't survive the loss of another loved one.

"Everyone is all right, but Liam just brought me a note. I'm sure it's nothing, but the writer says he's going to hurt our sons."

Patrick hesitated. He had no more sons, and was aware of it every day of his life. And then with a pang of guilt he realized it could be Thomas or Liam. "I'll be right there, Harriet. Don't you be openin' the door for a soul."

"Yes Da."

Harriet called to Liam in her sweetest voice, "Liam, 'ave ye found your book son?" Harriet wanted the boy near. She knew she couldn't live under the weight of any more heartache.

Spring 1919

Patrick's coffee

Patrick was half-asleep, but he could hear Mrs. O'Doul's rooster crowing next door. The sound transported him back to the County Kerry farm of his youth. As he tried to return to pleasant memories of Ireland, the images that emerged were cold and desperate, accompanied by the pain of an empty stomach. Patrick's American stomach grumbled and he knew it was time to get up.

He carefully got out of bed, so as not to disturb Harriet. She had been sleeping fitfully lately. He suspected she was going through the change, though they never spoke of it. She was more sharp-tongued than usual, her features pinched. Harriet's inner demons plagued her without mercy. He hoped they might be kept at bay with a few more hours of sleep. In an effort to keep peace in the house he had taken to making the morning coffee.

Patrick stepped into his slippers and picked up his bathrobe from the chair by the bed, pulling it on as he walked downstairs to the kitchen. The morning air had seeped into the house making it damp and cold like a Boston fog. Patrick opened the backdoor and went out to the woodpile for some logs to stoke the oven. Despite being the month of May it smelled like snow. 'Aye it's Boston, anything's possible,' thought Patrick, as he stoked the stove with wood and lit the kindling. Soon the kitchen would be transformed, warm and pleasant.

He pulled down the can of Maxwell House coffee and scooped out five rounded spoonfuls into the percolator basket. He threw in an extra scoop at the end, enjoying the extravagance. He always suspected Harriet scrimped on the coffee. Her's was a nasty weak dishwater-tasting brew that Patrick never complained about, but threw down the sink when her back was turned.

The bare ceiling bulb cast harsh shadows about the room. With the first pink rays of sunlight Patrick turned it off. With the kitchen now warm and filled with the enticing smell of coffee, Patrick realized the one thing missing was eggs. He pulled out the big iron skillet, decided to splurge and took the bacon from the icebox. He knew Harriet saved breakfast meats for Sundays after mass.

"You live but once. And if today is the day...."

He wasn't going to worry about work yet. Thoughts about his job throbbed in him like a toothache. He pushed away his worries. He began to cook the bacon as the coffee came to a boil. He suspected it would not be long now before Harriet and Patricia would be down.

Harriet was the first blurry-eyed Kelly to appear in the doorway. Not yet fully awake, she began to complain, "Patrick Callahan Kelly what've you done? I was savin' that bacon as ye well know." But even as the scolding passed through her lips they curled into a smile. The kitchen was warm, the coffee smelled rich, and breakfast was on its way.

"Are you daft man? I always said so." She went to the breadbox and pulled out a fresh loaf she had made the day before. She cut it into wide slices and brought out honey and jam. Patrick kissed her on the cheek as she passed. She shrugged, "If it's to be our last meal we should eat like kings. Don't ye agree Da?"

"I do." With spatula in hand, he pulled out a chair at the kitchen table for her. "Have a seat while I finish your breakfast."

"And when was the last time you made me breakfast?" asked Harriet.

"It's been too long, maybe I should give up the police work and go in for being a short order cook. I know a place in Southie wantin' someone."

"You'd be goin' all the way to Southie for work? Is that so you can poison people you dinna kin?" She teased.

"Leave us say I figure I'd better try out my epicurean delights on strangers first."

"Epicurean delights is it now?"

Patricia shuffled into the kitchen. Her reading glasses were still perched on her head, where they must have sat all night. Her hair was unruly and her faced unwashed.

Harriet said, "Aren't ye a sight."

"My little princess" said Patrick hoping to avoid any fight that might spring up between mother and daughter, a volatile mix on the best of days.

"Good morning Ma, Da. Coffee please."

"Aye, the coffee, I almost forgot," said Patrick.

Spring 1919

Harriet stood and reached into the cabinet, pulling out three large mugs. "Let me," Patrick said. He picked up the potholder Harriet had crocheted and grabbed hold of the coffeepot handle to pour the steaming brew.

"Ta-Dah." Patricia blew across the top of the cup before sipping it.

The three Kelly's held their tongues while they drank their coffee as the golden light of morning filled the kitchen.

The Masses

"Greedy fools. Sent our boys into Russia to destroy 'communism', instead of fighting the Germans. Just because Lenin refused to shed the blood of his countrymen in order to appease the allies in their African land grab," said Max Eastman.

"Yeah, but we shouldn't discuss that, Max. We know more than the average Joe. They think their boys went to Paris. They don't realize how many found their way to Siberia and Petrograd," said Jack Reed.

"The Masses," said Max. "That would be a great magazine title. We'll speak for all the people. For the citizens without a voice." Eastman pulled a reporter's notebook from his pocket and began scribbling notes.

"Great Max, but lay off the altruistic crap. Let's just tell it the way it is. The industrialists made off with the loot during the war and now we're left with nothing but anger." Reed took a pretzel from the bowl on the table. He pointed at Max with it and continued, "The Masses. Aren't you afraid people will mistake it for a religious paper?"

"So what if they do? We're certainly proselytizing. It's the religion of Red."

"Right. What we need now is a lawyer. Someone to keep us and our converts out of jail."

Max turned to the bar. "Barkeep, how about another round for my friend and me?"

"Is that milk or water for your college friend there?" Several of the other patrons laughed at O'Malley's joke.

"You tell me. We'll take whatever you're serving today."

O'Malley pulled down a bottle of his best whiskey. His regulars would never pay for the good stuff.

"Here you go lads," said O'Malley bringing the bottle to the table. "There's plenty more where that came from." He slapped Max on the back, spilling his drink on to the floor.

Jack asked, "Could you bring us a few more glasses, so we can share some of this fine whiskey with your other customers?"

Everyone in the bar was paying attention now.

Bolshevism

Thomas was waiting in O'Malley's for his father to get off duty. The townie bar was full of off-duty cops, except for the two men seated in the corner. The quality in their jackets and the tailoring of their shirts showed they weren't from Charlestown. A half-finished bottle of O'Malley's finest whiskey sat in front of them, along with a few shot glasses.

Thomas moved to a table that was closer to the men, in an effort to hear the stranger's conversation. Visitors were discouraged at O'Malley's. If these two men had remained in the bar, they'd have to have a reason. The handsome gentleman wearing an embroidered vest and tweed coat was carrying on an animated conversation with Joe Nixon, a police officer who had experienced more than his share of heartache.

"That's what Max and I are saying," said the stranger. "That's what I'm saying. You make a deal with Frank McCarthy of the American Federation of Labor and sure, you'll get a pay raise and maybe a paid holiday or two. But the Industrial Workers of the World will treat you like men, like human beings. We're going to merge all the unions together. Make one big union that the capitalists can't ignore. The IWW is going to set the whole economic structure of this country on its ear and make the division of profits fair. In the end we're all going to be working for the same thing. A healthier society. A place where each and every one of us can bring up our children with pride."

"And how many wee ones 'ave ye at home?" asked Joe Murphy, still covered with soot from his shift at the fire station. "Most of these lads have between five and ten children apiece. That is, the ones they know about." The men at the bar laughed and nodded.

"Excuse me?"

"Ye heard me man. Done a lot of labor with your hands 'ave ye? Seen a lot of babies through their dyin' years and then later through their growin' years?" Jack Reed and Max Eastman didn't respond.

"Nay, I dinna think so. What's more, I don't want to hear your Red rot. Just drink your drink and pipe down."

"Give 'em a break," said Thomas Kelly. "The man's right, but his argument's weak. He doesn't know he needs a sledgehammer for the likes of you. What the gentlemen are saying is that the IWW will watch out for your safety, ensure you make more money, and provide you with a job where no one can fire you because they don't like your looks. Except maybe you, Lou Connahan. You're one ugly son-of-a-bitch." A few men at the bar chuckled.

One called out, "What's different in what these lads are sayin' versus that AFL fellow, Tommy? It all sounds the same to me."

Thomas stood up and addressed the men who were listening, "Let's call a spade, a spade. These men are Bolsheviks." The room quieted, chairs scraped against the floor as their occupants strained to see a real Red. Thomas turned to Reed and Eastman and asked, "Do I misspeak, gentlemen?"

Jack answered, "You're right mister. That is, unless you're contemplating having us lynched."

"As you can see," Thomas continued, "they have no horns or tails, but they do spout a policy that this administration and businesses find frightening. In fact, more terrifying than our recent plague or the war. They speak of shared profits. Making every business one that's owned by the people."

"Horseshit. What blarney are you spoutin' lad? We're police officers. There be no profits in what we do."

"Don't be a dolt, Fred, these men are talking about eliminating your jobs." The men began to shout epithets at each other, as a dozen conversations broke out.

"Hear me out," shouted Thomas, raising his hands above his head. "Get the blood out of your eyes. If we followed their logic, there wouldn't be a need for policemen because there wouldn't be any poor. You lunks wouldn't have any warehouses to protect, or anarchists to chase down because you'd own as much as old Mr. Chatham up on Bunker Hill. We'd all be equals. I want you to stop and consider how much of your time this past week was spent protecting some rich man's wealth instead of helping people?" A murmur passed through the crowd.

"That's right. Most of you are earning a few pennies of overtime for standing in front of the houses of prominent citizens to ensure no one throws a brick or bomb into their window. The question is, why are people throwing things? It's because they work for those men and don't earn enough to feed their families." Thomas turned to one of the bar's regulars.

"Joe, you work in Chinatown right? You've seen how those sweatshop owners take advantage of the women. They're nothing more than slaves, chained to their sewing machines without ventilation, sanitation or a living wage. That's what these two men are getting at. They're saying you can sign the AFL's agreement, but you're still working for the rich man. But now you've got to pay the union too. These men here are saying that the rich man's success should be your success."

"Have you gone daft Thomas? Your Da'll kill you, he hears you spoutin' this rot," said an old timer.

"Not likely Mr. Kennedy. Do you all know where my brother Timothy died?" The room went silent. Evoking the name of the dead was a serious matter. "I know you're aware he died in the war, but where?" No one ventured an answer.

"In Russia," Thomas paused for effect. "Our government was more afraid of Bolshevism than the Kaiser. As were all the ally countries and Germany too. Everyone stopped fighting each other for a moment and went after the Bolsheviks because they posed a greater threat to capitalist concerns, without which there could be no war. They needed to protect the interests of a group of men that represent less than one percent of our country. Those rich bastards sent our American boys to die in a war in Russia that most of us were never told about." Thomas's face reddened with emotion.

Spring 1919

"I'd listen to what these men have to say, because it'll not be long before your bosses tell you to shut them up. These two are more dangerous than the Krauts, or the poor, or the man set to break into your house. These are the men who work to ensure you are treated with dignity and respect and for that they will be damned to hell."

Thomas sat down and the bar erupted in conversation. Max reached over and shook Thomas' hand, "Quite the speech, mister. Can I buy you a beer?" Thomas was angry. Angry for the waste, for all the wrong decisions made by Wilson. He needed to get out of there.

"No, but thanks. I need to go walk off some of this steam. I'd recommend you leave before these tough guys decide I was full of Tommy Rot and they string you up after all."

With that, Thomas went to the bar and caught O'Malley's attention, "Tell my Da I'll see him at home."

Curtis's decision

"Discipline. Discipline is what these men need," said Chief of Police Curtis as he read the reports on his desk. "A raise indeed. They should feel honored to be on the force."

"I believe they do chief," answered Sean Connor, his aide. "All they want is for you to go out to some of the station houses and see the conditions for yourself. Also, I have confirmed that the men haven't received a raise in five years. They chose to have the money go towards the war effort. Almost all of them had sons in the war."

"Fine. But why complain now? They should stand proud. Things are getting better. I'm sure we'll address their needs in the coming years."

"But sir, with the post-war inflation, they can't feed their families. Most policemen are making less than twenty-five cents an hour, and that includes men who have been on the force for ten years. Consider Patrick Kelly," said Connor, pointing to the dossier on Curtis's desk. "He's served on the force for almost twenty eight years and he's making less than my cleaning lady. What's more, he has or had six children."

"You pay your cleaning lady too much. What do you mean had?"

"According to the records one son died in the war. Another came back without a hand, but died in the molasses incident and two more children died of the flu so he's down to two children and a grandchild."

"And that's my fault? If he isn't happy he should go get a job somewhere else."

"Sir, I think you're missing the point. These men take a great deal of pride in their jobs. The Boston police force has been credited as being the most efficient and least corrupt force in the country for several decades now." Connor leaned over Curtis's desk and stared straight into Curtis's eyes. "Sir, the men simply ask that you inspect a couple of the station houses. If you don't perceive the buildings to be below code, then they'll accept your decision."

"Nonsense," said Curtis slamming his hand down on the desk and standing up. "I'm the Commissioner, the Chief of Police. I won't have some rabble telling me what to do." He riffled through the papers on his desk, forcing Connor to step back. "One of these station houses is almost a hundred years old. I'm sure it has some peeling paint. Why don't the men just repair it? This is their problem, not mine." Curtis walked over to the window and took in Scollay Square. Two police officers were assigned to the square yet Curtis saw a questionable element lurking there.

"Look at that. Look at that man. Tell me he doesn't look like a pickpocket or a Red. Probably has a pipe bomb in his coat pocket. But are the officers doing anything to move him along? Why no. One is helping an old man across the street and the other is talking to children. Ridiculous. I tell you, the police are overpaid for the duties they perform." Curtis turned away from the window and glared at his assistant. "And don't you ever take the side of the police force against me if you intend to keep your job. This is none of your business. You're excused."

"Yes sir," said Connor. He had told Thomas Kelly he would determine the mindset of the Commissioner, but he was disappointed by the message he would have to share. A fight was coming and while he sympathized with the police, he knew he could serve them better by keeping his job.

Spring 1919

Liam's illness

Liam sat among the weeds in the tiny backyard, where one sickly tree grew tall in an attempt to reach the limited sunshine that found its way between the row houses. Harriet stood on the stoop outside the kitchen door watching the boy. He appeared to be in an opium fog. His little hands stroked a single blade of grass over and over again. He neither smiled nor frowned. He was oblivious to all that was around him.

Patrick came up beside Harriet and placed an arm about her waist.

"Hello, my Galway bride."

She stood motionless and did not respond to his touch.

"Patrick, have ye noticed anything odd about Liam?"

"Other than he's four? Isn't that odd enough for ye old woman?"

"No, not that. Not the four-year-old shenanigans. No, I mean this," she pointed to the child who remained deaf and blind to his grandparent's presence. "There's something wrong with him. He goes into these stupors. I don't know what to make of it."

"Come now, the lad lost his parents not more than five months ago. Hasn't he the right to mourn?" Patrick felt a sharp pang of guilt and removed his arm. The loss of his eldest son was still painful. At times, the memory of the day took his breath away. "That should be more than enough," he repeated.

"No Patrick, it's something else. The boy cries for his parents. He's sad when he thinks of them. This is somethin' different. This is deeper, a melancholia. I saw it in Ireland. In those poor souls that felt they'd never get out, that their fate was to starve to death. They resigned themselves to it."

"What are you saying? That little Liam is depressed? You be wanting to take him to a psychiatrist now?"

"I didn't say that, but I want to talk to someone who knows about the Spanish Flu. I've heard tell that some people who had it, who had it even a wee bit, ended up with a lingering unhappiness. A brain fever of sorts."

"Nonsense," said Patrick unwilling to let any more disappointment enter his house. "The lad just needs some fresh air and sunshine. Here now, I'll be takin' him over to Bunker Hill and we'll play in the field."

"I hope you're right Mr. Kelly. I hope you're right." And in a louder voice she called out, "Liam Harry, it's time to come in for dinner." The child did not respond. "Liam Harry, you get in here right now." She said it with all the sternness she could muster, attempting to keep the worry from her voice.

After a moment Liam glanced over and saw his Nana and Granda. He seemed not to recognize them and then as his eyes focused he beamed a smile at them. Patrick saw his son Patrick Jr. in the boy's face while Harriet saw her first born, the son she had abandoned in Ireland. The couple reached for one another, unaware of the source of the other's pain, but comforted by each other's presence.

Scollay Square

"Murphy, what do you make of it?" asked Patrick as they left the commissioner's office.

"Don't know Patrick. I'd say we're heading for a fight." Murphy stopped to strike a match against a lamppost and lit his cigarette. "Hot one today, ehh?" The two men paused to take in the bustling activity in Scollay Square. "I know if O'Meara were still the commissioner," Murphy continued, "this needn't have happened. Our boys weren't trying to do wrong. Police forces across the country are unionizing. The AFL and IWW are the only choices I know of; you'd think Curtis'd be pleased we didn't go Red."

"But what about the men Murph?" asked Patrick. "One of those boys is mine. Eight good officers put on suspension. How are they to feed their families?"

"I'm sure all of the precincts will chip in a little somethin'. If we hadn't been so bloody honest all these years we could have been putting a few dollars away for a rainy day."

"Nay, it's been a pleasure bein' a clean cop," said Patrick. I hope that Curtis doesn't break the spirit of the force. We're the best. You know it, I know it, and so does every other state in the Union. Nothing beats Boston's finest for honesty, integrity and courage."

Murphy threw his cigarette to the ground and stamped it out

with the heel of his boot. "You don't have to sell me Kelly, it's fine bunch of lads we have. But we need a lawyer. Powerful forces are gathering behind Curtis and I believe he and those above him are going to use our simple complaints to gain national attention. If we're going to keep our good names and our jobs we'll need a lawyer. What's Thomas doing these days?"

Patrick never thought of his son in the context of his work. Thomas moved in grand circles outside the sphere of the police department. How old it made him feel to be asking his son for help.

"It's a pip, he left the international swells to do labor law. I never thought of it, but I guess we're a walkin'-talkin' labor issue, aren't we Murph?"

"You bet your ass. Give Thomas a call and let's meet at O'Malley's tonight."

The worm

Thomas sat and watched the worm eat away at the otherwise beautiful apple. He thought of all the metaphors, rotten apple, how the worm turns, etc. Watching it was sickening and intriguing at the same time. The worm was at the heart of U.S. politics and the economy wrapping itself in the flag and shrouded with words like democracy and freedom. But like the apple, the heart of the country was being eaten away from the inside out.

Thomas considered his idyllic surroundings in the Boston Garden. Swan boats were pedalled across the small pond. Children played hoop, parents with infants cooed. Each mother and father interpreting the facial expressions of their child based on their own desires.

Is that not what the U.S. Republic is also designed to do? To interpret and put words into the mouths of its constituency? Didn't John Adams, and the other founding fathers design it this way, so that the average man could focus on putting food on the table for his family, and not worry about the complexities and intricacies of governing? To that end Adams had simplified government for the average man and left the difficult work to men of learning, the landed and the elite.

Brilliant as Adams was, in the end, all of the branches of government would lack the touch of its citizenry. With the ruling class in full command, Thomas was witnessing a government adrift in a sea of rationalization that allowed any atrocity in the name of commerce.

He had become a cynic. Too much time spent dealing with injustice had made him dour. Thank goodness for Helen, the sole bright spot in his life.

Thomas stood up. He had to shake this dreary mood before Helen arrived, because she'd pick up on it. Her lack of sight seemed to give her supernatural abilities to detect the many subtleties in his mood. Perhaps all she sensed was a change in breathing, an inaudible sigh, or the quickening of the pulse. Thomas didn't know all her tricks yet and often fell prey to her awareness of an emotion he possessed, but which he had not yet found the words to express.

This was the sort of thing that made her magical. Helen never ceased to surprise him. If she had a flaw, and he almost believed none could exist in so perfect a person, it was her devotion to the church. A fringe group called the Swedenborgs had transfixed Helen and she spent every free moment supporting their ministry. Actually, he was jealous, but he would never tell her that.

Then, as if on cue, she approached him, carrying a charming lace parasol that stood out against the new green leaves. Her hat was neat and well proportioned, making her a good two seasons out of fashion. Her dress, while modern and loose fitting, was belted at the waist giving the impression of a Gibson girl.

Annie was beside her in a dark gray, non-descript dress. She blended into the background. There were times Thomas was so dazzled by Helen that Annie seemed to disappear. These days Annie was kind enough to leave them alone, on one pretense or another, and Thomas would, in his own clumsy way attempt to communicate directly with Helen. In truth it didn't matter what he said for he was sure Helen knew his heart and he hoped that she held a similar regard for him.

There were impediments to their union, but in the end, he suspected the most unforgivable would be a Yankee in love with a Southern belle.

Spring 1919

Suffragists

"Ma, what am I to do?" Patricia sobbed, head on her arms leaning over the kitchen table. Harriet feared the worst and assumed her daughter pregnant.

"What is it dear?" asked Harriet in a surprisingly gentle voice.

"Ma, they've hurt my sisters."

"What?'" asked Harriet confused.

"They've beaten and brutalized my sisters. They forced suffragists on hunger strikes to eat, by forcing hoses down their throats and gagging them with porridge. Two women died. Good women, friends of mine. Why Ma, why?" Patricia let out a wail and Harriet comforted her. Both women were radicals. Harriet willing to let the fervor for temperance take her to places she didn't even recognize in herself. Patricia doing the same with her passion for the vote.

"They be afraid of us, daughter. Men nary understand us. They don't know what we can do and it frightens them. They know we're fearless but they don't know our limits. Can we defeat them? Yes. Will we? Yes.

That's why they hurt your friends. They wanted you to quit but seeing your success they became brutal. Most of your friends will survive. You frightened them. Now you must finish the job."

For the first time Patricia became cognizant that her mother was not just her mother. Harriet Kelly was a woman of politics. She knew how the world worked and how to get what she wanted in the context of a bigger agenda. Patricia and her mother were the same sort of woman. All these years she had thought of her mother as a cold fish and equated her with President Wilson. Now Patricia could feel Harriet's fire.

It was Harriet who broke the spell.

"I have to set the table for dinner. Go get yourself ready and make sure Liam washes his hands."

Liam's music

"Mrs. Kelley come in, and this must be Liam." The matronly woman bent her knee to speak to the boy, face to face. "Liam, your Nan here tells me that you've quite the ear for music. Have you ever thought about playing an instrument?"

Liam wouldn't look at her.

"Go on now, answer Mrs. Cavanaugh," Harriet scolded.

"No Ma'am."

"Your Nan has some shopping to do and is going to leave you with me for an hour. I thought I could show you around my music room. What say you to that?"

Liam shot Harriet a worried glance. She hadn't meant to leave him there. Liam didn't like being out of sight of a family member since his parent's death, but she understood Mrs. Cavanaugh's logic. Liam would never admit to liking anything in her presence.

"Yes love, for just a moment. I won't be gone long and Mrs. Cavanaugh has many wonderful instruments for you to play while I'm gone. You won't even miss me."

Liam rushed to his grandmother and grabbed at her skirts. He showed his bravery by not whimpering when she pried his fingers from the cloth and handed his fist to her friend.

"You be a good boy now. I'll be back in two shakes of a rabbits tail."

"Don't you worry about a thing Mrs. Kelly. Liam and I will have a good time."

Once the door shut, with Harriet on the other side, Liam began to cry. But Mrs. Cavanaugh was not deterred.

"Liam, come with me for a moment, there's a window in here and you can watch your Nana walking to the market." The ploy worked and Liam followed her willingly.

They entered a large room with tall ceilings, paneled in maple. Upon the walls hung every type of instrument imaginable. There was a bassoon, trumpet, clarinet, banjo, two guitars, a violin, and in the center of the room stood a grand piano facing one direction and a harpsichord facing the other. Between them stood an elegant harp. Liam forgot to go to the window, entranced by the objects.

"How about we try out each of these instruments and see if there isn't one that takes your fancy?"

Liam nodded. She took a Celtic pipe hanging in a holster down from the wall. She handed it to Liam and indicated where to blow. With the first peel of sound the boy's eyes flashed. He looked up at Mrs. Cavanaugh to determine if it was all right. Her smile reassured him. They went around the room making a sound on every instrument until finally, they ended up at the piano.

It was like the elephant in the room. He had approached it from every side and it seemed menacing, it so big and he so small. Mrs. Cavanaugh helped settle him on the stool and placed his hands on the keys, forming a C chord. With the first vibration of sound that reached the air Liam smiled with satisfaction. Mrs. Cavanaugh knew beyond a doubt that Liam had discovered his instrument. He and the piano would form a life long friendship.

A matter of love

Thomas arrived with a bouquet of white peonies and lavender. He relished purchasing flowers for Helen, an event that went beyond mere color and included the senses of smell and touch.

Annie Macy answered the door with an all knowing grin, "Mr. Kelly, fancy seeing you here. Miss Keller is indisposed. Would you care to sit with me in the parlor?"

"It would be a pleasure," Thomas said, attempting not to show his disappointment that Helen was not ready to receive him.

Annie ushered him into what had become a familiar room. The two women had taken up residence in a suite at the Parker house. Their parlor overlooked the busy street below. When the windows were open, one needed to yell to be heard above the din. Today was cooler and thankfully the windows were closed.

"I've been meanin' to ask you some questions young man," said Annie.

"What is on your mind Mrs. Macy?"

"Your intentions." She pointed to a chair, indicating that Thomas should sit.

"Mrs. Macy, I assure you my intentions toward Miss Keller are most honorable. The more time I spend with her, the more certain I am that we belong together."

"Then you'll be askin' her to marry you?" Annie and Thomas's eyes met. The question was indiscrete.

"I believe that discussion will be between Helen and myself."

"Aye, I suppose it shall. However, I want to know why ye love her? You're a good lookin' young man with a promising future. Why should you be interested in a middle-aged deaf and blind woman?"

Thomas stuttered, "How…? Isn't it obvious…? After all, Mrs. Macy, you live with Helen. If anyone in this world should know how extraordinary she is, it would be you."

"Aye, I know what a handful she is and that she possesses a gift to share with world. But why do you love her is what I'm askin'?"

Thomas blurted, "Because we are one and the same. She can move mountains and wants to. To me, Helen is a radiant beauty. Hers is a beauty of the heart and soul. There is no one like her. But I believe the real question Mrs. Macy, is why would Helen want me?"

"Aye, now there's a question I've asked myself and Helen many times. So far I haven't an answer that satisfies."

Thomas realized his pleading eyes must have looked pathetic, "Please Mrs. Macy."

Taking pity on him Annie Macy responded, "Well, Helen would say that you see her; that most men want her because she is a novelty or an inspiration. But you alone see her."

"What does that mean?"

"Best as I understand it, Helen seems to think that you can sense her feelings, understand her desires for improving the lot of humanity. She believes that together you make up two halves of a puzzle and that you can help one another accomplish the deeds set before you in this life." Thomas blushed.

"You needn't be blushin' in front of me young man because I know better. You see I'm an Irish woman. And while ye may have been born here in America your parents are both from the old country. Meanin' they carry the fear in them, and you've inherited it as well. It's a fear that affects the way you see the world and the decisions you'll be makin'."

"I beg your pardon. My father is fearful of nothing. He is a fine police officer. I think you are mistaken Mrs. Macy."

"I may be wrong about why Helen loves you, but I'm not wrong about the fear that clings to the Irish. We're all afraid, afraid that the landlord will steal our homes, afraid our children will starve, afraid for our own survival. These are not flights of fancy lad, these are real fears that the Irish have faced for centuries."

Thomas's throat was dry. He opened his mouth to speak, but it was Annie who continued.

"Thomas, I believe you will hurt my Helen because she cannot understand the fear born within you. She may see your spirit, but I see the cloud that lives above you, the shadow that you shall always live beneath.

I do not doubt that you will provide for my sweet bird. You will make piles of money to stave off your Irish financial insecurity, but you will resent our Helen for the effort, despite the fact she doesn't give a damn about money. Just look around. Do ye think we can afford this suite? Or the Parisian clothes on our backs? Of course not, but Helen lives for today and let's tomorrow work itself out. Ye know that is not how you or your kin are. Each of you worries about today and tomorrow and some far off future that will never come. I say you and Helen are nothing alike and a fish and fowl will find no home together."

Annie gave Thomas a hard look that preempted any response. "Mr. Kelly, you will do what you need to and Helen will do as she pleases, for she does love you with all her heart. She sees in you a great statesman. A man who will help the world understand that each and every person is the same. I only hope that ye can find in yourself a wee bit of the hero that Helen worships in you."

Before Thomas could speak Annie abruptly stood up. "I'll go see what's keeping our Helen."

Harriet's confession

Every Friday Harriet went to the Haymarket to buy produce. She always enjoyed passing through the densely populated North End and attempting to identify the cooking aromas of the Italian neighborhood. But as she crossed Commercial Street on this warm day the overwhelming smell of molasses slapped her in the face. She looked down and saw the offending substance bubbling up through the cracks in the cobblestone street. The stench and realization that it was here, where she stood, that her dear son died, caused her to feel faint. She forced her legs to move, reliving his experience in her mind, each step more difficult than last. Emotions engulfed her, just as the wave of molasses had consumed her son.

Patrick Jr.'s darling face swam before her. She recalled his sweet disposition, certainly not inherited from her. She had been so relieved when he had returned from the war. Losing his hand was a small price to pay, compared to the losses of so many other families. But his freak death at home had caused Harriet to refortify the walls around her heart.

She leaned against a building, overcome, as sadness and regret swept over her. Usually her anger, the key component to her internal fortress, held the engulfing emotions at bay, but today she was caught off-guard and her emotions threatened to overwhelm her. She shuffled forward in search of sanctuary.

Part of her mind stood outside of herself. She barely recognized the disheveled, shrunken, old woman, walking down the street, hunched over, a mere shadow of her matriarchal self. Yet this was Harriet. With each child lost, the disappointments and bad decisions weighed her down further, attempting to destroy her spirit. Her anger had kept her alive and even that was seeping away, leaving only recrimination.

She reached the courtyard of the Old North Church and went inside to sit in a pew. She mused over the lie. The Old North Church burned down during the Revolutionary War. But the tourists didn't know any better. She wondered, 'Is life the lies we tell each other and ourselves?'

Harriet was overpowered by remorse and self-pity. In that moment, she was willing to join a silent cloistered order. But the silence, she knew, would be filled with the voices of her dead children, which threatened to drive her mad. Even now, images of Timothy, killed in Russia, came to her. She had reared him like the others, but she had never liked him. He was cruel, bitter and willing to take the easy road like her first husband. Never inclined to put in a full day for a full dollar, Timothy worked all the angles.

Spring 1919

When his number was called for the draft she felt certain he would go AWOL and was surprised when he appeared in their Charlestown doorway dressed in uniform. "How do I look, Ma?" He had said, turning like a girl in a new dress. "I cut quite the figure, huh? Those girls in France won't know what hit them."

She realized, as he spoke, that he was going to war to have fun. The lack of morality which war brought would suit Timothy. In her heart it was good riddance and she was sure God would make her pay for such sinful thoughts against her own flesh and blood.

And then there was her youngest, little James, although he was not so little. A strapping youth, already playing football and tall enough to make the basketball team. He was the pride of the neighborhood. A friend to everyone. The neighborhood girls would hang outside the Kelly's door, in hopes of a glimpse of him. And he was kind to them all. He never let his popularity go to his head. He took after Patrick, his father, and would have dedicated his life in the service of others. When he and Erin took ill with the flu, Harriet never considered that they could die. They were both so young and vibrant.

Erin was as strong as an ox. While not a beauty at sixteen, Harriet could see that her daughter would grow into a handsome woman. Erin was practical to a fault and she'd have made a good wife for a husband of ambition, maintaining the home fires while he went out into the world to make a name for himself.

But now, both were gone, before having fully blossomed. One day they appeared to have a cold and the next they were dead. Their bodies were removed and taken to the car barn. Patrick would not let her go there. He told her that there were tens of thousands of bodies there. That it was a nightmare of epic proportions and he wanted to save her from the horror of it.

But Patrick had faced it everyday. Sometimes he would have to take the bodies from the homes. There were just so many dead. Between September and November alone, over 100,000 people had died in Boston. Soldiers were arriving home to sit at vacant hearths.

"Are you all right, Ma'am?" A young minister touched Harriet on the shoulder. Certainly he could see she did not belong. Probably assumed she was a tourist, as Irish and Catholic as she was.

"Are you all right? Do you need some water or a doctor? You're not well." It slipped from his lips before he could check himself.

"I'm fine. Just a bit faint. I came in to pray. I hope that's all right, this not bein' my church."

"Ma'am, God hears all our prayers wherever they're said. I'll get you some water."

Harriet was relieved when he left. Harriet felt as if her black mood could engulf the world. Four of her American children dead before their time and Harriet was about to suffocate from guilt as she forced herself to recall the two wee ones she had left behind in Ireland. The two, that by now, were probably grown, with children of their own. Or who may have died of famine, disease or the cruelty of their own father. Her evil husband. As his image surfaced in her mind a moan escaped her lips. The minister returning with the water heard it.

"Sister, is there something I can do for you? Please let me call a doctor. Or a priest."

She almost laughed at the irony of the situation. This was a dark time. Death was all around them and the minister worried over the moan of an old woman.

"Nay, ye be attendin' to your own."

With that she stood and took herself out through the doors. Hunched and beaten she went out to face the day. Harriet's life was full of misery. She could not enjoy the future or the past, but lived instead in a state of perpetual purgatory.

Liam's secret

Liam's teeth ached, but he didn't want to complain because the dentist hurt him. Besides, his Nana had assured him all these teeth were going to fall out anyway. Meanwhile he would just stay away from sweets and the other foods that it hurt to eat.

To forget his discomfort he practiced the piano. He kept hearing music in his head, but when he tried to play it – it never sounded the same. He would describe it to his teacher and she would tell him to focus on the classics, which he did. The piano came easy to Liam and

Spring 1919

he found that there was not a piece of music that he couldn't easily pick his way through. His fingers were still too short to stretch across an octave, but he made do.

However, the music in his head gnawed at him. Something inside of him knew it was important, that the sound was original, that it was his. One day he would surprise everyone.

WASHINGTON DC

The role of women

Emmet sat alone in the parlor of his parent's house. Viewing the room with the eye of a stranger, he noted that his parents were well-to-do. Quite near the top rung of colored society.

He reached for a piece of lace that hung over the back of the sofa. He recognized the exquisite detail of his mother's lace work. He didn't know the name of the pattern; perhaps it was Filet, Cluny or Floradora. He did know that his mother was an unstoppable force and that women like his mother kept men from being shiftless. Hell, based on what he had seen in the war, it just might be that women were responsible for keeping the world in one piece. Men, black or white, couldn't resist going out and pitting themselves against one another. Women made a civilization. Women were why men had evolved.

As he sat musing, Kay arrived home. Seeing him in the parlor, she brightened with joy. Emmet found himself touched by her sincere pleasure at his presence. Kay's spirit was irrepressible and untarnished. With so many dreadful images seared into his memory, Emmet realized it was his sister's smile that truly brought him home.

Kay dropped into a chair across from him without ceremony and began removing her hatpins and hat.

"So what are you up to, big brother? How come you're sitting here in a dark room by yourself? Why aren't you outside? It's springtime or hadn't you heard?"

"I'm just pondering the nature of men and women."

She let out a low soft whistle.

"And what have you postulated, professor?" She sat back, after freeing herself from her large straw bonnet festooned with ribbons and feathers.

"That women are the civilizing force in the world."

"I like it. Tell me more."

"For example, you take a young man and put him in a room or an apartment and he might get himself a bed. A coffee cup. Perhaps a chair and small table. After a few years a bookcase." Kay appeared puzzled. "Now you take that same apartment and put a woman in it and by the end of a couple of months it's fully furnished with chairs, sofas, pots, pans, lanterns, artwork and even things like this," he held up the edge of the doily on the back of the sofa. "These subtle things make an apartment a home. Men don't know how to make homes. They know how to build them and destroy them, but they don't know how to make them come alive."

"What you're saying, brother dearest, is that we women create life." She grinned as she recognized the multiple meanings in her sentence.

"Exactly. Women put the living into existence. The reason to strive. Perhaps even the reason to kill."

"Oh, no you don't. You're not pinning war on us. What about that white woman, Jane Addams. She's better known than the President of the United States. She lost everything trying to stop the war. So did lots of women. They fought so hard they lost their prestige and reason. No big brother, women hate war, we know it for what it is, the opposite of creation, and therefore, the antithesis of who we are."

Wilson in denial

"What 'colored problem'? What are you sniveling about, Colonel House? If I had a problem with the colored, I'd know about it, wouldn't I?" Edward House had been Wilson's trusted advisor since he took office. As Wilson put it, House was his better half, his humanity. But lately House didn't seem to understand any of Wilson's initiatives. They were always at odds.

"Sir, you've had other, perhaps more important, things on your mind," responded House, attempting to give Wilson an out.

"Damn it to hell, that's what I'm telling you. The Paris talks fizzled into nothing, drifted right down the Seine, thanks to you. Now I've got to go back and finish your job. They all but kicked us out of their country. Said they needed a break."

"Yes sir, I know. But there are items that need attending to here, domestically. You have several significant concerns, that I believe will come to a head by summer."

"What are you talking about?" An agitated Wilson threw a stack of papers on his desk. He hated the fact that he would have to return to Europe. Edith had already told him that she would not join him on this trip. The thought of being without Edith crushed his spirit. "You've taken your eye off the ball, Colonel. The League of Nations is your number one priority. I need Congress to support me on this. How many senators do you have lined up?"

Colonel Edward House was a diminutive man. He stood at the window staring down Pennsylvania Avenue. He looked at the sheep on the front lawn and wondered when the gardeners would be back from the war. He hated the smelly animals although the tourists loved them. He prayed that the plague or a bullet hadn't taken the last of the men with botanical interests. Why did everyone enlist?

"Edward, are you listening to me? Where do we stand with the Senate?" Wilson's voice was shrill. He wasn't going to hear a single word House had to say.

"They're against you, sir. They don't understand your Fourteen Points and they believe the League of Nations will put the country further into debt. Here at home, sir, we're facing a serious...."

Wilson cut him off. "Good God, man, if we don't have a League of Nations we won't have a world. The way these spoiled monarchs are dividing up the pie, they're sowing the seeds for another war."

House observed his Commander-in-Chief and saw that Wilson's

eyelid was twitching again. In a moment the great man would crumble into his chair in a fit of melancholy.

"May I fix you a drink, sir?' asked Edward.

"Now that's the first sensible thing you've said, but let's have Benjamin fix it, he knows what I like."

House was startled to realize the colored man had been standing in the room the entire time. His stillness made his black suit and white gloves nearly invisible.

"Yes sir." said Benjamin as he moved to the bar. House noted that the aide poured bitters and added a powder, leading the Colonel to wonder what medicines Wilson was secretly taking.

Benjamin brought the concoction to Wilson, who was now sitting at his desk with his head in his hands, just as House had predicted.

"Your drink sir," said Benjamin evenly.

"Thank you," was all Wilson could manage. He drank the liquid in a single gulp and made a sour face afterwards.

"Can I get you or Mr. House anything else sir?" asked Benjamin.

"No, we're fine. We won't be needing you for the next few minutes. Why don't you wait outside the door."

"Yes sir."

"Go ahead House," Wilson said, with an audible sigh. "Tell me about my problem with the negroes."

"They're being strung up."

"Excuse me?"

"And not just in the south, but also in the north."

"Why? And what are we talking about? One or two bad apples?"

"No sir, thus far there have been seventy lynchings and the number grows every day. The men returning home believe that the colored are taking their jobs. They are lynching soldiers who are still in uniform."

"What?" Wilson shook his head from side to side. "Soldiers are stringing up blacks that have committed crimes?"

Now it was House who wanted to sigh. "No sir, out-of-work white men, some of whom are neighbors of yours, are stringing up innocent negro soldiers, men who fought bravely overseas."

"What are you talking about? How many negroes did we have in the war?"

"Approximately three hundred and fifty to four hundred thousand. Most served with distinction, twenty-five were awarded the Congressional Medal of Honor. In France, the Tuskegee men were requested more often than any other division."

"You don't say?" It was obvious that Wilson was no longer listening. He appeared to be in a fog. "What should we do about all this, House? I'm sure you have an opinion."

"I do. I believe you should show your support for the working negro by publicly acknowledging their deeds in the war. Perhaps with a statue, and also by allocating funds for their colleges."

Wilson roused himself at the mention of college. "What's that you say? What does a negro need with a college education? Now I know we had one or two at Princeton, both good men, but I suspect it was just to show we could produce a Frederick Douglas or W.E.B DuBois, like Harvard. I don't see any harm in educating the colored through grade school, but beyond that, what's the point?"

"Because it's the right thing to do Mr. President. You've thrown support behind any number of white schools. Why not some negro schools?"

"Nonsense, what good will it do to build up the hopes and dreams of a black man when he will only be able to work as a manual laborer. Ridiculous." Wilson took off his pincer glasses and rubbed the bridge of his nose.

"If the violence gets worse," said an exhausted Wilson, "call out the National Guard. Otherwise ignore it. Let the local authorities take care of their own."

Colonel House wanted to protest, but he knew that when it came to the colored, Wilson's southern heritage came to the forefront.

"There are several other important domestic items," House continued, "the labor unions, ratification of the Nineteenth Amendment, the escalation of organized crime around prohibition and the Red Scare." Now Wilson stood up and went to the window to gaze at the sheep, a smile appearing on his lips.

"As for the unions, to hell with them. Let the factory owners shoot them for all I care. The suffragettes are on their own as well.

Spring 1919

I've hated that group ever since that horrific march when I took office in '13. I'd have vetoed the Amendment if I didn't think it would cost me votes. I may need them if I run for a third term. Prohibition, same thing. Let the cops take care of it. I did veto that bill and Congress overrode me, so let them deal with it. And what was your last point?"

"You need to put a leash on Palmer. The Attorney General has no right deporting American citizens. There'll be an outcry the likes of which you've never heard, Mr. President. You must fire him."

"Not on your life, House." Wilson said it with a calm not typical of the high-strung President. House was more certain than ever that Wilson was taking opium to relieve his stress.

Wilson continued, "Palmer is a bulldog, but he's my bulldog. He'll obey my commands. Right now I want to give him and his pup Hoover some free rein."

Wilson crossed to the divan and stretched out, resting the back of his hand over his eyes. "Now, if that's all, House, I need to take a nap."

"Yes, Mr. President."

House exited the room, closed the door and snapped his folio shut. Benjamin nodded, making House jump.

"How do you do that Benjamin – make yourself invisible?"

"Years of practice sir."

"Benjamin, do you mind if I ask you a personal question?"

"I won't know until you ask sir."

House chuckled, spoken like a true politician. "Benjamin, have you been to college?"

"Yes sir. Graduated Howard University in 1892."

"And yet you work here as servant. Why?"

"I majored in political science sir." And with that, Benjamin gave House a knowing smile. House nodded and left the building, certain Wilson didn't even know Benjamin's last name, much less that he possessed a college degree.

Louvenia the Inventor

It was just past midnight when the explosion shook the house.

112

"Terrorists!" shouted Ben.

"Louvenia," said Claire in return.

They raced into Kay's bedroom, to find it empty. Then Emmet's. He too was missing.

"Let's go downstairs and make sure the house isn't on fire," said Claire.

They descended into a cloud of smoke.

"Claire, go back upstairs and collect our valuables. We'll need to get them out of the house before it burns down."

"Just a minute, Ben." Claire groped her way along the hall until she reached the kitchen and the doorway to the basement. She called out.

"LOUVENIA?" Claire was relieved when she heard the faint and rueful voice in response.

"Yes, Momma."

"Is this your doing?"

"Yes, Momma."

"Are you all right?"

Louvenia emerged from the cloud of ash. She hugged her mother. "Yes, Momma, I'm all right. I'm sorry to have frightened you. I've been..."

"I know dear, you were working on an experiment."

Louvenia nodded. Claire's eyes stung from the particles still suspended in the air. "Lou, you go open the front door. I'll find my way to the backdoor and open it."

Benjamin stood frozen. He hadn't known, hadn't even guessed, that his daughter might be behind all of this.

Still gripped by fright he roared, "Louvenia, what is the meaning of this? Are you building bombs in our basement?" He was serious. What would the neighbors assume except the same thing? Everyone was on the alert for terrorists.

Claire brushed past him as she opened the side windows. "Don't be ridiculous, Ben," she said. "If you paid more attention to your daughter you'd know what she was working on. Our Louvenia is very talented." She didn't say it, but Benjamin heard, 'the smartest of all our children.'

Spring 1919

Benjamin cringed. He was old-fashioned enough to believe inventing was for men. That it should have been one of his sons that was given this gift. Daughters were supposed to sew and cook. But in his house everything was turned on its head. The women, including Claire, had full lives outside of the home. And all he could do was bellow.

Kay appeared on the stairs just above where the dust hung in the air.

"Is everyone okay?" she asked.

"Where have you been young lady? And where's your brother?" asked a suspicious Claire.

"Emmet's not here? I was in my room, where else?"

Claire had never thought her daughter would lie to her straight-faced. She was certain she knew the answer, but instead replied, "Get down here and help me clean up this mess."

Louvenia, standing in the hall, turned to follow her mother into the kitchen. Benjamin reached out and took her hand. "Louvenia, come into the parlor."

"Yes Papa."

Louvenia's face was covered in a grey mask of ash. The chalky substance caused her skin to appear white, but her unmistakable negroid features would never let her pass no matter how fair her skin. They sat facing each other.

"What were you doing downstairs?" he asked in a calm voice. "What just shook the house? Are you all right? Are we in any danger of the house falling down or burning up?"

She placed her hand over his. "No Papa. I'm working on a heater for the house and I just didn't give it enough exhaust and it exploded. The worst of it is the big mess in the basement, but I'll attend to that." She smiled and dust fell from her cheeks.

"I thought you were making improvements to the icebox?"

"I'm working on that too, Papa. I have about fifteen inventions in development. All of them to improve efficiency or remove the drudgery from household chores." Claire entered the parlor. Louvenia smiled wickedly.

"I want to try to put Mama out of business."

"You do that child and the world will stop spinning," said Claire. "Rich people will always need their lives cleaned and organized."

Lou said, "I know you're right Mama, but my inventions may make your life a little easier."

"Louvenia, you've not answered me," her father broke in, "what exactly just got me out of bed?"

Claire patted Louvenia's arm silently, communicating that she should stay and talk with her father.

"I'm working on a way to heat the house in the winter. At present we have the fireplace in the living room and the stove in the kitchen to keep us warm, while the rest of the house is freezing.

Kay walked through to the front door with a bucket full of ashes, "You've got that right sister, I can see my breath in my room."

"I'm working on a mechanism that will allow us to heat all of the rooms equally. So that you could pass from room to room and it would always be the same temperature. Ultimately I'll have each room with its own controls so an individual can set the warmth to his or her pleasure. You know how Momma likes it hot."

"Louvenia I've never heard of such a thing," said her father, "What gave you this idea?"

"Poppa, have you been to my room in the attic this winter? It was the ice on the inside of the windows. That's what gave me the idea."

Benjamin remained awed at the creative capacity of his daughter. She was the best educated among them, with several advanced degrees, but there was more to it. Louvenia could pluck ideas from the air and then form them into objects of physical substance. Like an alchemist of old. Straw into gold, that was his daughter.

He silently thanked God that she was all right. And asked himself and God once again, 'Why couldn't she have been a boy'?

Kay's escape

As the house began to rumble Kay found herself halfway out the window, her feet dangling, looking for a foothold. She was sneaking out for a few hours to listen to Duke. He was sitting in with a new band and Kay had heard the trumpet player could blow some hot licks.

Spring 1919

Sitting in the dark with a handsome black man was just the way she wanted to spend her Sunday evening. And then her foolish sister tried to blow up the house.

"Damn," muttered Kay under her breath, as she hoisted herself back up over the windowsill. Certainly all of Washington saw her hanging there, as the busybody next door ran from her house into the street, to find out what had caused the noise. One day Louvenia would actually do it, and lay them all to waste.

Dr. Allen's cure

Emmet couldn't sleep. Nightmares still haunted him. He'd hoped that when he got home and into his own bed, they'd stop, but tonight was no different. Once again he put on his clothes and wandered out into the street, half hoping to run into another soldier he could talk to. Instead he found an all-night billiard hall and went inside to play a game. A dandified little man was sitting beside one of the three tables, wearing a light brown flannel suit.

"Can't sleep mister?" he asked, with a Jamaican accent.

"No, I guess I'm still keyed up."

"Not to worry friend. In my bag here, I've got the cure to all your ailments. The balm for your aches and pains, the antidote for your dreams, the sunshine that dissipates your rainy day."

He held up a small vial of dark liquid. "In this bottle, for a mere $1.50, I have a drink that will bring you the glow of peace. Right here before you, I hold the answer to eternal bliss. Just two swallows of Dr. Allen's elixir and you'll be seeing golden fairies." He handed the bottle to Emmet. Emmet held the glass container in his palm like an exquisite gem. Then he reached into his pocket for the money.

"Perhaps you should grab several bottles friend, because after prohibition, I'll be charging $3.00 apiece for this liquid happiness."

Emmet knew he was being hustled, but he hadn't slept in days. The notion of slipping into blissful ignorance appealed to him more than his concern regarding the addictive properties of opium.

"Sure pal, give me three bottles. I could use some sweet dreams tonight."

A war request for Louvenia

Lou was excited about a referral from her chemistry professor. A white man, Bud Rawley, was coming to see her to discuss a project. She didn't know Mr. Rawley, but she was certain he had money and that was what she needed to continue her more complex experiments and move her lab out of her parent's basement.

When the knock came at the door, she was ready.

"Mr. Rawley? Please come in." Lou had been expecting an older gentleman and was surprised to find that Bud Rawley was no more than thirty, impeccably dressed in a hundred-dollar suit with spats. He wore a ruby ring and his tie sported a large diamond stickpin. Mr. Rawley's most notable feature, however, was his flaming red hair.

"How do you do? Miss Louvenia Johnson?"

"Yes sir. Please come in and have a seat." Lou ushered Buddy into the parlor. She had set out tea, along with cookies. The cookies were her mother's suggestion.

"May I offer you some tea, Mr. Rawley?"

"That would be delightful." Bud Rawley had asked all over Washington for a chemistry whiz kid who understood fiber composition. Everyone recommended the same person, Louvenia Johnson. The fact that she was colored did not surprise him. Howard University was graduating first-rate chemists. But the fact she was a girl came as something of a shock. Bud Rawley was used to working with men.

"So, Miss Johnson, Professor Moen speaks very highly of your work and your experiments. He believes you're the next Albert Einstein of chemistry."

Lou laughed and hid her smile behind her hand. "I'm sorry Mr. Rawley, Professor Moen may have mislead you. Although I have a fondness for science and it appears, a knack for formulas, my real expertise is in mechanical engineering. But how may I assist you? Moen says you have a unique challenge."

Buddy filed away the fact Louvenia had other talents he might be able to leverage. For now, they would discuss the problem at hand.

"Did Mr. Moen give you any specifics?" he asked. She shook her

117

head no. "Well I have ammunition plants throughout the South and the Midwest. One of my plants makes cannons. During the last war we had difficulty with the bags of powder. In some instances we experienced as much as a fifty percent failure rate. I need to fix this, Miss Johnson. With your knowledge of chemicals and fiber, everyone I've spoken with claims you'd be the perfect candidate to address the issue."

Lou's mind immediately began attacking the problem. She could see that moisture was the real enemy, causing the fiber to deteriorate rapidly with exposure. Before postulating further she stopped herself and asked, "But Mr. Rawley, the war is over. Why do you need to solve this problem now?"

Buddy forced himself not to smile at her naïveté. He knew that she was already at work on the problem and he was certain she was the right person for the job. He decided to be direct, "Miss Johnson, there's always a war."

"That's ridiculous. We just fought the Great War, the war to end all wars. I doubt there'll be a need for another. Mr. Rawley, I believe you had better retool your factories for peace and prosperity." Realizing she was talking herself out of a paycheck she added, "Perhaps there's some other application for which this material could be used?"

Buddy smiled broadly and said, "You let me worry about the orders, Miss Johnson. Will you help me with my problem?"

They talked for hours. By the time Buddy left, he was certain Lou would solve the problem quickly, if given the appropriate resources. He also knew he was getting her services for a song. He was not interested in taking advantage of her, so he would have his lawyers add bonus incentives that she would easily achieve.

Madame Walker dies

Claire had been absent from the table during dinner. She sat in the hallway on the phone, but barely spoke. Ben, meanwhile, grew angry. "Claire, your food is getting cold!"

He was tempted to go get her and demand an explanation. The girls were nearly finished and hadn't stopped jabbering throughout the meal. Something about fabric that Benjamin couldn't follow, he assumed it was about a dress. Emmet, as usual, had not joined them.

Benjamin was irritable. He no longer liked his job and worse yet, he'd lost respect for his President. He needed a change, but he didn't know what.

For the first time Benjamin realized that W.E.B. DuBois might be right. Booker T's isolationism theory was not going to work. The powers that be could, at any time, interfere and kill his people. The changes required would be massive and needed to be carried out through the courts. Perhaps he'd quit his job and go to law school.

Ben's thoughts returned to Claire. "Claire, get in here." He threw his napkin on the table and his daughters stopped their conversation just long enough to determine his bad mood was not aimed at them.

He lumbered down the hall to collect Claire. She was just hanging up the phone, tears streaming down her cheeks.

Ben's mood changed swiftly upon seeing her face. He realized something serious had happened and spoke with concern. "What is it, Claire? Has someone died?"

She nodded, unable to speak. He went to her and held her close. He and his family had experienced too much death for one year. "Who is it Claire?"

She shook him away, almost like a dog shaking off the rain. "Madame Walker's dead, Ben. I'm aware you didn't like her, but A'Lelia is my favorite cousin and she was devoted to her mother."

"I know dear." Benjamin was relieved that it wasn't someone closer to home.

"But Ben, there's more." She paused and he became anxious. "Could we step out for a moment, maybe go over to The Heavenly for coffee? There's something I need to tell you."

"Yes, of course, but I must say this all sounds very mysterious."

"Let's just say it'll be a surprise."

Benjamin went into the dining room where the girls had started on the Jello dessert. Their conversation ceased when he entered. "Your mother and I are stepping out for a moment. We'll be back shortly. Please clean up the dishes in kitchen."

The girls smiled. "Taking Mom out on the town, Dad?" asked

Spring 1919

Kay.

"Nothing of the kind, your mother has just received some bad news and we're going to discuss it." Before they could ask, he held up his hand for silence. "We'll talk about it later."

Claire was waiting for him in the hall, her coat already on. She was holding his coat out to him.

"Let's go dear," he said, offering her his hand.

Louvenia and Emmet

Emmet stepped into Lou's lab in the basement. The room was full of tables and upon each one stood an experiment. There were beakers, bunson burners, wires and every sort of measuring and calibrating device strewn about. Her work area appeared to be a mad house and yet he suspected there was logic to the chaos. Louvenia never even heard him come down the stairs. She started upon seeing him standing in the doorway and dropped the beaker of solution she held in her hand. Emmet bent to help her clean it up.

"No problem Emmet. The liquid is inert."

"And that's supposed to comfort me?" He asked half in jest. "What types of chemicals are you working with down here Sis?"

"All kinds, depending on the project," she answered while picking up the pieces of glass.

Once she was satisfied the largest shards were accounted for she ignored the puddle of liquid that remained on the hard packed dirt floor. "Would you like me to show you what I'm up to these days?"

"I'd love it."

"I'm limited by the size of the lab. It restricts the types of projects I can consider. That being the case let's start here," she pointed to the bench against the wall. Emmet had a vague memory of his father's tools hanging there and wondered where they were now.

"This experiment is more or less a lark, something I work on in my spare time," She pointed to a thin metal briefcase that had a glass lens on one side and an eyepiece on the other.

"I give up, what is it?"

Louvenia picked it up as a cameraman might, holding the long lens in her hand and bringing the eyepiece to her face. She turned a makeshift crank with her right hand.

"I know it isn't an original idea, it's a refinement on the movie cameras they currently use to make flickers. My camera is smaller and more agile for news men and women to take into the field." She handed the camera to Emmet. "It's light and easy to handle, able to work in low light situations."

Emmet tried to use the contraption and failed, but the lab held many more wonders. "What else are you working on?"

"Over here," she walked a few feet and stood in front of a wooden pallet. Upon it sat several barrels of scrap metal. "I am figuring out a problem brought to me by one of the dock workers. Try lifting that pallet."

He dutifully tried to lift a corner and was surprised he couldn't budge it. "How much does this thing weigh?"

"Somewhere between 400 and 500 pounds." She reached up to wires hanging from a pulley in the ceiling. She hooked each of the four wires to the metal rings embedded into each corner of the pallet. Then Louvenia handed him a metal box with three buttons.

"Push the green button." He did as he was told. And to his amazement the load lifted off the ground in a smooth movement, without the slightest hesitation.

"I'm limited as to the size of the loads I can work with here in the basement, but I'm certain this mechanism will lift loads ten times what I have here." Louvenia took the controls from Emmet and with equal precision lowered the pallet back to the floor.

"I'm impressed Lou. We could have used something like this in the war. I can't tell you how many times I was asked to lift really heavy things."

Lou smiled at his appreciation. "I believe my hoisting device will have many uses across all industries. I'm fortunate that the gentleman I'm building it for didn't require that I give up the patent or copyright." She walked to the far end of the basement and Emmet followed.

"But it's this invention over here, I think, that'll make us all rich." Louvenia pointed to an ash-covered box in the corner. She beamed at it as she would a winsome child who had just properly recited its multiplication tables.

Lou asked Emmet, "What is it that you hate most about winter?"

"I don't know, the snow, the cold, the shivering."

"Exactly. And what of chopping, stacking and bringing in fire-wood all year, not to mention picking out coal for the oven."

"Yeah. I sure didn't miss those chores while I was away. What have you done? Found a way for coal and wood to walk into the house and jump into the fire?"

"Sort of, stand back for a moment," she motioned for him to move away from the box. "I scared Father to death with this. I've had, well, a few mishaps." She turned a valve on a green tank sitting four feet from the box. Then she leaned down beside the box and with a long match ignited a flame that in turn lit several gas jets.

"Emmet could you please flip the switch to your left?" He walked to the wall and did as he was told and heard the sound a fan come on.

"Give it a minute and then come over here." The two stared at the box, which made low rumbling sounds. The room filled with the smell of dust and gas. "All right," said Lou, "Place your hand here."

Emmet did so and was surprised to experience warm air passing over his hand. He considered his sister. "How did you do that? What is this thing?"

"It's a gas heating furnace. People will be able to use it to heat their entire house from one central location. By installing heater vents on every floor and a duct system people will say farewell to cold winter days for good."

Emmet considered Louvenia with a new sense of pride and wonder.

"Are you a genius, Lou?" he said it as a joke, but as soon as the words left his mouth, he realized it might be true. The question turned Lou into the awkward little girl he had known growing up. She looked down at the floor, covered her smile with her hand and said, "You silly."

"Seriously Lou, this is really something. Do you have a good lawyer?"

Louvenia regained her composure. "Yes Emmet, I have a terrific lawyer."

"Good. I ask because I met a great chap in the Army, a Charles Hamilton Houston. He's gone on to Harvard Law School, but I know he'd do me a favor if I asked him."

"Thank you for the offer, but I'm using Aunt Walker's patent lawyer. He's been a great help in explaining the patent process to me. Did you visit Aunt Walker when you were in New York?" Louvenia gestured toward a couple of nail kegs for them to sit on as they talked.

"I kept meaning to get up to her new place. I hear it's quite the palace."

"You truly missed something. But then you probably saw more than your fair share of palaces in Europe."

Emmet wasn't ready to talk about what he had seen during the war and instead asked, "So what are the potions on the table there? Are you building a still?"

Lou grinned. "I'm creating a fabric out of polymers, a completely synthetic fabric." She went on to give Emmet all the science behind her discoveries. He didn't understand any of it, but he was happy to be home. Louvenia and Kay's enthusiasm for life was intoxicating. He was beginning to absorb the fact that he had survived the war and now it was time to celebrate.

Claire's decision

For a few brief moments from the time she had taken the call and heard of Madame Walker's death to the time she was eating her ice cream sundae, Claire saw herself as a free woman, running her own show. A'Lelia had asked her to come and help her manage the Madame Walker empire. A'Lelia told her she could have any position, at any location. The very thought of it had excited Claire. She was ready to move beyond domestic servitude and put her business degree to good use.

But Benjamin threw cold water on her dreams. He mentioned that his work was stressful and full of plotting politicians. He said that it was not the time to make big changes, having just lost Roy and June.

Claire could have argued her way around the politicians, but she saw some sense in what he said about the children. Claire still had not been able to bring herself to go into June's room for more than a minute. She was afraid of something, perhaps fearful of letting loose the intense emotions she felt around June's death. She knew everyone on her street shared a similar loss, but it provided no comfort. Perhaps Ben was right, perhaps she was tempted by A'Lelia's offer as a way to avoid facing her wounds.

Tesla's visit

Louvenia was working part-time at the Smithsonian and there were still days she would pinch herself, not believing her good fortune. She didn't need the money. She earned plenty with her inventions, but just being around the discoveries made by the great minds of the last century continuously inspired her.

She walked over to the Tesla coil and shook her head gently. She whispered under her breath, "What a disappointment."

"Are you disappointed in my work, the politics that destroyed me, or in my own lack of vision?"

Lou turned to discover a tall man with wild hair standing behind her. Nikola Tesla. The great man himself.

"Mr. Tesla how do you do? It's an honor to meet you sir."

Tesla laughed good-naturedly, "I can assure you Miss, it's not been viewed as an honor by most. What's your name and what brings you to stand before Tesla's folly?"

"My name is Louvenia Johnson. I am also something of an inventor, and I work here at the Smithsonian."

"So Miss Johnson, have you come to see if there are any scraps left on the bones of my original idea that you can pick off and call your own?" Lou's eyes opened at the accusation. "Don't misunderstand me, Miss Johnson. I'd hold no malice toward you. There have been so many before you who have tried. It would take an extremely creative mind to conjure up yet another discovery from my original work."

"No sir. I was here to marvel at the elegance of your design. And wonder once again how Westinghouse could choose Edison's design over yours. Your solution to electricity would have saved money, reduced the risk of accidents and was in every aspect, superior."

"Ah, but I didn't know Alfred E. Smith, the governor of New York. Nor did I offer to wire his house, stables and lawns with lights. I sold my project on its merits, simpleton that I am. You know why Edison is great?"

"He has excellent men working for him?"

"Yes that's true. I was once one of them. But no, he is great because long ago Edison stopped being an inventor and became a politician and a marketing genius. His publicist works night and day to sell the Edison image of inventive, reliable and safe. You never read anything about his brutish nature."

"I'm aware of Mr. Edison's failings," said Lou. "I may be working for Miss Beulah Henry out of New York."

Tesla lifted one of his bushy eyebrows, impressed. "So you really are an inventor Miss...?"

"Miss Louvenia Johnson, sir."

"Miss Johnson, you would be fortunate to be working with Miss Henry. She's one of the greatest minds in our country today. Perhaps the world. If she were not colored and had Edison's publicist, she would be known as 'the mother of invention.'" He stepped closer to Louvenia, "So Miss Johnson, what is your area of specialty?"

"Mechanical engineering."

"Ah, so you work for the military?"

"Not exactly, but I suspect there will be more government contracts in my future."

"Do you have a good lawyer?"

"Funny, that's exactly what my brother asked me."

"He's right, a good lawyer will enable you to keep your patents after you sell your designs to the government. That way you can go on to sell them to other friendly countries and buyers."

"Thank you for the advice Mr. Tesla. And you sir, what are you working on these days?"

Lou had hit a sore point and Tesla visibly withdrew. He began walking away and replied over his shoulder, "I'm working on staying alive, Miss Johnson. Simply staying alive."

Spring 1919

Palmer notices Garvey

"Sir, the man is dangerous," said J. Edgar Hoover.

"Garvey?" asked Attorney General Palmer.

"Yes sir."

"Don't be ridiculous, Mr. Hoover. He's an over-inflated baboon."

"I don't think so sir."

"But the hats and the faux uniforms alone scream charlatan. Who's going to take him seriously?"

"The 50,000 people who went to hear him speak in Harlem yesterday."

"What's that you say?" asked Palmer. "How many people? Where exactly?"

"50,000 colored people standing on the sidewalks and in the streets for the sole purpose of catching a glimpse of the man."

"Was there no other spectacle, a parade, circus event or something to cause all those people to turn out?"

"No sir. Just Marcus Garvey."

Palmer didn't hesitate. "Put a tail on him. Add him to my daily reports. I want to know what Mr. Garvey has in mind."

"Yes sir," said the young Mr. Hoover. The trace of a smile crossed his face as he left Palmer's office.

Benjamin and DuBois

"Benjamin, it's so good to see you again. I've missed our talks since we sailed back from France together," said W.E.B. DuBois as he gripped Benjamin's hand.

"I don't get to New York with any frequency," said Benjamin somewhat taken aback. He hadn't noticed it on the ship, but now, standing on terra firma in the heart of DC, Benjamin recognized the voice of a politician when he heard it and DuBois spoke with polish.

"But Benjamin, there's so much going on at the NAACP right here in your own backyard," DuBois held out his arms to take in the bustling office where they were standing. DuBois stood in front of a simple wooden desk within a glass office. Beyond were twenty to thirty people, mostly young, busy with papers at desks and tables.

The room was stacked with books and papers everywhere. The office hummed with activity.

"Things are heating up here. We at the NAACP anticipate that DC will be the flash point of a great race debate. I'm planning on staying for at least a month. You must promise we'll see a lot of each other while I'm here." DuBois was as smooth as any Louisiana politician and to Benjamin's keenly astute eye, the Louisiana politicos were the finest. DuBois offered a cigar, but Benjamin shook his head no. Benjamin grew tired of the gracious front. He sensed that the sincere talks they once had during the crossing were lost, and that DuBois now thought of him as nothing more than an asset to be utilized.

"What do you want, E.B.?"

DuBois dropped into the chair beside Benjamin.

"Why Benjamin, whatever do you mean? I was just hoping to get to know one another better now that we're in the same city."

"DuBois, I live and breath politics. I stand in the Oval office eight hours a day. I know the prelude to a sales pitch. Let's have it."

DuBois made a face that looked like he had sucked on a lemon. He appeared comical, but Benjamin was in no mood to laugh.

"All right Benjamin, I'll get to the point. You have the ear of the most powerful man in the country, maybe the world. You must be aware of his inclinations regarding the passage of the Pan African Act. Benjamin, as a colored man, you know that lynchings are on the rise. We must put an end to it, and you Benjamin, may be able to help."

"I appreciate that you were brief sir, but I can assure you I'll not betray the trust I have with the President. To do so would put my job and my freedom in peril." Benjamin leaned toward DuBois over the arm of his chair and added in a whisper, "In case you haven't noticed, this administration is locking up its citizenry at the drop of a hat. Have you not read the Sedition Act?"

Benjamin continued in a low voice, "Anyone who speaks out against the administration gets five to ten years in prison. If you're against its policies and hold with ideas like suffrage, socialism, equality of any sort, fair wages, actually anything that's not related to the League of Nations, you can be put in jail without redress. I suggest, Mr. DuBois you tread lightly. In the end you must remember Wilson is from the South, the Deep South."

DuBois pulled a small silver cigarette case from his jacket and offered one to Benjamin who refused, but not before noticing DuBois smoked French cigarettes. DuBois lit up and took a long pull.

"Benjamin you're right. We're crazy to believe we'll make any significant impact with this President. However, we cannot stand by and watch negro men and women be hung from the street lamps of our cities. I'm not asking for the world here, just fair treatment for the colored. I'm tired of following the approved dictums of Booker T. Washington's separate and unequal. The law is no longer acceptable. Jim Crow has allowed the white population to objectify us and to treat us as second class citizens."

DuBois stood up and glanced out the window toward K Street. "And I'm sure you know my opinions about Mr. Garvey. He wants to have us all go back to Africa. The notion that the Europeans will give control of Africa back to us, shows the man is a simpleton."

"Yes, but one who has captured the imagination of our people."

"Exactly, and that's because they cannot imagine a set of laws that applies to blacks and whites – equally. I'm talking about overturning the Jim Crow laws."

"I know the argument E.B. I have children. I'd like to leave them something better than this, but there are powerful forces against you. Your nemesis at the moment is not the President, but Attorney General Palmer. Wilson is focused solely on the League of Nations. His neglect, has allowed a viper into the heart of our nation. E.B., don't underestimate my warning about Palmer. If he's not already infiltrated your organization he will. And his goal will be to destroy you and everyone who follows you."

DuBois considered his staff, hard at work. Something in DuBois's expression, made Benjamin realize that the man was a leader. He was a man who could command absolute loyalty. Benjamin's warnings would serve as inspiration, not a signal of defeat.

"Benjamin, that's why I've asked you here. You know these things. You know more than I realized. I need your help, Benjamin. Whatever you can give me." DuBois let the rest of the sentence go unsaid, but it was clear. DuBois wanted Benjamin to forget his oath of secrecy and provide intelligence regarding the infiltration of the NAACP and other government activities designed to bring down the colored organization.

"E.B.," Benjamin stood up and held out his hand. DuBois reached for it and covered it with his left in an act of sincere appreciation.

"I'll do what I can," said Ben.

Emmet on the Mall

Emmet was discouraged. He'd been home for four months and couldn't find a job. He had briefly found a position sweeping floors at a tannery, but the business closed within two weeks, leaving him and everyone else at the tannery out on the street. Now in late June the long Washington Boulevards were full of tourists and men out of work. With the war over and the government closing up shop for the summer there were hundreds of applicants for every job. Emmet thought the roving young men who had taken to the streets were akin to packs of wild dogs in search of prey.

"Hey you." Emmet heard a man call out behind him. He thought nothing of it. The voice was full of bravado and he suspected it was a youngster wanting to show off for his girlfriend.

"Hey you. Colored boy. What's you doing in these parts?" Emmet heard snickering. There was more than one. A chill ran down his back despite the warmth of his wool uniform.

"Ain't you heard me boy? Whose uniform you wearing? Did you steal it?"

Emmet knew he was going to have to turn and confront them. He also knew that in the rules of engagement a man should only begin a fight in which he was certain of its outcome. Emmet considered his location. He was on the Mall near Fourteenth Street. St Joseph's church was six blocks north. Even if he sprinted, the chances were good that they'd catch him as soon as he reached Constitution Avenue, because he'd be delayed by the traffic. If he turned and confronted them, he doubted that reason would enter into the conversation. If there were five or more of them, he didn't stand a chance. He wished he carried a gun, but his father wouldn't hear of it.

Spring 1919

"Boy, you better turn around. I won't be askin' you again."

Emmet was near the Washington monument. He could run to it and plead with the park guards for assistance. But the chances of their support were fifty-fifty at best. Emmet stopped and slowly turned. As he did, he was relieved to see that there were just three of them. Sailors, all juiced up on homemade hooch that they'd probably been drinking since their ship dropped anchor. They were big guys, broad across the chest and stout. Each had forearms the size of torpedoes. He suspected they were gunnery mates.

"Are you talking to me?" Emmet asked in an even tone.

"Who the hell else? What's you doin' here boy?"

"Walking home. Is there something I can help you with?"

"Yeah, are you the nigger everyone is looking for who raped that girl?"

Emmet saw the two young men behind his accuser slamming their fists into their palms, ready to pummel Emmet with any word of denial or acknowledgement.

Emmet answered, "I'm not sure if you read the paper today, but the young woman in question recanted her claim. She explained that she lied to get out of trouble with her family because she'd been out late." Emmet gave a slight smile. "Girls will be girls you know."

"I don't know nothin' about that. I do know I've got a sister and if you laid a hand on her..." The three drunken sailors nodded.

"Where are you from?" asked Emmet trying to engage the men.

"From none of your damn business. You saying you want to attack my sister?" The men stepped forward, almost in unison.

"I was just trying to be polite. Can I help you find something here in Washington? I grew up here and could direct you to any part of town you might have an interest in."

"We aren't goin' to be interested in any place a darky knows about," the sailor sneered. Then his eyes lit on something over Emmet's right shoulder and he nodded. Fear rose in Emmet. He didn't need to turn to know that more white soldiers were coming up behind him. Without another word he bolted north towards the White House.

The chase

Emmet ran fueled with the adrenaline of fear. He reckoned that there were ten to twelve young men chasing him. They yelled obscenities and told people they passed that he he had attacked the white girl. Others joined in the pursuit. Emmet believed he could outrun them. If he could get to the White House gate he could find shelter within. The guard might even recognize him from visiting with his father. The challenge would be crossing Constitution Avenue. The traffic would be heavy and he'd have to dodge horse drawn carriages and automobiles.

Emmet rounded Constitution and almost ran into four more sailors. The men behind Emmet shouted, "Get him" and the new recruits joined in the pursuit. One of them was slim and fast. He caught up to Emmet easily. He lunged for Emmet's feet and toppled him in the street. Clouds of dust rose from the skirmish on the dirt road. In two heartbeats the sailors were on him. They beat him with their fists and feet. The bile in Emmet's mouth made him realize that he was going to die. He could smell fear on the men. They were reduced to their most base instincts, unable to stop themselves from beating him to death. There were no police in the city that would stop this act of violence.

Emmet thought of his father and for the first time the adrenaline subsided enough that he simultaneously felt the kick to his groin and his nose being broken. He deeply regretted that his father must endure the pain of losing another son. He thought of his sisters Lou and Kay and smiled.

"Is that nigger smiling?" shouted a sailor covered in blood. "You like this boy? We've got more to give you."

The beating continued. Emmet no longer felt the blows. One of the men found a stick, another an iron pole. They broke his bones at will. Emmet could hear the cracking. He thought of his brother Roy who had died in the war and sister June who died of the epidemic. Sweet June, he would be happy to see her again. Emmet left his body to the mob and went unconscious.

The sailors were disappointed that he was still breathing, and not satisfied that Emmet had suffered enough, although they had broken

131

almost every bone in his body. A corporal stopped a passing car, went into the trunk and secured its portable gas tank. A soldier took it and poured the contents over Emmet. The original sailor, who shouted at Emmet, pulled out a cigarette and lit it. Before blowing out the match he threw it on the young black soldier still wearing his medals for bravery. Emmet lit up like a bonfire. The pack of men had to step back the blaze so powerful. The driver of the automobile sped away, not wanting to be part of the gruesome scene, his wife crying in the seat beside him.

"Henry, what was that about? Why did they set that soldier on fire?"

"Mildred, it's none of our business. You just keep your eyes straight ahead and forget you ever saw a thing."

The two dozen sailors stood around the burning body in a daze, as the firehouse alarms began to sound.

Summer 1919

BOSTON

O'Malley's bar

"A toast to the greatest Irishman alive, Michael Collins!"

"Here, here," replied several of the men in the bar.

"Damned if I'll drink to the man," said Frank Keehan. "He's a bloody murderer."

"For fuck's sake Frank. You're a good customer so I won't be throwin' you out for sayin' that. But I'll be askin' you to keep your feelin's to yourself as to Mr. Collins."

"O'Malley, the man is a terrorist. He's killing civilians. He's rippin' the country apart."

"Aye, but he's got the English listenin'. We've been at it for seven hundred years and this is the first time they've taken us seriously. After all, how's it different, what Collins is doin' versus what we did here in America to get rid of the English?"

"The blood of the innocent is on your head O'Malley. I, for one, will no longer drink in an Irish Republic Bar." Frank Keehan left in a huff, but the dozen men remaining took up the conversation.

"He's got a point," said one man taking Frank's place at the bar.

"He's got no point at all. He's either with us or not," said O'Malley.

Summer 1919

"Go easy on Frank," said another regular. "He lost his sister in one of Collins' raids. He's hurtin' somethin' fierce and you remember he used to be in here raisin' money for the cause. Now he feels responsible for the lass's death."

Many in the bar crossed themselves and said a small prayer for the lost girl.

"I'm sorry to hear that," said O'Malley. "God can strike me down if I don't mean it. But it was bound to happen. We knew we'd lose some of our own. I'd even venture to say Frank's own sister would rather die and meet St. Peter than to live under the English boot."

"You can't be sayin' that, O'Malley. You're just tryin' to justify your position," said Patrick Kelly.

The men at the bar turned to listen to Patrick. He had the respect of these hard drinking men. He was a man who could be counted on, a police officer who didn't take sides, and wasn't corrupt.

"Patrick, I was only sayin'…"

"Aye, you were sayin' that the end justifies the means. I'd like to see a free Ireland as much as any man here. But I'm with Frank. The killin' of innocents is over the line. If they were part of the army then they'd be soldiers, but a young life, that hasn't yet decided where it stands shouldn't be used to justify another death. Ye know I've lost children, grown children and if you told me I could have just one of them back if I became English I'd not hesitate. Not for an instant." The room was silent. "Besides O'Malley, you should stick to being a barkeep, my glass is empty."

The men at the bar laughed and O'Malley pulled another pint. "So Patrick, I guess that means you'll not be donatin' to the cause? You're aware President de Valere is in town with Harry Boland raisin' money."

"You can count me out, O'Malley. All I need is to be contributin' to a radical group these days with Commissioner Curtis about our necks. No, I'll leave you to your politics, gentlemen." Patrick downed his beer and went out into the bright summer day.

Memories of Timothy

Thomas Kelly couldn't help but nod off on the train to New York

City. He pulled out his Parker fountain pen several times, to begin writing a letter to Helen, but the rhythmical rocking of the train worked against him. On the way to New York he had meant to read Chief Justice Oliver Wendell Holmes paper on the right of civil servants to strike. Despite his father's constant reassurances that the police force would never strike, Thomas could feel the coming of a brawl, just as he had as a child, when he would seek out his younger brother Timothy in a bar. Tim was always ready for a fight. There were nights Timothy went out to pit himself against the world.

Thomas had known Timothy's dark side. It was always a little too ready for the fight, itching to take on the biggest bruiser in the bar in an attempt to what? To be put down?

For the first time, Thomas wondered about the precise circumstances of Timothy's death in the war. Did he charge a hill of machine guns leading a doomed attack? Thomas suspected that might be the case. He and his family would never know unless tales came back to them. The Army would say no more than that he had died in the service of his country.

Liam practices

Mrs. Cavannaugh was pleased with Liam's progress on the piano. The lad had a good ear. But every now and then he would begin playing combinations of chords and notes she had never heard before. Nothing she had ever played.

She knew not to admonish the child for his creative pieces. Instead she encouraged him to write down the notes if he could, and praised him for his original melodies. She needed to get him in front of someone who could evaluate his talents. She suspected he was an original.

"Liam, play me that tune you wrote last week. How did it go?"

And without hesitation Liam's little fingers played notes that seemed so discordant as to be contrived. He was developing a language of music and she would help him as best she could.

Summer 1919

Patricia and Jack

"Mr. Reed, my brother Thomas is full of nothing but praises for you," said Patricia as she sat beside the handsome man on a bench in the Boston Gardens.

"And he also speaks well of you," replied John Reed. This surprised Patricia. She never thought of her brother speaking kindly of her. She always thought he considered her too radical, too fringe for compliments.

"Really?" she replied.

"Truly, he believes you should be the next President of the United States. That you have more common sense than Wilson does. And more heart than Teddy Roosevelt, God rest his soul. Which is why I insisted on meeting you. I couldn't continue my life without meeting such an extraordinary woman." His smile was beguiling. Patricia found herself wanting to kiss him. She shook her head to clear it and the feathers on her hat fluttered.

"Forgive me for saying so Miss Kelley, but are you aware that feathers are passé? Ribbons are the thing these days. Women's heads are adorned by frumpy hats that look like gunny sacks."

"And that's precisely why I've not changed with the fashion, Mr. Reed. I like my feathers and broad rimmed hats. At a minimum, they keep young men at a distance," she gave him a flirtatious smile. And without a moments hesitation, Jack Reed leaned over and used the ample brim of her hat to steal a romantic kiss.

"Miss Kelly," he said pulling away from their momentary tryst. "I congratulate you for not being a slave to fashion." She blushed slightly.

Patricia stood and held out her arm wanting to know more about this bold and audacious man, "Come Mr. Reed. Tell me of Russia." They spent the day together filled with admiration of each other's commitment and ambition. They were two of a kind.

Patrick at Bunker Hill

Patrick Kelly Sr. and Greg Yeats, one of the suspended officers, strolled around the Bunker Hill Monument. The monument's strength and height inspired Patrick. He didn't like going into it, but he liked the history behind it.

"I wish I'd been here then," Patrick said out loud.

"When?" responded Greg.

"It must 'ave been somethin' to live here when the British owned the town. When they forced families like yours and mine to board and feed soldiers. When they treated the locals like second class citizens."

"Aye, sounds a lot like Ireland, ehh?" said Greg.

"I suppose you're right. And I suppose O'Malley is right about Michael Collins not having many choices in getting the English's attention. It's just that..." Patrick trailed off.

"It's against everything that we have worked for – our motto to serve and protect," said Greg finishing Patrick's thought.

"That's it in a nutshell. So what of you, lad? How are you keepin' yourself."

"I've got a security job at a local bank. But did you hear? Eddie's drivin' a milk truck."

"You can't be serious."

"So help me God," said Greg with a grin.

"But you're okay? I mean, I'd be devastated to leave the force. It's my family."

"I didn't have as many years in as you, Kelly. But I know what you mean. I wore the uniform with pride. I don't like seein' what's happening. It ain't right. I'm just wantin' my due. Fighting Curtis is easier for me with just a few years into the force than someone like you who's so close to his pension."

"So you say, but I do appreciate your sacrifice. I've contributed to the fund goin' 'round for your families. Are you receivin' the money?"

"Patrick, stop worrying about me. We're fine. We just need to get us a union and be done with it. I don't care if it's the AFL, IWW, or our own union. We just need someone to watch out for us – six years without a raise against 500% inflation. We'll starve at this rate."

"I kin what you're sayin'. I don't understand why Commissioner Curtis doesn't. You'd think we were askin' for money from his own bank account. I'm afraid we're in for quite a battle. I'm sorry, son. You'll let me know if you be needin' anything?" Patrick put a strong hand on Greg's shoulder. "You nary think twice about ringin' my door bell on Alston Street."

"Thanks, Patrick."

Patrick gave the young man two more pats on the shoulder and turned up the hill to head home.

Anti-Saloon League rally

The woman sitting beside Harriet could barely contain her excitement. She commented under her breath, "We've waited a long time for this." Harriet didn't respond, intent on listening to the presentation being given from the podium.

Poking Harriet in the ribs, the woman leaned in and whispered, "Everything they say about Congressman Hobson must be true ehh? He's quite the looker." The woman jutted her chin towards the speaker and winked at Harriet.

Harriet observed the handsome man with the southern drawl on stage. She didn't trust good looks. She felt they corrupted the bedecked and Harriet was confident that Mr. Hobson had been corrupted long ago. 'The Great Destroyer' as he had come to be known, could be the destruction of the cause if he didn't watch his step. Yet, there on the dais, he was saying all the right things, how drink kills five times as many people as war. That liquor turns the black man into a brute and the nature's noblemen into killing machines.

While the purpose of this meeting was to bask in the success of the passage of the Hobson-Sheppard Resolution also known as the Eighteenth Amendment, Hobson and his colleagues were introducing something new. Something Harriet had heard rumor of, The Volstead Act that would put the Eighteenth Amendment into effect immediately, instead of several years from now.

"Will you...." the woman began.

"Shhh," said Harriet intent upon the speech. The woman huffed, but remained silent.

Hobson continued, "Scientific research has demonstrated that alcohol is a narcotic poison, destructive and degenerating to the human organism, and that its distribution as a beverage or contained in foods, lays a staggering economic burden upon the shoulders of the people, lowers to an appalling degree the average standard of character of our citizenship, thereby undermining the public morals and the foundation of free institutions, produces widespread crime, pauperism and insanity, inflicts disease and untimely death upon hundreds of thousands of citizens, and blights with degeneracy their unborn children, threatening the future integrity and the very life of the nation." Hobson went on to spell out the articles of the Eighteenth Amendment, that included the end of selling or manufacturing liquor in the U.S. or its territories, except for sacramental and medicinal purposes."

Hobson looked out over his audience and continued, "I'm sure you all know the Amendment by heart, but it's Senator Volstead who has enabled us to see our dream become reality sooner than later. We will, this month, submit to the congress his Amendment H.R. 6810. Mr. Volstead has confirmed its constitutionality and we believe H.R. 6810 will pass the Senate without resistance. Ladies and Gentleman we may have a dry country by September 1919!"

Harriet imagined God nodding in confirmation that everything she had worked for was right and good.

Patrick at the game

"So Patrick, what do you think of the union?" asked Jim McInnis, as he took a bite of his hot dog. McInnis was the Mayor's right hand man and he had been sent to take Patrick's temperature regarding a pending strike.

Patrick's eyes didn't leave the game. He was hoping to see Babe Ruth hit a home run. The Babe had the best home run hitting record of anyone in the American league. There was half a chance the Red Sox would make it into the playoffs this year, thanks to Ruth.

"What's that you say, McInnis?" asked Patrick. "What union? There isn't a union, last I heard."

"Don't play coy with me Sergeant Kelly. You know what I'm talking about, the AFL union. Are you for it or against it?"

The Red Sox infielder, Red Shannon, hit a double and the crowd rose to its feet.

"Watch the game, will you McInnis? Is this why you brought me here, to carry on about the union? Don't we have enough of this talk around the station? No one can do their job any more for talk of the union." Patrick heard a crack and turned fast enough to see the ball fall just short of the green wall in left field. A single by Frank Gilhooley. Ruth was up next and the Red Sox were down 6-3. A home run by Ruth would tie the game.

"Hey," said McInnis. "Isn't that Caldwell pitching? The guy who got hit by lightning while on the mound?"

"Aye, and you know he continued that game and beat the Athletics two-to-one."

"Kelly, listen, just tell me if you'll walk out with the rest of the boys if a strike is called?"

Patrick turned to face McInnis, "I dinna kin. I work. I do my job. But I can tell ye I don't like how Curtis is handlin' things, but beyond that…" There was a loud crack and the crowd erupted. Men were slapping each other on the back with joy. Babe Ruth had hit a home run and the game was tied.

An angry Patrick Kelly roared at McInnis. "Now look at what you bloody well made me do. I missed the shot I came here to see. A Babe Ruth home run and you made me miss it. Shut your face you lout and sit down while I at least watch the man take his bases." The fans remained on their feet as Ruth took his time rounding third base. Once Ruth was back in the dugout, Patrick flew into McInnis.

"What do I think of the union? I think it's grand! Listen here, I've been on the force for more than twenty years, working over seventy hours a week. That's nothin' compared to the eighty-five hours most of the younger men work. They make the awesome salary of twenty-five cents an hour. And after twenty years do you know what I get? Twenty-nine cents an hour and the luxury of working during the day when there are fewer troublemakers about. Have you been to a station house lately? They're filled with vermin, rats, and fleas and most lack runnin' water. Do I believe in the union? Yes sir. It's about time. I can't feed my family because of the war profiteers, the same men who took one of my sons and maimed the other. If it weren't for the flu killin' two of my other children my family would have starved on my wages. As it is, my wife takes in laundry." Patrick stood up abruptly.

"To hell with you and your free tickets, McInnis. I'd rather not have to sit next to a man like you, turncoat that you are."

Patrick dramatically ripped his ticket in half and threw it in McInnis' face. Patrick knew the man didn't deserve it, McInnis was only doing his job, but it felt good. Besides, Patrick wasn't about to leave, he just went up to the bleachers to watch in peace. The strike was coming and there would be plenty of time to ponder it in the days to come.

Thomas waits for Helen

He knew when she had entered the room by the scent of her perfume. He wondered if blind people always wore distinctive aromas, in order to quickly identify each other. Helen's scent was not overpowering, it was like her, unique and unforgettable. He had imagined it was the smell of southern magnolias. Thomas was in awe of everything about her. She made his puny complaints about life inconsequential. Helen seemed not of this world, her spirit always gay, her ability to see past shortcomings, her infinite willingness to give without any expectation of receiving. No, Thomas was certain Helen was an angel sent as an example for mere mortals.

Her accomplishments were so great they humbled even the most erudite. Besides writing best selling books, performing to sell out crowds and traveling throughout the country, she also attended to the simple things. Her hair was poetry. Her clothes fashionable and always spotless. Helen's ability to focus on a person in conversation, rapt as if there was no one else in the world, made those who talked with her believe they had an important purpose.

Thomas waited for her with great impatience. He had splurged and purchased a box at the symphony so that he could be near her. She loved music and tonight they played Beethoven, her favorite. Having been banned so many months during the war, along with Brahms, he knew it would provide a special treat.

Summer 1919

Revolutionaries unite

"Patricia, you have visitors," yelled Harriet, over the sound of the Victrola. Liam had been playing records all morning. Mostly classical, but right now dance music blared. Harriet hated it, but she tolerated it, since music brought Liam so much pleasure.

"What Ma? Who is it?" Patricia called from upstairs.

"And how should I know?" Harriet put the tall man and plump woman in the parlor. As an active member of the Women's Christian Temperance Union Harriet knew politicos when she saw them and the two in the parlor were seasoned campaigners – which probably meant they were hungry and tired and would appreciate a cup of tea.

Patricia came bounding down the narrow staircase, curious to know who would show up at her door unannounced. She was quite surprised at the stature of the couple standing in her parlor.

"Mrs. Goldman, Mr. Eastman," said a flustered Patricia. "To what do I owe the honor of your visit?" Patricia fretted for a moment about inconsequential matters. Did she get all her hair up? Were her shoes buttoned? Was her dress clean? "Liam stop that racket," yelled Patricia. As she collected herself, her manners resurfaced, "Has my mother offered you refreshments?"

"Yes, thank you Miss Kelly," said Emma Goldman soothingly. "Please Miss Kelly, come join us." The trio sat and Emma spoke, "I do apologize for catching you unawares, but we were in town for the Communist Party meeting. Have you heard?"

"What?" asked Patricia.

"That Jack Reed has started the first American Communist Party this week in Chicago. They wouldn't let him or his followers into the Socialist Party convention so Jack took a delegation into another room and began the first legitimate Communist Labor Party of America, the CLP for short. He's quite the..."

"Revolutionary?" Patricia offered, as Emma nodded and smiled.

"Yes, it was Jack that insisted we meet you. He said you were a woman more dedicated to the cause than even myself," Emma paused, her gaze piercing Patricia, "and perhaps it's vanity, but I just had to meet you."

"The honor is all mine. And I believe Jack may have exaggerated.

146

Emancipation and women's rights are my primary activities. I have dedicated body and soul to those causes."

Emma's eyes never left Patricia. "Nonsense, the vote is the opiate of the masses." Harriet's mother had just come in with a tray of tea and cookies. She grunted at Emma's comment, as she bent to set down the tray.

"Do you not agree Mrs. Kelly?" asked Emma.

Harriet stood and smoothed her apron. "You only get what you take by force in this country. You have to have backbone. Passing all the laws in the world won't do a thing if you aren't willing to back them up with muscle."

"Ma," protested Patricia.

Max Eastman chimed in, "No, I believe your mother is right, Miss Kelly. But Mrs. Kelly, are you advocating violence?"

"If that's what need be," Harriet folded her arms across her chest in defiance, ready for a fight.

"I agree with you," said Emma, "But I must confess I'm surprised by your position, considering you're a policeman's wife. How does your husband feel about your anarchist leanings?" Emma smiled, but her face remained serious.

"My husband's opinion need not concern ye. Now if you'll excuse me, my grandson needs my attention." Harriet left the room. The remaining three searched for a conversational thread to retrieve.

"That's my Ma," said Patricia in explanation.

"And a fine woman she is," said Max. "I'm quite certain I'd never want to be on the other side of any issue she takes as her own."

"Kind of reminds you of someone, doesn't she?" Emma said as she poked Max in the rib with her elbow.

"Ah, the mirror rarely recognizes its own reflection."

Patricia could tell the two were a couple and had been for many years. They had faced danger together and spoke in the short hand of those who would give full measure for each other.

"How may I help you, or is this simply a social visit?" asked Patricia.

Emma again leveled a stern gaze at Patricia, "Miss Kelly, is there truly such a thing as a merely social visit among revolutionaries?"

Summer 1919

She winked at Patricia and continued, "Now that Jack has got himself a party, we're going to need some candidates to run for office. Your name appeared on everyone's short list."

Patricia took in the significance of the comment.

"What office did you have in mind?"

Max responded, "President."

"That's right. President of the United States," added Emma. "Now there's a job you could sink your teeth into."

"And you could make your Ma secretary of war," quipped Max.

"I'm not sure if you're serious or not," said Patricia, "but I do know the last man who ran as a socialist, much less a communist, found himself in jail. Is still in jail and will be for more than ten years, thanks to Wilson. I'm not sucker enough to believe that Wilson wouldn't do the same thing to me. He has no love for the Suffragette movement, so getting a women's rights activist and a communist at the same time would be too sweet a dish for him to pass up."

Emma studied Patricia for several minutes. Patricia did not squirm under the scrutiny, but held her ground. Finally Emma spoke, "You're right my dear, this would be a suicide mission and Jack underestimated you. Your brand of courage should not be wasted on this goose chase. However, if we were to come to you with a solid, legitimate offer, would you consider it?"

"Yes," replied Patricia.

"Good then," said Emma and stood, prodding Max to his feet with her walking stick.

"Come along Max, let's leave Miss Kelly to save the world. She just might have the pluck to do it."

Prohibition begins

Harriet Kelly picked up the lumberman's axe, raised it over her head and swung it down hard at the massive oak barrel. The beer keg represented a tangible threat to her and her children. The blade cut through the long bands of the barrel, rending its integrity and spilling beer into the room. Enthusiastic on-lookers cheered.

Harriet stood tall and proud. She imagined herself as an avenging angel, her sword (the axe) ready to slay any dragon (liquor manufac-

148

turer or drunk) that should cross her path. She liked the image. Harriet had given every extra minute of her life for the past ten years to fight for the Eighteenth Amendment. She woke early, before her children were out of bed, to distribute pamphlets in the freezing cold. She stayed up late to knit socks and mittens for fundraisers. She had even taken food out of her family's mouths; to save pennies for the cause, so passionate was her desire for a federal prohibition on liquor in America.

Harriet was besotted by the benefits this law would bestow. Women would no longer have to fear their husband's senseless brutality. Without the evil drink, most husbands could actually become dependable. Without the serpent alcohol coursing through mens' veins Harriet was optimistic that the country would get on the right track – stop fighting wars and start being productive. The elimination of intoxicants would improve the condition of all mankind.

"Congratulations, Mrs. Kelly," said a politician who made his way towards her from the throng of spectators.

"Why thank ye sir," she responded. She didn't want to talk to any lawyers or politicians right now. Harriet knew these buzzards just wanted to be associated with the success of the League to further their own careers.

She nodded to the man, turned away and walked toward a clique on the other side of the room. A tall, comely man in his twenties stepped into her path.

"I wanted to let you know, Ma'am, anytime you need help swinging that axe you just call me."

Harriet was pleased that a young man of drinking age was involved in the movement, showing that prohibition wasn't simply the cause of bible-thumping men and dried-up old women.

"Yes Ma'am, the more barrels of liquor you destroy the better for me."

"Aye the better for all of us," responded Harriet. "You're not familiar to me, do I kin your family?"

"No Ma'am, my name is Bill Curran," he took off his bowler with a flourish.

"What brings you here Mr. Curran?"

"Just to witness your success with my own eyes. To make sure that making alcohol illegal wasn't a nasty rumor. And, by Jove, I'd say you and your friends have done it. Congratulations."

"Aye, we have Mr. Curran," said Harriet with pride. "And quite the battle it's been. Thank goodness for the Women's Christian Temperance Union and the tenacity of the Anti-Saloon League for gettin' us here. But we ain't be finished yet, we still need the Volstead Act."

"I wouldn't worry about that. You should consider it done."

"I appreciate your enthusiasm, but we've been successful 'cause of the fact we have taken nothin' for granted. What type of work do you do Mr. Curran?"

During their conversation Bill had maneuvered Harriet to an out-of-the-way corner, so that they could speak without being overheard. "I'm in the distribution business."

"And what does that mean? Distributin' what?"

"Liquor," said Bill leveling his gaze at Harriet from beneath the brim of his hat.

Harriet began to laugh and then realized he was serious, "But you just offered to help me smash barrels."

"That's right, the more you smash the more I can charge for my product. You and your friends here are going to make me a very rich man. People are never going to stop drinking, but now that you've made it illegal, you've increased demand. Why just last week I opened six new speakeasies here in Boston. Unlike bars, women go to speakeasies, which means I have twice as many people to sell my booze to. I've got to hand it to you, I couldn't have come up with a better scheme if I tried."

"Why you be the devil himself. You're Lucifer here to test me. You won't win Mr. Curran. Good men, like my husband, will put you and your kind out of business and we'll have a sober society."

"I'm afraid not, sister. You've set free a genie that you'll not be able to get back into the bottle. You've started a pestilence that will last as long as you keep your law on the books. And trust me it'll become law. My friends and I will make sure of it. There's just too much money to be made, and if we grease the right palms even a veto from Wilson won't stop us." He pulled a toothpick out of his vest pocket and placed it casually in his mouth. "Yep, you opened the door to hell, Mrs. Kelly. Don't be surprised by what demons emerge."

Harriet froze at the sound of her name.

"Of course I know your name. You're one of our poster girls, you and Miss Stanton – the axe swinging sisters. Mark my words, history will label you both as dimwits for having allowed organized crime to flourish. In the past, crime didn't need to be so organized. It was just a loosely knit group of men who trafficked in prostitution, gambling and minor infractions. But you Mrs. Kelly, you've created a whole new opportunity to build an empire, one that will rival Caesar's. I'd like to shake the hand of the woman to whom I owe my good fortune."

Bill moved towards Harriet, but she quickly stepped backward, immersing herself in the crowd, unwilling to bring attention to the man or the conversation. She was sure he was lying, but now there was a kernel of doubt. What if the success of her passion was corrupted? She was startled from her thoughts by a hand on her shoulder. She swung around and was relieved to see that it was Patrick.

"Are you all right lass?"

"Aye, it's good to see you Da." Her eyes searched the crowd in order to point out Bill to Patrick, but the tall man was gone.

"I was in the neighborhood and thought I'd walk ye home if you're ready to leave."

"That'd be lovely. Thank ye for thinkin' of me."

"It's my job to watch out for my family. And I must confess this end of town has a few scurvy characters hangin' about. I'd just as soon ye not be walkin' home alone."

"Aye, I won't," she said.

He glanced at her sideways wondering why she didn't argue. For Harriet not to argue, no matter how minor the request, was out of character. Patrick encouraged her to talk the whole walk home, but she kept her thoughts to herself.

Summer 1919

Patrick to NY

Patrick felt discouraged. All that he had been, believed in, and lived by was being called into question. He had always been proud of his job, enjoyed the camaraderie of the force and at the end of each day, he felt he had done some good. Sure, he wasn't paid a living wage, but he didn't mind picking up an odd job here and there to make ends meet. As for the filthy working conditions, he had the good fortune of living near the precinct so he could go home to sleep when he was on extended duty beyond twelve hours a day. As a youth he hadn't minded the vermin, because he was so drunk by the time he tumbled into the cot at night, that even the fire alarm down the street at engine house fifty-two couldn't wake him.

What was happening now signaled the end of a way of life. Commissioner Curtis had broken a trust with the police force, something Commissioner O'Meara would never have done. O'Meara had been one of them. Curtis was going out of his way to make it clear that he was not sympathetic to the complaints of his officers. Suspending eight men with the threat of dismissal showed that Curtis didn't understand. The men were not demanding a union, they just wanted to have their grievances heard, and Curtis was saying he'd have none of it.

The outcome, whatever it might be, would be bad. For the first time in his life Patrick considered another profession. If he had the stomach for it, he'd join the Murphy brothers and become a mortician. Now there was a lucrative business, but with the flu subsiding there wasn't even as much business for them.

'I've got to get out of town and clear my head,' thought Patrick. He considered visiting his brother in New York. Patrick had vacation time coming up, maybe he'd go see Cyril and forget about this mess. Cyril had recently made sergeant. Perhaps he'd have some advice since his department had gone through the same union troubles. Cyril would be a good man to talk to.

"Harriet," Patrick shouted, "We be packin'. We be goin' to New York for a few days. I'm off to cable my brother."

Harriet never heard his words. By the time she made it down the stairs Patrick was out the front door and she wondered what her husband was shouting about now.

Helen says goodbye

The day was warm, very warm. Thomas ignored his discomfort and steered Liam towards the shade of a willow tree. From there they could see the swan boats being gently paddled back and forth across the small pond of the Boston Gardens. Except for the heat, it was a glorious day, the flowers smelled sweet and every blade of grass was a vibrant green.

Thomas found himself imagining how he would describe the color to Helen when she arrived. She hadn't met Liam yet, but Thomas was certain the sensitive boy and Helen would hit it off. A squirrel tentatively approached the boy and his uncle. A stranger scared it away as he called out Thomas's name.

"Mr. Kelly?" Thomas nodded. "I'm afraid Miss Keller will not be able to join you today. She sends her regrets and asked that I deliver this note to you."

"Thank you," said Thomas flatly. Without opening the note he knew it contained bad news. Thomas reached into his vest pocket to tip the messenger.

"No sir, that's not necessary. It's my pleasure. Anything for Miss Keller."

"Thank you again."

Thomas stood. He wanted to pace. He absorbed information better on his feet.

"Come on Liam, let's go to the frog pond. You can splash in the water there."

"Yippee," shouted Liam as he began to takeoff his shoes.

"No, not yet. We have to cross Charles Street first and you must hold my hand as we cross.

"Oh, Uncle."

"Don't you, 'oh Uncle' me. Just do as I say."

Thomas grabbed Liam's hand roughly. Then he relaxed his grip as he realized he was taking out his own dread of the letter on the boy.

Thomas couldn't possibly know what was in it, and yet, he knew Helen. They were in love. He was certain of it. Thomas was planning on asking her to marry him this weekend. Perhaps she sensed it.

At the gate Thomas looked both ways before crossing the busy thoroughfare, filled with carriages, carts and cars. The dusty road was a riot of movement and color. He held Liam's hand tighter.

"Come along boy."

A few steps into the street, Liam lost a shoe. A car full of people was bearing down on them and Thomas had to scoop Liam up quickly and move toward the middle of the street to get out of the way. Just as he began his first stride for the other side, Thomas looked in the opposite direction to see a thoroughbred with rider in a full gallop coming toward them. He felt his adrenaline kick in and in a continuous motion, lept in two large bounds to the other side.

A breathless Thomas set Liam down hard on the grass.

"Now you stay here, while I go back to get your shoe."

Thomas was angry, but not at Liam. He was already wondering what he could have done or said differently in order to keep Helen. He dashed out into the street and was almost hit by a fire engine, as he retrieved the boy's shoe.

Thomas returned to Liam, heaving him to his shoulder while holding both the shoe and the letter.

"Now let's get those feet wet."

As Liam splashed in the water, Thomas read the words neatly penned on the scented lavender stationary.

> *My Dearest Darling,*
>
> *I know you've already surmised that this missive holds bad tidings. Sweetheart you are in many ways more sensitive to that which is not seen than I. But I'll not digress into my thoughts about you, of which there are many. Instead, I must steel myself and tell you I have been called home. My mother demands that I spend the rest of the summer with her. I harbor uncharitable thoughts and believe that her true purpose is to separate me from my true love. And while a few months are nothing to wait, I must now take stock of reality.*
>
> *Thomas, you've a brilliant future before you. One full of astounding accomplishments. You must have a sighted guide to secure your success. A political asset. I imagine her to be a*

woman who could charm a bird from a tree. This is who you must marry, to ensure your advancement, and enable you to make the world a better place for us all.

My mother is wrong in that she believes I cannot be a good wife. I'm certain I will be, but my husband shall be a teacher or writer. Someone who I can count on and support, but who will not need me to guarantee his prosperity.

Now darling, I can hear all of your rebuttals to my words, but I must insist that you weigh them carefully. Once you do, you'll know I'm right.

Thomas, I shall always love you. I hope years from now our paths will cross again and we'll share with each other the adventures of our lives. For I am certain, our stories will contain great deeds. Especially yours, my love.

May God keep you always in his graces, as I shall treasure you in my heart.

Yours,

Helen

Involuntarily Thomas crushed the letter in his hand, but he could not part with it. He knew what she said was true. Yet he rejected it. He felt rejected. Thomas demanded an answer from God. And in response, his eyes fell upon Liam playing in the fountain. Laughing and enjoying the other children. Liam whose life had been shadowed by tragedy could still smile and enjoy the moment.

Thomas knew that one day he would fall in love again, but for now, he would put all his energies into his career. He'd make Helen proud.

New York

Harriet and Patrick in New York

The trip was good for them both. Staying at his brother's crowded
Bronx apartment was the low point, but Harriet and Patrick spent
time together, sharing their interests with one another, which they
had never done before. He attended a temperance rally with her,
while she listened to the speeches of the IWW leader William D.
Haywood with him.

They enjoyed each other's company as they took in several
vaudeville performances at the Grand Palace in Manhattan, where
the Blind Boone Concert Company and Eubie Blake played. They
laughed at the jokes and marveled over the dogs that would jump
through rings of fire. Harriet wondered why she and Patrick had
never gotten to know each other. How could they have lived together for thirty years and never shared joy or even simple frivolity?
Harriet feared she was to blame, always so serious, and stingy, saving pennies and out to protect the world from itself. She saw herself
as a harpy to come home to – no wonder Patrick spent so much time
at O'Malley's pub. If she had the choice she'd go to O'Malley's too,
to escape her sour moods. She swore, when they got home, she'd
sweeten her temperament.

Summer 1919

"A shame about the Red Sox and the Yankees being knocked out of the World Series," said Cyril, Patrick's brother. Too bad neither of us has Ty Cobb. The man might be an asshole, but if you bat .384 for the a season, it just doesn't matter if your personality stinks. He's a baseball giant."

"I still wish the Red Sox had made it. It's a real tragedy," Patrick replied. "Can you believe how well Ruth's been hittin'? Twenty-nine home runs. That's really somethin', and his pitchin' arm is gettin' better too."

"Aye, that's why I'm happy he's coming to work for us next year. And not as a pitcher, but an outfielder."

"What are you sayin'?" said Patrick in disbelief. "Harry Frazee would never trade Ruth away."

"He did, I guess he believes Carl Mays will be enough or maybe he just didn't have a choice. He sold Ruth for $125,000 and $300,000 in loans. Your Broadway producer must be on his last legs because I'm with you, Ruth is just reachin' his stride."

"I swear to Almighty that I'd stop bein' a Red Sox fan if I didn't love 'em so."

"Patrick, you come down and visit your old pitcher anytime you want. We've liked having you and Harriet here. Why don't you two move here after you retire? There's a lot more opportunity in the Bronx than in Boston. And while we didn't get the union we wanted we didn't do half bad. We make twice as much as your force and the perks are better too."

Patrick knew what his brother meant by the perks. The city was full of graft and it spilled into the pockets of the average policeman, making it much easier to get by.

"I'll speak to Harriet. We've had a good time. And you know Boston just isn't what it use to be."

The next morning they awoke to headlines about the Boston police strike. Riots had taken place throughout the city. Seventy were injured. Eight people were dead.

"Cyril, I should get back."

"I wouldn't if I were you, big brother. You go back and you'll find yourself in the middle of it. Forced to choose sides. I'd wait it out.

Send a telegram and extend your vacation a few days. You have the time coming, don't you?"

"I do."

The brothers didn't realize that the riots would go on. That the famous, wealthy and prestigious of Boston would sign up as volunteer policeman. Nor did they know about General Order 119, which cancelled the vacations of all officers, including sergeants.

Meanwhile Harriet and Patrick had a honeymoon. They went to the Statue of Liberty and toured Central Park in a horse drawn carriage. They even stayed in town two nights at the Plaza. Patrick dipped into his savings and felt it worth every penny. For the first time in their marriage Harriet and Patrick fell in love. They made a point of avoiding the newspapers. They didn't decide to return home until they received a telegram from Thomas that insisted upon his father's return.

As the couple said goodbye to Cyril's family, Harriet and Patrick felt a twinge of regret in leaving.

"Come back and visit us you two," said Cyril, with a wink to his big brother. "Patrick, you consider what we discussed."

Patrick gave his brother a bear hug and whispered in Cyril's ear, "I will, brother. We may be comin' back to stay. Thank ye."

BOSTON

Boston riots

When the police agreed to strike, they believed they were part of a general strike that included the telephone workers, the Women's Garment Union, and the firemen. All the union leaders had said, "If you go, we go." But when the time came, the labor leaders began to falter, leaving the uniformed policemen to stand alone in their petition for fair treatment.

As the clock struck 5:00 p.m. the police strike became official and the Boston Commons filled with unsavory characters. Dice games flourished in the open. The most wretched members of humanity appeared. It seemed as if they had been hiding in the trees waiting until it was safe to come out. Patricia was alarmed at the lawlessness she saw in just a matter of hours.

The shiftless and disenfranchised had come together on Washington Street. While Commissioner Curtis remained in his office, the band of irate locals proceeded through the shopping district shouting anti-police rhetoric. All of Curtis's recruits: athletes from local colleges, soldiers itching to exercise their hero status, blue bloods and out-of-work laborers stood at Scollay Square, three blocks away, unaware of the gathering horde.

Summer 1919

With the first sounds of broken glass on Tremont Street it was as if the starting gun for the Boston Marathon had been fired. Looters began shattering store windows throughout the downtown district. Haberdashers were the primary targets.

Patricia had planned on taking Liam to the Boston Gardens to ride the swan boats, but halfway through the Commons she sensed they should go home. Usually she would have retraced her steps and gone up to Park Street to catch the trolley, but today she felt safer walking over to Charles Street. The prison, as seen from the train stop, had guards with guns.

The morning paper

In two days the rioting was over. The storeowners claimed $750,000 in damages and theft. The politicians blamed it on the police. Not a word was printed that explained their side of the story. Even the AFL leadership left town. The police force stood alone.

Massachusetts's governor, Calvin Coolidge's words, 'There is no middle ground' and 'That way treason lies' were seized and printed in every paper across the country. Coolidge was credited with something new, called 'the sound bite'. For the first time he was considered presidential material. The little known governor nicknamed 'silent Cal' had become a celebrity.

Thomas was heartsick. His father had dedicated his life to the force. Thomas didn't know how his father would handle this treachery heaped on top of his other losses.

"If only he'd come home sooner..." And then the front door banged open and his parents entered.

Liam flew down the stairs into the arms of Patrick, "Granda you're home!" The little boy kissed his grandfather and gripped him about the neck.

"And you've no sugar for your Nana?" asked Harriet, good spirited.

Thomas met them in the hall, as his parents set down their grandson along with their bundles and cases.

"Da, have you seen the papers?"

"Aye son, it'll be all right. Whatever it may be, it will be all right."

Thomas knew not to argue. If his father had picked up the Boston

162

Globe, he would have registered the smear job already underway. The Boston Police were now responsible for every ailment in the city including potholes and unpaid taxes. Finally, in an unprecedented action, everyone not on duty that day was let go.

Thomas was prepared to shout down the unfairness and yet, once again, it was his father who saw things clearly. Patrick had a plan.

WASHINGTON DC

Wilson's riot

Benjamin stood at the hall window in the East Wing of the White House. The sky was an ominous orange. Smoke hung over the city.

The Washington Post had printed false information about a young white girl being molested. Even though the editor knew the story to be untrue, they had also printed a notice encouraging all white men who were angry (over the concocted incident) to gather at the market just before sunset. With the tension that already permeated the city due to the lack of jobs and the summer heat, the district was about to catch fire.

Each day ships disgorged as many as fifteen thousand more soldiers onto the docks; men without direction or prospects. They were a disillusioned mob. They had once heard of great profits being made in their absence and initially assumed they would return to a life of ease. At the very least they hoped for something that could help them forget what oafs they had been for going to war in the first place.

Soldiers were returning home as factories were shutting down or reducing their shifts. The rage these men now felt was easily directed at the colored population. Throughout the country, south and north alike, men and women of color were being lynched for no reason. They were blamed for the lack of jobs, for the war, for the loss of hope. 'A heavy burden, even for a black man,' thought Ben.

And what of the President? Benjamin had worked for Roosevelt and Taft. He was fully aware of how difficult the job of running the country was and he went home nightly relieved it was not his cross to bear. But he also saw how the personality of the President shaped, the country for better or worse. He believed Woodrow Wilson had lost his way.

Before going to Europe, President Wilson had had a passion for the American people. But diplomatic defeats in Europe led Wilson to turn his disappointment into a denial of the needs of his constituents. Personally, Benjamin tried not to expect much from his President. He had not faulted Wilson for not acknowledging the loss of his children, even Emmet. But now Benjamin felt that Wilson's lack of awareness extended far beyond Benjamin's own personal tragedies. The President was out of touch with the losses of the American people. Wilson was no longer with them, but against them.

Every time his aide, Colonel House, approached Wilson with a domestic policy issue, Wilson waved it aside with the response, "I have much bigger things to attend to. My job is keeping the world a safe place. Let the states take care of their own. That's why we have state government."

For the first time, Benjamin saw that even Edward House, Wilson's closest confidant, was losing patience. The world might not know it, but without House, Wilson governed without a heart.

Benjamin could hear the two men arguing in the next room.

"No, House, we need to talk about that upstart President from Ireland. He wants to meet with me. I'm going to need the Irish vote to be re-elected. Do you think I should meet with him while this terrorist Collins is running around Ireland killing Englishmen and civilians? Doesn't it send the wrong message to the Red terrorists here at home?"

House had been facing a painting on the wall, with his back to the President. When he turned, Wilson was surprised to find the

Colonel was red in the face. House spoke, but his words faltered. "Mr. President, what about the District, sir?"

"What about D.C.?" Wilson sputtered with anger. How dare House redirect the conversation, "What the devil are you talking about?"

"The District of Columbia is not a state, sir. How do you expect them to take care of this city, which is on the brink of exploding into race riots? Are you aware that your own assistant, Benjamin, lost his son to a brutal mob last week? This city is a powder keg about to explode. What are you planning to do about it?"

Wilson's face became expressionless, except for the tic over his eye. House knew that Wilson, was dismissing him, rather than engaging in a confrontation. "You disappoint me," said Wilson turning to read the papers on his desk. "Such thin metaphors and clichés. I know you can do better than that."

House held his retort in check, unwilling to anger the President further. Wilson had reached his limit, his eye and cheek twitched insistently. Both House and Benjamin knew that Wilson could handle no more. Since Wilson had no other advisors, if House were to leave, the President would have only his wife Edith to turn to for guidance.

"Very good sir," said House, "Let me know if you should need anything." As House left, Benjamin entered the Oval office, certain House would not return and that Wilson was too stubborn to call him back. Benjamin's heart sank with the knowledge that every American citizen was now left more vulnerable.

The White House

That evening Benjamin watched the city burn from the hall window of the Executive Mansion. Bands of white men were prowling up and down Pennsylvania Avenue in search of prey. The age, sex, and culpability of their victims was irrelevant. Only skin color mattered.

Isaac, the Wilson's house servant of thirty years, quietly appeared at Benjamin's side. "I ain't seen nothin' like it. Heard tell of things like this, carried out by that group in the South, the ones that wears the sheets."

"The Ku Klux Klan," Benjamin said flatly.

"Yeah, them. They were quite a menace after reconstruction, but I haven't heard of nothin' like this since I was a child." Issac shook his head.

"They aren't wearing sheets this time. They're wearing U.S. military uniforms. Most of them are from the Von Stueuben, which docked in the Washington Navy Yard two days ago. Why aren't their superior officers taking control of this situation?" Benjamin was angry. He knew the Secretary of War and Defense. He had served him coffee. The Admiral knew the names of Benjamin's sons who went to war. Where was the Admiral now? Why wasn't the President calling out the National Guard as House had recommended? A chilling thought crept into Ben's consciousness, but before he finished his thought, Isaac spoke again.

"Haven't these boys had enough of killin'? Enough of war? If they'd attack innocent American civilians, makes you wonder what they did 'over there.'"

Benjamin's face grew hard, the tendons in his jaw stiffened. "Isaac, were you with the President in Georgia or did you join him after he took his position at Princeton?"

Isaac turned away from the window to consider Benjamin. "Since Wesleyan University. Mary and I met him in Boston. Why do you ask?"

What Benjamin was thinking was treason, according to the Sedition Act. Uttering a word against the President would land you in jail. If Wilson knew what Benjamin was thinking right now, he'd be jailed for life.

"Nothing, Isaac. I have to go home and make sure my family is safe."

"Is you crazy? You goin' out in that mess? You know they've strung up thirty-five black men this year. You lookin' to become number thirty-six?" Isaac's face was a mixture of anger and fear. Benjamin wasn't sure if Issac was actually worried about his well-being or about the President's reputation, should Benjamin be strung up.

"I'm going, Isaac."

"Wait. What was your question?" Isaac wanted to stall him. The worst was not yet over outside. If Benjamin left tonight he probably wouldn't survive the walk home.

"Maybe you should come over to my house. We live nearby on K and Twelfth," offered Isaac. But Benjamin wasn't listening. He shook off his black jacket and handed it to Isaac.

"Would you put this away please? The President is in a foul mood. It's better if he thinks I've already gone."

"Of course," said Isaac. "Be careful Benjamin."

Benjamin reached out to Issac and the two men shook hands. Benjamin left the White House that evening with one burning question, 'Is the President a racist?' He had accepted that Wilson was an ignorant white man, but a white racist cracker, that was something else.

Claire at home

Claire was beside herself. None of her family were at home. Her husband was late and there was a war at her door. She kept the lights out and watched innocent neighbors being attacked from her second floor window. She prayed Kay, Louvenia and Ben had found safe places to hide.

The thought made her sick. She heard herself say the words, 'a place to hide'. Why should she or anyone else in America need to hide in their own homes? What had gone wrong? Why was this happening? Were negroes so hated by the white race?

She considered the town of Boyle, Oklahoma, now four thousand strong, which Booker T. claimed to be, 'the most enterprising and interesting of negro cities.' Maybe he was right. Perhaps she and her family should move to one of the fifty all black Oklahoma cities, away from the random violence of whites. But how would that assure their safety? Couldn't the whites storm those towns any time they wanted? The laws passed in Okfuskee County, forcing all black citizens to move, proved that nowhere was safe as long as negroes did not have a voice in the making of laws.

Claire was too afraid to think clearly about such things. Her mind was a jumble of dreadful scenes, each ending with a member of her family bleeding and alone.

"Momma?"

169

Summer 1919

Claire jumped at the voice behind her. "Louvenia, is that you?" The two women rushed into each other's arms.

"How did you get here? Where were you?"

"I was at the Smithsonian. I had to walk across the Mall to get home," Louvenia began to cry. "Momma I saw such dreadful things, such horrible things. How could people be so cruel? How could they hate so much?" Claire held her daughter tightly and rocked her. She knew not to ask any questions. Too much violence had already been brought into her home.

Benjamin on the streets

Benjamin nodded at Pete, the old guard at the door, as he walked through the lobby.

"Ben, you're not going out there? It's dangerous. I've been watching people get their heads cracked all day long and it's getting worse. Why don't you bunk here tonight?"

All Benjamin knew for sure was that he had to get home to protect his family. "Pete, you've watched violence being perpetrated and you've done nothing?"

"Hey, I'm just a glorified door man, I can't do anything about it," said Pete with a sullen expression. Then he perked up, "I did call the police. I asked them to station men on all the street corners around the White House." Benjamin's anger was near the surface now.

"Bully for you," muttered Ben. "Good night Pete."

Benjamin pushed through the door. He was attired, as always, in his brown wool suit. He wore highly polished lace up shoes and a straw boater with a brown ribbon decorated by a small red feather Claire had added for color. Thinking of her made him smile and then worry because he knew she was home alone and there was no telling how far the violence had spread. He hoped that Kay had stayed at the theater with friends, avoiding the hostilities.

Benjamin turned right, heading down Pennsylvania Avenue toward Thirteenth street. He lived five blocks from the White House, but they were long blocks. As he passed the Treasury building he heard a man yell.

"There's one!"

170

They were already upon him by the time he realized he was the target. A blow to Ben's head sent his boater flying and forced him to his knees. Then he felt his ribs crack beneath the impact of a wooden bat. In a flash, Benjamin knew he was going to die, a senseless death. He would die disappointed in himself. "Claire" passed through his lips.

"What did he say?" asked one of the four uniformed thugs.

"Don't know," answered another. "I think he's calling you a girl's name."

Benjamin felt the bat land across his back. He fell to the ground hard and his head hit the pavement, knocking him unconscious. Two of his attackers caught sight of moving prey and ran over to join a group of men who were forcing a young colored man to the ground.

"Let's step on his head 'til he's dead," suggested one of the soldiers. The sky was red with blood and the men had little imagination. So they began taking turns grinding their boot heels into the young man's head. Most of the attackers wore army uniforms, as did the black man beneath their feet.

Benjamin came to and heard a whistle in the distance. He had a vague sense that someone was kicking him. The sound of the whistle drifted closer. He saw shoes inches from his face. A familiar voice floated down. Benjamin noted that the shoes were meticulously polished.

"You idiots," said the police officer. "Get away from this man. This is the President's aide. Are you nuts? Are you wantin' to be put in the brig for the rest of your lives? Get out of here fast before I have you brought in."

The policeman stood by Benjamin's head to prevent any more blows. The boys snarled and whined like beasts denied their freshly felled game.

Benjamin heard one of his attacker's voices. "Hey, let's go finish up on this nigger who stole the uniform." The young men cheered and descended on the poor soldier who's eyes had already lost any spark of consciousness. Then Benjamin's world went dark.

Summer 1919

The Howard Theater

"Kay, you need to come home with me."

"Yeah, right. My Momma would tan my hide good if I went home with you." She laughed and started for the door.

"Kay, I'm not kidding." Duke went to the door and put his large hand against it. "They're rioting outside. I came here to find you. I suspected you would be here and not realize the danger. They're fighting all around your house. You can't go home."

At first, Kay thought he was making up a story and then she realized he was telling the truth. She rushed for the door.

"Let me out. I need to know if my parents are all right."

"Come home with me. We can call from there. Your reputation is safe, my mother is home and she'll take care of us. Trust me Kay, you cannot go home until this over. They're killing blacks all over the city, men and women." Duke said it for effect, he didn't realize that it was really true.

"I trust you, Duke." She held out her hand to him, and he took it. Turning out the lights so that their silhouettes would not appear in the doorway, they rushed to the back of the building and traversed the alleys until reaching the safety of the Ellington residence.

Benjamin at the White House

He awoke with a start. "Where am I?" Benjamin tried to sit up, but discovered he was strapped down.

"What's going on here? Why am I tied down?"

A doctor stood nearby, conversing with an older nurse.

"Mr. Johnson, you're suffering from broken ribs, a severe concussion and possibly a broken back. You'll need to lay still until I can get you to the hospital for x-rays."

"No sir, I need to get home." Benjamin could say the words, but he wasn't sure that his body could carry them out.

"We'll have someone go to your home and make sure everyone is well, but for now, you'll wait here in the protection of the White House, until we can get you to the hospital. Nurse, please administer the sedative."

"No, I need to know…" Benjamin didn't finish the sentence.

"It's a mild sedative, specifically to relax the muscles that were recently abused. I'll be able to wake you as soon as we receive word. Where do you live?"

Benjamin slurred his address as he fell off to sleep.

The doctor turned to the nurse. "He doesn't know it's morning. I hope his family survived."

Wilson and the National Guard

"What is it? Don't you know I am not well?" Wilson spit the words at the secret service agent who had entered his office unannounced.

"Yes sir, but I thought you might want to know that there's rioting going on throughout the District even in front of the White House."

"I'm sure it's just a few high spirited sailors."

"I beg your pardon sir, but it's a bit more than that. Dozens of people have been killed and hundreds injured. Your aide Benjamin Johnson is downstairs. He was pulled in off the street. A group of soldiers attacked him in front of the Treasury and left him for dead. His back may be broken, sir."

"What are you saying? The Treasury building is fifty feet from the White House!"

"Yes sir. The city's not safe. Please stay away from the windows."

Wilson walked to his desk and picked up the phone. "Get me the National Guard."

Kay and the scout

Kay returned to her classes a few weeks after the riots, but rather than going around to the student union to play piano as she often did, she headed home. Her mother needed her.

"Kay, aren't you joining us?" asked her friend Florence. "I hear there's a new piano roll in the union called the Charleston Rag, by Eubie Blake. Come on Kay, you could write the lyrics." Florence was young and slim like Kay and full of life. She wanted to be an actress, but excelled in chemistry. Kay often thought that thirty years from now she would hear Florence's name mentioned in association with an important scientific discovery.

"No Florence, not tonight. I need to go home and be with my family."

"Oh, I'm sorry Kay," she said, with real compassion. "How are your parents doing? Is your dad better? I'm sure all of you must miss Emmet something awful. He was such a good man."

Kay wasn't ready to talk about Emmet. Even now the mere mention of his name brought tears to her eyes.

"Thank you Florence, but I've got to go. I'll see you in class tomorrow." Kay turned and walked briskly down the path to the bus stop that would take her into D.C. She hadn't any chores to do at home, but she wanted to be near her mother. She liked to get home first, so that Claire didn't have to face the empty house. Kay would start up the Victrola or get the piano going so that their home was full of light and music. Emmet's death had visibly aged her mother, even more than the passing of June or Roy.

It was late in the afternoon and already it was getting dark. The bus moved slowly through the dusk. Now and then Kay glimpsed the occasional horse drawn carriage heading for an outlying farm.

A white man sitting in front of her said out loud, "Beautiful country you have here." He turned and smiled at Kay. He was slick, in a city sort of way.

"I'm Clifford Miller," he said, introducing himself.

"Kay Johnson."

"Are you from around here?" asked Clifford.

"Yes. And yourself?"

"No I'm here visiting a friend who had the flu. Several of his people died and I wanted to pay my respects. Did you lose anyone?"

Kay was taken aback by the abruptness of his question and yet she couldn't stop herself from answering. "My sister June died of the flu, here in D.C. I also lost a brother, Roy, who caught the virus while he was in the army in France. I lost another brother here."

"I'm sorry to hear of your losses. I was hiking in Appalachia when the flu hit. People there didn't know much about it. The fever didn't reached them until after I left. A returning soldier brought it home." Clifford shook his head, "I was fortunate, somehow the Spanish Lady missed my house. How did your other brother die?"

"He was killed by a mob just before the race riots in July," she said stoically.

Clifford looked at her with stunned disbelief. "I don't understand the south. Never did. I'm terribly sorry for your loss."

"I know, it's incredible. He survived the war and the flu and then he's killed just by walking down the street, in his own neighborhood. His death devastated my mother. The randomness of the violence destroyed her spirit."

"Then that's where you must help her. You're a vivacious young woman. It emanates from you. You must share that with your mother and father. Bring them joy."

Kay blushed, "I do my best, but actually I'm at sort of a rebellious stage of my life. I'm ready to move on."

"But you owe them so much. They've been there for you. For a short time you must do the same for them." He looked into her face. His light blonde hair was receding and he wore horned-rimmed glasses that accentuated his kind blue eyes. His skin was white and slightly yellowed. She couldn't guess his age. White people always looked older than they were. She suspected somewhere in his thirties or early forties.

"I'm sorry, but what is it you do? Are you some kind of psychiatrist?" asked Kay.

"No," he said smiling. "I'm a talent scout for the Orpheum Vaudeville circuit. I travel all over the country scouting out acts. That's what took me to Appalachia, I wanted to find something unusual. You know, singing dogs, people who play piano with their feet, that sort of thing."

Kay sat bolt upright, "You mean you're looking for vaudeville acts?"

He laughed. Every woman he had ever met had aspirations for the stage. That's why he almost always told them he was a traveling salesman, but Kay was different. He liked her and he suspected she might have talent.

"Don't tell me. You sing, right?" He said it in mock surprise.

"How did you know? Yes, and dance, play the piano and my best talent is that I can write lyrics to any song you can hum."

"Now that's unique. I'm not sure I am up to humming right now, but how about singing me a soothing quiet tune." Kay began to sing a verse of Daddy Long Legs. To his surprise she had a voice. A beautiful voice. Her control and timbre, were magical. When she finished singing, he had barely enough control to restrain himself although he really wanted to sign her up right there on the spot.

"That's a wonderful set of pipes you have. What are you studying in school?"

Disappointment filled Kay's eyes, "You didn't like the song?"

"I didn't say that. I asked you what you're studying in school, and when are you scheduled to finish?"

"I'm studying literature. I'm to be a teacher. I have two years left." She sat back, defeated. For the first time, depression hollowed her cheeks into a sullen expression.

"What if I give you my card and when you graduate you come see me, before you start teaching."

She didn't believe him. "Sure Mister Miller. You'll be my first call."

"Should be. I'll start you at $25 a week." And he smiled.

"What!" she shouted. "My father doesn't make that in a month and he works for the President! Are you serious?"

"Very much so. I didn't mean to tease you Kay, but I've seen a lot while traveling around this country. I don't mean to pry, but I assure you that if you were to leave school and home now you'd break your mother's heart. No mother can stand to lose four children in the same year. And to be honest with you, I'm not sure the time is right for you either."

Kay sat back, chagrined. She knew he was right.

"Keep up your practicing. Become an excellent pianist and excel in your studies. Vaudeville will wait for you. And meanwhile, keep my card." He handed her his card and then reached into his jacket pocket and pulled out a worn little brown book. "Tell me your full name Miss Kay."

"Kay Talbert is my stage name, but my real name is Kay Ruth

Johnson. Let me give you our phone number."

"All right, shoot."

"North East 8-7754. Just in case you have to fill an act while you're in town."

They both smiled, knowing they would meet again. The Capitol building rose up before them.

"This is my stop, Mr. Miller. I hope to see you soon."

"The pleasure will be all mine Miss Johnson."

Wilson in a new light

The President's mood continued to worsen. It was apparent that the Senate was not going to rubber-stamp the League of Nations. Wilson began to growl and snap at everyone around him.

"Benjamin, bring me some tea."

"Yes sir." Benjamin had returned to work only days after the attack. His injuries caused him to move slower.

"Wait a minute." Wilson removed his glasses and looked up from his desk which was covered with papers. "Benjamin, sit down for a moment. I'd like to speak with you."

Benjamin grimaced at the thought of sitting. Getting into the chair was not a problem. It was getting out. Besides, the President rarely spoke with people these days. He was more inclined to pick a fight. But Benjamin was in no position to argue, so he sat against the wall in a straight back chair.

"No, come here to the couch." Wilson pointed to the divan near the center of the Oval office. Benjamin knew his reprieve would come only if someone rushed in with a message that the building was on fire or a war had broken out.

"Benjamin, you were here in July when those awful riots took place, weren't you?"

Benjamin said nothing. Choked up by the fact that his own boss was unaware of the death of his son, much less his own brush with death.

Wilson put his glasses back on and began rustling the papers on his desk.

"Yes sir."

"Were they started by foreign nationals? Communists, as the young Mr. Hoover thinks?"

Ben's astonishment at the question left him speechless.

"Well?" the President peered up over his wire rims.

"No sir, I do not believe foreign nationals had anything to do with the riots."

"That's what I thought. All right, you may fetch my tea."

Benjamin left, stunned, disgusted. His disappointment existed on so many levels that he could barely find the words when, later that night, he tried to explain it to Claire.

They sat in the parlor. Benjamin was silent for a long time. Claire was making lace waiting patiently for Benjamin to speak.

"Take your time dear," she said gently.

"You know I've always given the President the benefit of the doubt. I've always felt, that deep down, he loved the country and its people."

Claire set aside her lace, as Benjamin continued.

"I may have been wrong, Claire. He might be the heartless brute so many have made him out to be. An egotist who cannot see beyond his own sphere of influence."

Claire remained still, letting Benjamin's chagrin fully settle into the room.

"I had such high hopes for him. Yes, as time progressed, I realized he was not going to be a man of the people. That he was preoccupied with foreign policy so much, that he ignored the trouble here at home. I never thought he was unconscious, but he's completely unaware of the pain and stress of the American people." Benjamin rose and went to the fireplace, his face turned away from Claire.

"And I'm not talking just about the negroes, but everyone: the factory workers, the American Indians, women, policemen and returning soldiers." Benjamin paused, his eyes pooling with tears. Claire wanted to go to him, but she knew he was not done yet. He shook his head as if trying to clear it.

"I'm sorry, Claire. I can't work for the man. He's making bad decisions for the people of this country and I can no longer stand by as his step-and-fetch-it servant and watch him destroy everything that I admire and am proud of."

"What is happening specifically, dear?" She wasn't sure why she asked, but she felt Ben needed to get it out. His frustration had been building for months, and speaking about it might bring some relief.

"The most appalling things are coming out of the Attorney General's office. Palmer is mentally unbalanced. He sees espionage and traitors everywhere. He's ready to deport every legal alien in the country and rip parents from their children. Deny citizenship. Revoke citizenship from others. He is paranoid about Communism. He acts like it's the religion of the devil. I can understand why J.P. Morgan and the Rockefellers would dislike it, but why should Palmer care? And his new junior henchman Hoover is a weasel. I tell you Claire, Palmer is damaged in a way I haven't figured out yet, and he is out to injure as many people as he can to feed his demons."

"But Ben dearest, what triggered all of this?"

He stopped. His heart raced in his chest and there was a roaring in his ears. He knew exactly what started it. But he was afraid to speak of it, for if he did, his anger might explode into a violent physical rage, ending with his fist through the wall.

Instead he answered, "I overheard Hoover with the President the other day talking about discrediting Garvey to make him out to be a thief and cause the movement to turn against him."

Claire said nothing, but was shocked by the revelation. Benjamin never shared conversations from the Oval office.

"Mr. Hoover has collected incriminating evidence on a few men and is blackmailing them into sabotaging Garvey by discrediting the Black Star Line. You know that I'm no fan of Garvey. I think he's an arrogant fool. Left alone, I'm sure he would fail on his own. But our administration does not feel that's fast enough. They have agents and collaborators on the payroll, posing as Garvey's staff, set to over-pay for inferior ships. They want to bring a lawsuit against Garvey to discredit him in the eyes of his followers."

"Why?" asked Claire. "I mean, why did they need this to happen faster? Granted, Garvey isn't the sharpest tack in the box, but he has done some good. Why him?"

"I've asked myself that same question over and over. Why? Why break the law and spit on the constitution in order to bring down a man who, through his own ignorance, will bring himself down. I believe it's because they're afraid. Afraid of anyone with power. Personal power, power from constituents, power of knowledge, power through might. But most of all, they're afraid of the power generated by people when they band together in an effort to accomplish something. These men are afraid of the power given to each American citizen simply because they were born American. Independence is not something they can control, and they feel the need to control everyone and everything. They're afraid of our freedom."

Claire and Benjamin sat in silence as the clock on the mantle ticked off the minutes.

"Ben, what is it you are saying? That another government, run by the intelligence agencies, is forming, behind the one that the average citizen knows? A sort of shadow government?"

"Precisely. I'm worried Claire."

Claire pondered the implications. "But the President won't survive another election. I know he's talked about running for a third term, but I don't think his party wants him. Won't the next man in office clean up all this subterfuge?"

"As long as he knows about it and is smart enough to do something. Yes, maybe then." Benjamin seemed to relax a little at the thought. He sat up straighter, his shoulders less hunched.

With a sense of relief he repeated, "Yes, I suppose you're right."

They were quiet for a long while. Until eventually Claire went to him and sat on the arm of his chair – "Ben I love you. I'll follow you anywhere. I support your heart's desire. But I don't want to grow older with you regretting your life decisions. This is your time Ben, you're 54. What's your contribution going to be?" She kissed the top of his head and pulled him toward her. She could feel the change in their lives taking shape around her.

Hoover's report on the riot

Benjamin knew that the path he had chosen was a precarious one for an American negro. He lived in the middle class of America, working as an aide to the President. But Benjamin also belonged in the upper middle class of well-educated men of color. Ben's peers maintained fine homes, elegant cars and brought up their sons and daughters to be pillars of black society. They did not socialize with whites.

Benjamin had always prided himself on his ability to live in both worlds amicably. He often thought that upper class blacks would be astonished to know how whites perceived the negro race without class distinction. But today, as Hoover, a man not yet thirty, read his report on the status of the negro nation to President Wilson, Benjamin changed his mind.

"Excuse me, Mr. President," said the young Hoover. "But shouldn't we ask your man here to leave. He is, after all, one of them."

Wilson hated it when anyone told him what to do, especially this pip-squeak. In other circumstances he might have agreed, but the arrogance with which Hoover presumed he could dictate the President's actions raised Wilson's ire.

"Benjamin will stay. He's my trusted and loyal servant and I assure you, young man, he has heard reports far more sensitive than yours without incident."

"But...," Hoover was cut off by Attorney General Palmer who sat next to him.

"Go on, Mr. Hoover," said Palmer, not wanting to diminish the message they were delivering.

Hoover began, his report detailing the brutal death of a young soldier two weeks before the riots, by a handful of sailors on leave. Benjamin slowly began to realize that Hoover was talking about Emmet. It was impossible that Hoover didn't know that Benjamin Johnson was Emmet's father. Benjamin became sick to his stomach, shocked at how a human being could be utterly devoid of empathy. Suddenly he couldn't remain in the same room with this demonic spirit.

Benjamin snapped, "Mr. President, I should step out."

Wilson scowled, "Fine. I'll call you when I need you."

Hoover continued with his presentation, unphased. Out in the hall Benjamin now clearly recognized that Hoover was a man that had ice water running through his veins. He saw enormous implications in the fact that Palmer had chosen Hoover to start watching American citizens. Palmer was developing an agency that was operating outside of the constitution, right under the nose of Congress.

Although Benjamin found Hoover to be a repulsive human being, he knew that Hoover alone was not to blame. The President had turned his back on the American people and it was he who should be held accountable for unleashing this plague on democracy.

Over the years Benjamin had made too many excuses for Wilson. Too many concessions, while believing, this man of great intellect would awaken to the turmoil within his own country. Benjamin could no longer forgive Wilson. The President had allowed an evil, in the form of Hoover, to corrupt the government's system of checks and balances that were put in place by the founding fathers. Wilson had abdicated. For the first time Benjamin blamed Wilson for the death of his sons. If it had not been for Wilson's actions, both Roy and Emmet would be alive today.

Benjamin was angry and he decided to place the blame where it belonged. He would sue his employer. He would sue the United States Government for negligence and then the Washington Post for murder. Benjamin would not let Emmet's life be forgotten.

Benjamin and the NAACP

Benjamin stood for a long time outside the doors of the NAACP offices. What he was considering doing was suicidal and he was not certain he wanted to associate the good name of the organization with his cause. However, in the end it would be the organization's decision to participate, not his. He climbed the spotlessly clean stairs. This pleased Benjamin because it meant DuBois had not abandoned all of Booker T. Washington's edicts.

"Benjamin, I can't tell you how sad I am for your loss," said James Weldon Johnson, field secretary of the NAACP. "I heard you were injured as well. How are you feeling?"

"Thank you for inquiring, James. I still have a bit of a limp, but the doctors say I'll be fine."

"It's good to see you Benjamin," said W.E.B. DuBois as the two men hugged. "I would like to introduce you to Walter White. He's our latest secret weapon."

"How do you do, Mr. White?" As Benjamin took in White's blonde hair and blue eyes he asked, "Excuse me, sir, but is your last name really White?"

"I swear on my grandmother's sweet soul."

Benjamin shook his head. "I'm glad you're on our side. I read one of your recent anti-lynching law exposes. It was excellent."

"Thank you for your generous praise. Let's hope I can write with greater force in order to stop these atrocities. No father should walk through those doors carrying your burden."

"Amen, brother," said DuBois. "Let's get down to business. Benjamin please step over here to our makeshift conference room." The men retired to the end of the room and sat at a kitchen table surround by a collection of mismatched chairs.

DuBois began the conversation, "As I understand it Benjamin, you want to sue the Washington Post and the U.S. government for your son's wrongful death?"

"That is correct."

"Interestingly, the Post would be an unwitting supporter of our cause because they did such an excellent job documenting what happened that night. I must ask you to reconsider your suit against them. I believe we would fare better having them as an ally rather than an enemy. When we bring the case against the government, the Post will want to cover it in order to sell newspapers. We want them sympathetic to the case, so that they will influence public opinion in our favor. If we make them a co-defendant they will use their paper as a pulpit to declare their innocence and discredit your complaint."

"I've thought of that E.B., but remember, the Post instigated the riot. Had they not printed a place and time for people to meet this might have all been avoided."

"True Benjamin, true. But Emmet was not killed on the night of the riots. You almost were, but not Emmet. Emmet died because a group of sailors felt free to kill a black man without consequences."

Benjamin's hand involuntarily formed a fist.

"I'm sorry, Benjamin. I don't want to make you relive the experience, but you need to know that if you go forward with this case, it'll become increasingly unpleasant. For instance, the defense will attempt to discredit Emmet, by making him out to be shiftless. They will suggest that his death was in someway his fault."

Mr. White added, "They may even manufacture witnesses."

"What do you mean?" asked Benjamin.

"In similar cases, the defense has produced white female witnesses that accuse the deceased of having molested them. This almost always causes the jury to come back with a 'Not Guilty' verdict."

"But these women would be under oath. Doesn't that mean anything?"

"Not to someone who's hungry. The war left a lot of widows without a breadwinner and with babies to feed. The rise in prostitution in this country is increasing at the same rate as lynchings. Make no mistake Benjamin, people are angry and they're hungry. They want someone to blame. That's why Emmet was killed. Our mission today is to show that lynching is not a way to overcome that frustration."

Benjamin felt like he was going to throw up. While he was committed to this course of action, he realized for the first time, that he would have to discuss his son as an object, not the flesh and blood little boy he had raised. The curious boy with the sweet smile. Could he go through with this?

"Benjamin, do you need a moment?" asked James Weldon Johnson.

"No, I'm fine. Let's proceed."

DuBois picked up the thread, "If you were an average man I'd tell you not to take this course of action. But Benjamin, you are not the average man. You are highly educated with an exceptional perspective and are well respected in your community. And you work for the President of the United States."

"E.B. we cannot involve the President."

"Trust me Benjamin, I don't want to pull the President into the case. He's already shown his mind by turning on the very people who helped vote him into office. We're nothing more than another minority group he has chosen to abandon. We have a different plan for you to consider. James, could you please outline our strategy for Benjamin?"

"Gladly E.B.," said Johnson. James Weldon Johnson had worked for Teddy Roosevelt as consul to Puerto Cabello, Venezuela. He was an artist, writer and a lawyer and had friends in high places. Benjamin knew they wouldn't win this battle, but he felt compelled to let the world know how his son died, hoping that by exposing his loss, lives might be saved.

A gig with Duke

"Kay, I have a gig tonight over at the Washington Hotel. You should come and sing with my band."

"Really? Do you mean it Duke? Do you really mean it?"

"You have a terrific voice. You just need to get it out there so more people know about you. We're getting started around 7:00pm."

A shadow of doubt passed over Kay's face.

"What's wrong? Do you have to be somewhere?"

"What will I tell my parents?"

Duke leaned back in his chair. "Tell them that you're with the great Duke Ellington. Soon to be the king of the big bands."

"And they'll say, 'Duke who?'" she teased. "Don't worry, I'll come up with something. You can count on me being there."

Duke enjoyed Kay and he was glad to be giving her this break. Especially because soon, he was going to have to tell her that he was engaged. The wedding was set for December.

Claire and Duncan Phillips

Duncan Phillips was devoted to his wife Nancy and to their children. He was a prominent figure in Washington and his home on R Street was on the outskirts of the city. They liked living in the suburbs, far from the noise and dirt of downtown. Cheap land allowed them the luxury of a very large home, which they filled with art.

Once a year they journeyed to Europe and spent a month or two in France visiting the galleries. In France, Duncan had discovered Picasso, Van Gough, Seurat, Vuillard and his beloved Bonnard. He could never get enough of Bonnard, relishing the large canvases depicting sunny days at Valins with his wife Misia. Vibrant pastel colors of pink and blue dotted the landscape.

The scale of Bonnard's painting influenced the Phillips' house design. To accommodate the magnificent canvases the halls were twice as large, so that an art lover could step back and appreciate the work.

"Duncan, I understand your love of this modern art, but couldn't you indulge in at least one Rembrandt or Renoir?," a visitor might lament. And Duncan would reply without smugness, "Art is in the eye of the beholder. You don't live here."

For twenty years he had collected works by artists who were rarely recognized in the established art community. Members of the National Gallery mentioned Duncan Phillips' name with slight derision, because he had gone his own way. But he and Nancy adored the paintings.

Slowly the couple had begun turning all the guest bedrooms into art galleries. Claire was passing through a second floor bedroom, now devoid of furniture, when she noticed a small painting of three men, two laying in bunk beds, the third sitting at a table playing cards.

"Do you like it?" asked Duncan from the hall.

"This picture reminds me of something Louvenia would have done when she was ten years old. The people are all flat and without dimension."

"Yes, but do you like it?" persisted Duncan.

"Not really Mr. Phillips, too gray for my tastes. It makes me think of prison."

"Close enough, these negro men are on a battleship. The picture was painted by a recent discovery of mine, Horace Pippin. The critics are labeling his work as 'primitive' since it's without depth. The difference is that here we have a grown man drawing like an eight-year-old, depicting a scene only an adult would recognize. It causes the viewer to pause, which is the most you can hope for from any work of art. I find it honest and invigorating."

"If you say so Mr. Phillips. I still have some old paintings of

Louvenia's that are very similar. Maybe you'd like those too."

Duncan laughed, "Maybe I would, Claire. Perhaps you should bring them around."

"Are you speaking of Louvenia?" Nancy Phillips asked, joining in the conversation. "How is she Claire? Still blowing things up?"

"Yes Ma'am, that girl of mine is going to burn the house down one of these days. That's why her father and I are encouraging her to rent a studio for her laboratory. There's no stopping her from inventing, so I'd just as soon she do it where she can't do too much damage."

"Wise idea. What is she working on these days?"

Claire became uncomfortable with the lengthy conversation. She had work to do, and while she enjoyed the Phillips, she knew that she would be judged on what she accomplished and not on the accomplishments of her family. "Gadgets mostly. New fangled electrical things that are designed to save time in house cleaning. Speaking of which..." Claire nodded towards the stairs.

"Of course, I'm sorry, Claire," said Mrs. Phillips. "I didn't mean to keep you. It's just nice to know what your family is up to. They are so accomplished."

"Thank you ma'am."

Claire took her leave and headed for the kitchen where the first set of party dishes awaited her.

As she left, she heard Mr. and Mrs. Phillips begin to argue. She didn't know what it was about, but she had noticed that disagreements were becoming more frequent in the Phillips' household.

Benjamin's mood

"When will they stop using us in their ads?" said Benjamin with annoyance, crumpling the morning paper.

"What's that, dear?"

"The white marketing people. When will they stop putting blacks in white uniforms and having us sell their maple syrup and cream of wheat?"

Claire came into the parlor, wearing a wide brimmed lavender hat. She turned to her reflection in the mirror, to make sure it was perched at a cunning angle before pinning it into her hair.

Summer 1919

"Where are you going?" asked a grumpy Ben, who shifted his concern from Aunt Jemimah to his handsome wife about to go out.

"I'm off to buy a new sewing machine. My old one is done in and the new ones have the ability to do so much more, like tucking and quilting. I don't know if you've noticed, but your children need new clothes and I'm afraid neither of our girls have any knack with a needle and thread."

She sat down in the parlor chair across from him.

"And why is that?" asked Benjamin. "You're a genius with a bolt of material. Why haven't they inherited that from you? Will you be clothing them their entire lives?"

"I suspect their husbands will take care of that." Claire stood up and went over to pat Benjamin's hand. "Would you like to come with me and keep me company?"

"No, I want to read some of this material DuBois sent me. I'm behind in my reading. It'll be nice to have some peace and quiet." As she readied to leave he added, "Claire, why is it that our daughters don't have boyfriends?"

He asked it with such sincerity that Claire felt her heart clutch. Ben was worried for his childrens' happiness.

"They will dear. We've raised them to be smart and independent. They haven't found the right men yet. They need spouses who will want them to succeed in their own careers, not just as supporters of a husband's career."

"Claire, was I the right spouse for you? Are you happy?"

"Now isn't the time for this conversation Ben. We've had a very hard year. A year of tremendous loss, but we still have each other. As long as we do, we can survive anything."

Benjamin sprang up and went to her. He held her so tight she found it hard to breathe.

"If something should happen to me Claire, I want you to know that I believe myself to be the luckiest man in the world to have shared this life with you."

"I know, darling. We'll get through this year. We must. And who knows what opportunities might await us?"

Benjamin walked her to the front door.

"You be careful out there," he said kissing her on the cheek.

"I will. I'm only going four blocks, don't worry. I'll be home in time to play you a game of Pit before dinner."

"It's a date."

Benjamin closed the door behind Claire and the emptiness of the house descended upon him. He resisted the temptation to run after her and instead, sat down in his chair to finish his reading.

Kay's costume

The tailor had done a beautiful job on her costume. Kay couldn't have been more pleased. The off-white dress was elegant, yet modern. Daring, yet demure. The loose fitting bodice was covered with glass beads that formed the subtle design of an egret. The dress moved with her as she walked and turned, swishing slightly and making a pleasant rustling sound. The hem of the dress draped just below her knee leaving a clear view of Kay's calf. On her size five feet were one-inch high sling-back heels made of gold silk.

Tonight she would be singing with the Duke at the Washington Hotel, but next week she would debut at the Orpheum. Kay had secured the fourth slot, not the best spot, in the ten act line up, but at least it wasn't the opening act where they put losers and dogs. Duke offered to be her pianist and play a song she had written, dedicated to her brother Emmet. The blues piece always brought her to tears.

She considered herself in the mirror and was pleased with what she saw. She looked like a star.

"This is for you Emmet," she said to her reflection. "Tony, please wrap the dress. I'll wear it tonight."

"You'll slay them."

"We can only hope."

Louvenia's patents

The patent attorneys at Victor J. Evans Company, on Ninth Street, were so used to seeing Louvenia, that all of the secretaries knew her by name. Lou was the most organized of their clients, always bringing the properly filled out forms, complete with models or sketches to support her evidence of conception.

"Miss Johnson, what have you brought us today?" asked Victor's son Paul.

"It's a gadget for the office. You've heard of the Acme's haven't you? They have those devices for holding papers together. They call it stapling." She didn't wait for a reply. "I've gone one better. I've made it so that the device will fit in your hand. The staples are thin and easy to remove. I've placed a staple remover right on the bottom of the device."

"What do you call it?"

"A stapler."

"But won't that sound like the Acme product?"

"No, they aren't calling it a stapler. However, this patent will need to be researched a little more thoroughly. The idea isn't completely original, but I've improved on the concept. Let me know what you can find out."

Paul picked up the device and pondered it. "May I?" he asked, pointing to several sheaves of paper.

"By all means, you'll find it's easy to use with just one hand."

Paul stapled the sheets together. The device held them fast.

"Now here's the best part. Separate them. The current solutions force you to rip the paper, but mine doesn't."

Paul did as he was told and it was true. The staple remover arm lifted the wings on the back of the staple without damaging the paper.

"We'll file this afternoon Miss Johnson, and then carry out our research later this week."

"Thank you Mr. Evans. Drop me a line at my home when you know."

With a nod Louvenia picked up her umbrella and exited into the rain.

Kay sings

"Who did you say we're playing for?" asked Kay, awed by the elegant ballroom. "I haven't been around this many white people since.... actually, I can't remember when."

Ellington laughed, "You don't get out much do you?"

She placed her hand on her hip, acting insulted and teased, "I beg your pardon?"

Duke recognized they were falling into their flirtatious patter. He liked this woman, but he needed to start making their relationship more professional, more about the music.

"Kay, here's the line up for tonight. If there is anything you don't know the words to, I'll have it on the music stand."

She saw the change in his demeanor and assumed he was nervous about the gig. Kay matched his seriousness and reviewed the songs they were to perform.

"I don't know this one song, Immigration Blues. Is it new?"

Duke leaned over her shoulder, having forgotten that he had added the piece. "Sort of. It's mine, an instrumental piece I've been working on. The host heard me play it a few months back and requested it. You'll be able to rest your pipes."

"Which brings me back to my first question. Who's throwing this bash?" asked Kay.

"Some guy out to impress a bunch of senators, their wives, and I guess a few military brass."

"I don't know about them, but I'm impressed."

"Yeah, Bud Rawley knows how to throw a party. I've played piano at some of his smaller venues. He's a real stand-up kind of guy. He pays well and tips generously. Men and women are drawn to him. He exudes integrity and mystery at the same time. A class act."

"Is he here? Can you point him out to me?"

"Sure, I'll introduce you." They walked over to a corner of the room where a small group had gathered. They were listening to a pear-shaped man tell a story.

"And then the Countess went to jump, but all the water in her moat had been drained to create a grazing pasture for the goats." The group of people laughed and the storytelling ambassador's belly jiggled with mirth.

Ellington approached a man standing beside the diplomat. He was well-built with coppery red hair. "Mr. Rawley."

191

Bud Rawley turned and smiled, "Yes, Mr. Ellington, what can I do for you? I must say, I am looking forward to hearing you play this evening. It will be a treat. Some of my guests are all atwitter, anticipating your performance tonight."

"Thank you sir, I hope not to disappoint them. Meanwhile I'd like to introduce you to our singer this evening. Miss Kay Johnson."

"How do you do Miss Johnson? It's a pleasure to meet you. Are you from DC or do you hail from elsewhere?"

"No, I was born and raised right here."

"Did you attend Howard University with Mr. Ellington?"

"I haven't graduated yet, but the rest of my family are Howard alumni."

"Very good. I'm so impressed with the education Howard offers. I find myself working with its graduates over and over again. Is there any chance that Louvenia Johnson would be a relation?"

"As a matter fact, yes. She's my sister. How is it possible you know Louvenia?"

"Your sister and I are entering into a business partnership. I'm trying to entice her to move to New York where she could be closer to my factories."

"New York?" said Kay, startled by the idea that her sister would have a reason to move to New York before her.

"Fear not, Miss Johnson. She has refused me thus far. Your family ties here are strong. However, your sister's gift for invention is pure genius and I'll continue to work with her no matter where she lives."

"You're too kind."

"No, I'm not, just a good judge of skill and opportunity. As a singer, why aren't you in New York? I've finally got Duke to agree to move there once he ties the knot."

Kay and Duke's eyes locked. Bud realized he had said too much, "I better attend to my guests, but it was a pleasure to meet you Miss Johnson. I hope you and your brilliant sister shall end up in New York and we'll be good friends."

As Buddy left them, Kay found herself wanting to follow him, to walk down the hall and out the front door. She felt herself adrift. Her sister now overshadowed her dream of New York. What's more, despite the fact she and Duke had never made any commitments to one another, she had no idea he was serious about someone else. Serious enough to be engaged.

Duke could not imagine what was going through her mind.

"Kay, I'm sorry. I know that…"

"It's fine Duke. We'll talk about it later. For now, you'd better add my blues piece to the repertoire tonight."

Wilson's attack

The train was pulling into Denver and Wilson was reading the newspaper. His moods were increasingly erratic and while the speeches for the League of Nations gave him some hope, each address took a toll on his health.

Dr. Grayson entered the car and stood watching as Wilson struggled to focus on the print.

"Your good eye is giving you trouble, isn't it Mr. President?"

Wilson threw the paper down in disgust.

"Don't be ridiculous Grayson. I see just fine out of both eyes. It's that damn baseball commissioner. He's as weak as a blade of grass. The owners worry they aren't going to make enough money, so they cut the players pay and reduce the number of games in the regular season from 154 to 140. Then they add games to the World Series. Ball club owners are no different than the war profiteers. They're making twice as much money as ever before. This will be a stellar year for the club owners, with all the boys coming home."

"Mr. President, please try to relax."

"And are you ready for this? The Red Sox owner is in such hot water he's going to sell Babe Ruth, his single best asset, to the New York Yankees. What's going on here?"

Dr. Grayson took another tack to calm the President. "You miss baseball, don't you sir?"

"Yes, yes I do. I was never so happy as when I was pulling together games at Princeton. I should have been a player not a politician. If it hadn't been for these eyes." He placed his finger on his temple. He turned in his chair to stand, but as if considering the options he fell to the floor instead.

"Mr. President. Mr. President!" Dr. Grayson reached for Wilson's pulse and called out, "Agent Grisom." A secret service agent appeared at the door. "The President's not well. We must take him to his bed. Then tell the conductor to return to Washington immediately."

"Yes sir."

"Woodrow," wailed Edith who ran into the car, having heard the commotion. She fell to her knees beside her husband. "What can I do, doctor?"

"We must get him to bed. I'll be able to treat him better there. Try to keep his feet elevated."

Another secret service agent squeezed in beside the doctor and Mrs. Wilson. Edith stepped back and the men maneuvered the President down the small corridor into the sleeping car. Edith followed, sensing that the end was near for her beloved husband. All she could do now was keep him comfortable and tell him only the things that would keep him calm. She'd keep out the world that had turned on Wilson.

If he were to die, he would die a man who believed he'd been appreciated.

Fall 1919

BOSTON

Harriet's first

He was standing there, as handsome as ever, his hat cocked over his left eye, his sandy hair escaping from beneath the brim. He smoked a clay pipe, the business end of the stem nearly gone. He was watching pigs being loaded into a truck, amused by the frantic youngsters trying to corral the beasts.

Harriet knew she should turn away, and lose herself among the crowd at the Haymarket, but she was transfixed as if watching an accident and unable to stop it.

A man carrying a side of beef bumped into her, startling her from her thoughts. She, in turn, toppled a cart of oranges. The commotion caused Colin McGuire to notice her. When she handed up the last of the run-away oranges, he was the one who took the fruit from her.

In an almost tender voice he queried, "Erin?"

"It'd be Harriet Kelly sir."

"I don't doubt that you're Harriet Kelly in this place, but I kin you as Erin McDermott of Galway. My bride of three years who ran off and left me with two wee children." His voice began to rise. Vendors and buyers turned towards them. He sensed he was gaining attention and liked it.

Fall 1919

"Are you daft man? I'm Harriet Kelly from Wadsworth."

"Erin McDermott, or should I say McGuire, who in the eyes of God is still married to me." He hit his chest for emphasis. "Are ye at all curious what happened to your dear sweet children? Or are ye still a heartless wretch?"

"Be away with ye, I have no notion of what you're sayin'. My husband's a police officer and I'm about to call for one if ye continue this nonsense. For nonsense it is. What's it to me if some lass up and left ye? Ya must be quite a brute. Good for her." Harriet began to laugh. Without thought Colin backhanded her, hard, across the mouth, causing her to fall to the ground. The vendors rushed over to her. A man began shouting for a policeman.

Several men held Colin back, as he growled at her, "I'll be seein' you again, Mrs. Harriet Kelly." With that, he shook off the men and ran toward the West End.

Harriet needs a lawyer

Harriet knew she would have to tell Patrick. She'd kept her secret for three decades and now she'd have to admit to her unpardonable sin. She knew Patrick loved her and had been a faithful husband. He would take this hard. The fact that Thomas's father was alive and had not died fighting the English, as she had told Patrick would be a betrayal of his trust.

All these years she had repeated the story, how she had left Ireland, after her husband Colin had met with an untimely death as a member of the Sinn Fein. His crimes were severe enough that she was at risk of imprisonment so she took a steamer out of Dublin, pregnant with Thomas.

Patrick had never pressed her for details, assuming that revisiting the past would make her sad. And when she was in a foul mood, he assumed she was homesick or missed her first husband. Patrick was always especially kind to Thomas, even though he was fathered by another man.

Tears ran down Harriet's face on the long walk home to Charlestown.

She and Patrick had had five children together and four of them were dead, two to the flu, one to the war and another to a freak accident. Only Patricia had survived. Harriet had never revealed to Patrick that she had two children before their marriage. Eight children in all, a number to make any priest proud. The thought of the church brought more heartache. She was married to two men. This, Patrick would not be able to overcome. Bigamy was illegal and a sin against God. She needed a lawyer. She had to see Thomas. She would have to tell her son about his father and then, although he might be furious, she needed his advice.

Harriet exposed

"Harriet, how ..." Overwhelmed and heartbroken by this betrayal, Patrick could not speak.

Harriet knew there was nothing she could do to redeem herself. Thirty-two years as a helpmate would be washed away with a single lie. What's worse, now that it was out in the open, both Patrick and Harriet realized that the lie was the source of Harriet's bitterness. What drove her to win her temperance crusade. She had never been a pleasant person, always critical and sharp to friends and family. The source of her angst, the man that she had hated for most of her life, the man who had attempted to break her spirit at nineteen, was at it again. When would this devil be done with her?

"Patrick, there's nothin' I can say. I was young. He was as reliable as a broken stick, but more than that, he was...is a cruel man."

"Has Thomas met him?"

Harriet felt the question like a slap across her face.

"Thomas should have the choice," said Patrick.

"But he needn't be meetin' the villain."

After a long silence, Patrick spoke in a strained guttural voice, "Will ye be leavin' me for him? For Colin?"

Harriet was dumfounded by the question. She almost laughed. Had he not heard anything? Did he not realize that she'd run away from this man once, at great risk to herself and her unborn child, not to mention abandoning two other children because she loathed and detested Colin? She adored Patrick, loved him not just in a storybook way, but respected and needed him. How could he ask her this?

Fall 1919

How could he misjudge her so? Did their marriage mean nothing? Could it all vanish in one afternoon?

"Patrick I love ye, and have for almost as long as I've drawn breath. Ya know it to be true. I'm your wife, even if God doesn't recognize it as so. It's a fact. Even if ye leave me, I'll die the wife of Patrick Kelly."

A confused Patrick asked, "I leave? What are ye talkin' about? How could I leave? It's yourself who's been unfaithful and must return to your husband."

"Patrick, wild horses couldn't drag me back to that black heart. I'd not be goin' back to him even if God himself told me I had to. I'd sooner die."

Patrick nodded, but Harriet could see that he had gone somewhere else, looking within for balance. Harriet wished she knew that place in herself.

They sat in silence as the sun set. As the shadows gathered Harriet went to light a lamp. She jumped at the sound of Patrick's voice. He spoke decisively.

"Let us just be, Harriet," Patrick said. "Let us live through each day as it comes. I want ye to go talk to Father Dixon and see if it isn't possible to get your first marriage annulled."

"I'll see him in the mornin'."

"That's fine then," he said standing. "Let's go to bed, it's been a long day."

Harriet knew it would be a cold bed. That they'd not hold hands as they fell asleep, as was their custom, united as they faced the unknown. Instead, tonight, Harriet would be set adrift. Her demons free to descend upon her and rob her of sleep. But she wouldn't complain. At least she was still with the man she loved.

A visit from Boston's finest

The rap on the door found Patrick napping in the parlor. He roused himself, a little startled to be caught sleeping in the middle of the day. Pulling up his suspenders as he went to the door, he dragged his fingers through his hair.

"Yes?" Patrick responded, before seeing the young police officer on his doorstep.

"Why Patrick Kelly, aren't you a sight!"

The two men stood staring at one another for a long moment, both elated. Finally Patrick thrust out his hand to the policeman.

"Michael Doyle, how good it is to lay eyes you. And you in your new blue uniform. Come inside, come inside. Let's take a closer look at ya." The man, in his early thirties, followed Patrick into the parlor.

"The cap's a pip. It must be a lot easier than the old one to keep on your head. Especially for a flat head like yours." Patrick laughed and took a friendly swipe at the brim of the younger man's hat.

"Curtis got the idea from out-of-town, maybe New York. He felt the domed hats were out of style. But then he's never had someone try to bean him on the head. We're all wagering that the first of us that gets a blackjack over the noggin is going to miss those old hats."

"Aye, ain't it the truth. And the blue uniform is to highlight your eyes is it? It won't hide the stains like the black one did. But the cut of the jacket's so short. Curtis must have saved himself a bundle. You'll be needin' a coat to go with that fine uniform, or you'll be freezin' your bum off." The two men laughed, but the humor had already become strained between them.

"What can I do for you Michael? I suspect you aren't here to give me a fashion show."

"No, you're right Patrick. I wanted to tell you how much we all miss you down at the station. You got a raw deal. Everyone knows it to be wrong and we've all sent a letter to Curtis telling him so."

"That was a mistake, lad. You needn't get involved in my hardship. Curtis was out to make an example of us and Coolidge capitalized on it so he could become President. There's no turnin' back now. You don't want to be associated with the likes of me. You've a fine career ahead of ya."

"Have you found any work?" Michael asked chagrined.

"Nah, most of the boys haven't. And me at my age. I guess it's time for a second career ehh? In any case it's time to move on. Those boys who think we're goin' to be reinstated are dreamin'. Coolidge put an end to that by callin' us Reds."

"But what will you do?"

"Dinna kin. But I've got my eyes open and meanwhile Thomas has moved back and is helpin' out with the bills. You know he's switched from international law to labor law?" Patrick let out a big laugh and slapped his knee. "Considerin' all the strikes goin' on in this country, he sure picked the right business to be in – wouldn't ya say."

Michael's smile was pinched. Patrick could tell there was more to his visit.

"Out with it, Michael." Patrick said in a resigned tone. "They've sent you to do some dirty work haven't they?"

Michael couldn't lift his eyes from the floor, but continued, "Aye, Patrick they did. I wouldn't of come, didn't want to come, none of us did so we picked straws, and well…"

"Ye got the short one."

"Aye."

"Out with it, man. I promise not to take a swing at you. I'm sober as a priest. Give me your worst."

Michael took a deep breath and began, "Curtis has asked that we collect the brass buttons from your uniform."

"What? My brass buttons? What does the mule-headed ass want with my buttons?"

"Me and McNamara have to collect them from our division. Curtis wants the department to track down all 400 men that were let go. Each precinct has to pick a man to go 'round and collect 'em."

"And I'm the first?"

"No, I went to George McCullen first. You know he has five wee ones and his wife had already sold the buttons and I had to ask for the money. It was dreadful." Michael hung his head even lower with the memory.

The two men sat in silence for a moment.

"Michael Doyle, I recruited you. Knew your Da, knew your Ma. I think it's time you leave here. This is more than a fool's errand. You've insulted the memory of all the fine officers who've gone before us. If Mr. Curtis wants his damn buttons so bad, he'd better come get them himself."

"But…"

"But nothin'. Who does he think is? For that matter, what does he think he can do to me? Fire me? He's already done that. Now get out of here Michael, before I throw you out. If ye leave now, I'll forget you were ever here."

The younger office walked to the front door and turned, holding out his hand to Patrick. "May God be with ya."

"He is, son. It's Mr. Curtis who's goin' to be needin' some extra protection these days."

Patrick and the Lieutenant

Two weeks later Patrick was summoned to police headquarters. He noted even the smell of the place had changed. As if it had been given a good cleaning to get rid of the likes of him. He was shown into his old commander's office. Patrick's eyes rested on the familiar objects of a lifetime. The awards, trophies, photos of happier times shared between all the men of the twelfth precinct.

"Patrick, we want you back," said Lieutenant Cavanaugh entering the room and sitting at the desk across from Patrick. "We realize you weren't part of the strike. Besides, we need some seasoned policeman. Attorney General Palmer has us making a lot of arrests. Unfortunately, I won't be able to reinstate you at your old salary, position or seniority. You'll have to come back on as a recruit, but with the raises that are in the works you'll make about the same. I hope you'll consider the offer, Patrick."

Outwardly Patrick showed no emotion, but inside he was seething. He couldn't believe that the Lieutenant, a man he had served with for twenty years, could make such a humiliating offer. Worse yet, the Lieutenant believed this was a dignified proposition. Patrick felt ashamed and insulted, but he responded with, "I'll discuss it with Harriet."

"I'll need to hear from you by tomorrow. The Palmer raids are to begin next week. We're going to start cleaning out all of the areas where recent immigrants have settled. He's already got the boats docked in the harbor for deportation."

Patrick knew better than to ask, but he couldn't live with himself if he didn't know for sure. "Lieutenant, are these immigrants guilty of anything besides having come to this country?"

The broad shouldered Cavanaugh leaned forward over his desk and in the low voice of a conspirator said, "Not that I know of Patrick. I admit, it's the worst kind of rotten deal. The boys on the hill want to be rid of any labor agitators, immigrants who might know their rights, and ask for better wages, or working conditions, that sort of thing. I think the powers that be are wrong. These immigrants are the very people who work hard and never complain, but it makes the government look good arresting people who don't speak English. That way they can accuse them of anything and the poor souls can't defend themselves." Cavanaugh sat back and watched Patrick's face. "Does it matter to you Patrick? I always thought you disliked the garlic eaters. I thought you'd be happy to be rid of them."

Patrick fumed at the assumption that he was a racist. He knew that his answer to the Lieutenant, regarding coming back on the force, would be his backside walking out the door. But he remained composed enough not to say anything inflammatory in a moment of anger. Instead, he stood and said, "Let me get back to you, Lieutenant."

"You do that Patrick, you do that," said Cavanaugh, smiling, confident he had cut himself a good deal by bringing back a seasoned officer as a recruit.

NEW YORK

A proposition for Patricia

Patricia had never been to New York City. She had only read stories about it that made her both excited and nervous about being there. No one at home knew she had taken the train to the metropolis. She had told her mother that she was staying overnight with a friend in Cambridge.

She approached the receptionist as she entered the lobby of the building on Broadway.

"Your name please?" asked the no-nonsense girl.

"Patricia Kelly."

The receptionist brightened at the name, "Why Miss Kelly. Miss Sanger and the others are waiting for you."

"The others?"

"Come right this way."

Patricia was guided through a maze of desks and filing cabinets. She wondered what others? She had been so pleased to get Miss Sanger's telegram to come visit. Sanger had long been a hero of Patricia's. Emma Goldman and Sanger were good friends and it must have been Emma that had told Sanger about Patricia.

"Here you are Miss, the others will be right in. May I get you something to drink?

"No. I'm fine thank you." Patricia found herself in a small conference room with a round table surrounded by five chairs. On the walls were banners from parades demanding women's rights.

A tall-distinguished woman hurried in and thrust out her hand. "I'm Margaret Sanger. It's so good to meet you."

"The pleasure's all mine, Miss Sanger. I've followed your courageous work for years and I'm honored that you'd take time from your busy schedule to speak to me."

"Please call me Margaret. And I hope you don't mind, but I have invited a couple of friends to join me. Sort of companions-in-arms." Sanger called out, "Ladies, would you please come in?"

The two women were older, but full of life. They emanated power, despite their white hair and hunched backs.

Sanger began, "Miss Kelly let me introduce you to..."

Patricia finished her sentence for her, "Mrs. Victoria Woodruff and Miss Jane Addams. I'm so honored to meet both of you. Never in my wildest dreams did I think I'd ever meet two such famous women. Women who have accomplished so much for our country."

Mrs. Woodruff, now in her 80's, was still a beauty. She wore a brown velvet day suit trimmed in mink. She responded to Patricia's praises, "My dear, I fear you've put us on a pedestal. We're but simple women to whom God gave a mission."

Miss Addams, in her trademark plain black wool frock added, "Yes child, we're women who were given a task and although our time is almost up, yours is just beginning. We'd like to discuss plans with you, now that the vote is almost within our grasp."

Miss Sanger saw the confusion on Patricia's face. "I'm sure this is a great deal to take in all at once, so let's not race forward, but take it one step at a time. I'm afraid the three of us are sometimes described as mini tornadoes and we must be careful not to buffet you about between us."

The older women nodded. Patricia could only imagine how many times these energetic women heard complaints from men and women alike because they moved too fast.

Miss Sanger continued, "Patricia, as you know, Emma Goldman

and I have done a great deal of work on providing women with birth control information. We believe that the most important thing for a woman is to have control over her own body. Otherwise her rights are no better than those of an animal in the field."

"Now, now," Miss Addams warned, "We said we would keep our personal agendas out of this request."

"Yes, you're right Jane, I'm sorry." Sanger continued, "In any case, the last time Emma and I were jailed for handing out leaflets we had time to catch up. She mentioned having met you through Jack Reed in Boston. Emma was quite taken by your commitment and suffragette verve."

Patricia blushed at Jack Reed's name, but knew that these women could care less about her private life. "I'm surprised she'd remember me. As I recall, Mrs. Goldman did not think much of a woman's right to vote."

"That's another matter. However, she does recognize a woman who can get things done. And she told me you were just that sort of woman."

Jane Addams took up the discussion, "A few days ago I came to Margaret with a proposition. While I may no longer be able to sway presidential elections I do believe I could be of some assistance in getting a congresswoman elected. With women having the vote it'll be important to have more women running for office."

"We have had several already," Patricia reminded her, "The honorable Martha Hughes of Utah, Frances Klock of Colorado and, luckily, Jeannette Rankin of Montana," said Patricia.

"Yes we know," said Miss Addams, "but women make up fifty-two percent of the population and at present represent less that one percent of the Senate and House. Over the next four years we would like to increase that number by at least ten percent, so we're looking for like-minded women to take up the cause. And Patricia Kelly, your name keeps coming up."

"Why me?"

"Well dear," said Miss Woodruff, "a seat is opening up here, you have no ties that we're aware of and you could move to New York. Miss Sanger and Miss Addams called me in to help because of my experience running for President, and, well, I have resources that may be of some assistance." Mrs. Woodruff paused and all of the women looked away from each other for a moment.

"To be candid, I'm selling my seat on the stock exchange and it should bring in more than enough money to effectively fund your candidacy."

Margaret Sanger reached across the table and placed her hand over Patricia's. "I know this is a lot to take in and it may come as quite a surprise, but we've thought it through and are 90% sure it'll work. That is if you're up for it. Is this something you'd have any interest in pursuing?"

Patricia turned her hand over in Miss Sanger's and gently squeezed. Then she stood up and said, "I'm your woman. I've dreamt about this day, but I didn't know how to make it a reality. God has sent the three of you to me. My mission is clear. I'm your humble servant."

Thomas and Patricia on the train

Patricia surprised her brother when she called him at his hotel in New York. She knew he was planning on returning home that evening and asked him if he would mind joining her back on the train. Thomas was happy for the company.

When she saw him on the platform Patricia let out a long whistle. "Hasn't my brother become quite the dandy? Since when have you taken to wearing your hair parted down the middle? And that's a store-bought suit. What's come over you, Thomas?"

Never able to win a battle of words with his sister, Thomas rolled his eyes in defeat. Then he pointed to their compartment. Patricia chuckled, pinched his chin and boarded the train.

Once in their seats Thomas hid behind his paper while Patricia tried to start a conversation. "So what about the White Sox scandal, Thomas? Do you think they threw the World Series?"

"Nah, the newspapers are just making up a story to sell more newspapers. And as long as it works, they'll keep making up stories."

"Aye, you're right there. Never trust what you read in the paper.

Especially those Hearst papers. That man doesn't make a distinction between truth and fiction."

"Pat," Thomas paused and stared out the window at the passing factories.

"Yes, what is it Tom?"

"How do you think Da would take it if I moved to New York?" He said it softly, but Patricia responded with a loud, "What?"

"I know, we're from Boston, but my opportunities are much better in New York. In three days I received two job offers and I wasn't even trying for a position."

Patricia began to laugh.

"Why are you laughing? Have you gone daft?"

Composing herself, she answered, "I was going to pose the same question to you. I too am considering moving to New York. I received an offer as well. A rather incredible offer."

"Do tell, Sis. Are you getting married?"

"Don't be silly. Listen, do you remember our talk last winter, when you told me I should run for president?"

"Vaguely."

"Well you're in good company. Margaret Sanger, Victoria Woodruff and none other than Jane Addams agree with you, except they recommend I start as a congresswoman."

"What! The Jane Addams? The woman considered the most powerful person in this country for six years running? Jane Addams of Hull House fame?"

"The one and only."

"But how did this happen?" asked Thomas.

"The credit goes to you big brother. Your introduction to Jack Reed, caused me to meet Emma Goldman who, in turn, told Margaret Sanger about me. She told Addams and Woodruff and now the lot of them want me to move to New York this month in order to meet my residency requirements."

Thomas didn't hesitate. "Do it. I'll help you convince the parents, but you must do it, Pat. This is what you've been working towards. This is what you should be doing." He leaned over and hugged her, "I am so proud of you, Sis."

"I'm not elected yet, but thanks. And what of you? What are these jobs you've been offered?"

"Nothing so grand as all of that. A labor law firm and an investment house both asked me to join them. Charles Schwab believes the stock market is about to explode and there'll be lots of money to be made now that the war is over. The Dow went up to one hundred and seven points today. It started in the eighties this year, so that's a thirty percent increase and they say it won't stop there."

"Tough choices: doing the right thing or making money," she teased.

Thomas laughed, but in truth he still wasn't sure which way he leaned. "Perhaps Da will have less of a hard time about you moving if I move to New York with you."

"Maybe, and who knows? Perhaps he and Ma will move too, if he can't get back on the police force."

"What they did to him was wrong. It was a rotten shame. But you know, I'm not certain he'd want to stay. Did you hear Palmer and his goons have made Boston's finest round up another group of innocent immigrants this week?" Then he became serious and leaned toward Patricia.

"Pat, I'm sorry, but I bet you haven't heard..."

"Heard what?"

"They arrested Emma Goldman."

"On what charge?"

"Being a Red I think. They're going to deport her."

"That's ridiculous. She's a U.S. citizen."

"Yes, but a naturalized one. I'm really sorry Pat."

The two rode in silence for some time and finally Patricia spoke.

"Yes, I'll be happy to move away from Boston. Every corner there holds some sadness. New York seems so full of hope and promise."

Her words made Thomas think of Helen and he added, "I'm with you Sis. I'm with you."

WASHINGTON DC

A script for Kay

"Miss Johnson it's so good of you to meet me," Jason Rothman said, as he stood to greet her in the dining room of the Washington Hotel.

"My pleasure, Mr. Rothman. Your note intrigued me. How did you know I was an actress?"

"I didn't, but I saw you two nights ago at Bud Rawley's party and was certain you'd be perfect for the lead in my new play."

"How exciting. Are you from the Washington area, Mr. Rothman?"

"No, New York. That's how I know Mr. Rawley. We came down on the train together."

"Oh, so you're not in the same business?" asked Kay.

Jason laughed, "Absolutely not. I'm merely a struggling playwright. I've had some small successes off-Broadway, but I'm still working to make it to the Big Time." The steward appeared, ready to take their order. "It's tea time. Would you like some tea?" asked Jason.

"Yes, please, that would be lovely," said Kay.

"A pot of Darjeeling with milk."

"Very good sir." The waiter left and Jason noticed there was only one other couple in the dining room.

"Don't people take tea here?" asked Jason.

"It's too hot. This is more of an iced tea type of town. Which reminds me. Why are you in the District?"

"I gave a short lecture over at Howard University to the theater department. I'm also doing some research in the Library of Congress for my new play."

"What's the play about?" asked Kay.

"A man who lives in the mid-west and works for a bicycle manufacturer. He falls in love with a beautiful, colored woman and they marry."

Kay tried not to appear shocked. If her father heard this he would have a fit.

Jason continued, unaware of her discomfort, "He ends up being falsely associated with the labor union that's trying to establish itself at the plant. People learn he has a mixed marriage and are particularly hateful. Management says he's a Red and drums him out of town."

"People can be that way," said Kay, as their tea was served.

"Thank you," said Jason acknowledging the waiter. "So they move to North Carolina so he can get a job in a textile plant. Only in North Carolina, it's illegal for them to be married. And they go through a lot of heartache until finally his wife leaves him. He's so distraught he goes out walking in the countryside and discovers a lynched black man still hanging from a tree. In solidarity our hero hangs himself." Kay instinctively raises her hand to her neck.

"What do you think?" asked Jason.

"I guess my first question is, what planet do you live on?"

"Excuse me?"

"What country, much less state, would let you produce this play?"

"I don't understand. What's the problem with it? It addresses real issues that are being faced everyday in this country. The problems of labor, racism, and ridiculous Jim Crow laws."

"Are you telling me you could get this play produced in New York?"

"I've already lined up a producer. Why?"

"Mr. Rothman, I don't know if you realize it, but Washington D.C.

is below the Mason Dixon line. And while that line might seem imaginary, I can assure you it's not imaginary to the people who live here. We pretty much keep to our own kind. With a play like that, we'd have another riot on our hands."

"That's my point exactly. We must bring to light the racist policies of our government, as well as the Red baiting of labor unions. I want my plays to mean something, Miss Johnson. I'm not interested in writing farces."

"Audiences will come to this play? I always thought theater-goers wanted to be entertained, to forget their troubles."

"You're right. This play will never be a box office hit, but it'll begin a dialog and that's what I'm hoping for."

"And your investors?"

"They're men of good conscience. You've already met one of them, Mr. Rawley. I've told Buddy all about the play. He loves it and will support it one hundred percent."

"If nothing else, you have me eager to visit New York. I can't imagine a town where people would be so accepting."

"I should warn you, Miss Johnson, New York isn't perfect." Jason took a sip of his tea, thought for a moment and then smiled. "But it's pretty darn close. Will you come? Will you do the play? We'll start rehearsals in two months."

"I'd need to check with my family. You see, Mr. Rothman, I recently lost a brother to the madness of the riots. While I have no qualms about bringing to light the recent atrocities and injustice, I'm not sure how my father and mother might react."

"I understand," said Jason with sincere chagrin. "I'm sorry Miss Johnson. I had no idea. Please accept my deepest condolences."

"Thank you Mr. Rothman. Would it be possible to send me a draft of the script? I assume you're still working on it?"

"Yes indeed, every day I'm rewriting scenes. So please remember that it's a work-in-process."

"I will Mr. Rothman, and thank you for the tea." Kay stood to leave. "I'm sorry. I have so little time today, but it's been a genuine pleasure meeting you."

"The pleasure was all mine. I look forward to hearing from you."

Fall 1919

Louvenia's results

"Miss Johnson, I was pleased to get your message. Have you solved my problem?"

"Why yes, Mr. Rawley. I also have some additional ideas for you."

"Do tell."

Claire interrupted them. "Excuse me. How do you do, sir? Has my daughter Louvenia offered you any refreshments?" Claire stared at Louvenia, certain her daughter had forgotten to ask.

"I'm fine Mrs. Johnson, thank you. Although..." he paused and pulled at the white color of his pink shirt. Despite being late autumn, the day was stifling, with the temperature in the nineties and humidity to match. "...actually I wouldn't mind a cool drink if you have one," said Buddy. Louvenia blushed.

"Ice tea or lemonade?" asked a vindicated Claire.

"Lemonade please."

As Claire walked out of the room Lou continued, unwilling to apologize for her shortcomings as hostess. Bud Rawley did not hire her for her ability to make lemonade.

"As I was saying, your factory has been using cotton to hold the propellant for your guns. They've made no allowances for the size of the guns or the amount of propellant. Unfortunately, if it rains, and the bags are exposed, the integrity of the bags and their contents will be destroyed by mildew. This is why you've had such a poor level of consistency."

"And your solution?"

"I have three." Lou stood up and went to the sideboard and brought over a tray, its contents covered by a piece of elaborately embroidered silk. She set the tray on the low table between them. With a small but noticeable flourish she removed the silk and exposed three bags, each the size of a hand, secured by a silk thread.

"My first solution and the one you're most likely to go with is silk." She picked up a bag that glistened in the afternoon sunlight.

"Mr. Rawley, your lemonade," said Claire, offering him a glass from a tray. "I just squeezed it."

Rawley pulled his attention from Louvenia to acknowledge Claire, "Thank you Mrs. Johnson. I hadn't meant for you to go to so much trouble."

"My pleasure."

"Momma," said Lou sternly.

It was obvious Louvenia wanted her to leave and Claire could see in Mr. Rawley's eyes that he was anxious to return to his discussion with Louvenia. Claire was proud of her daughter. In truth, she didn't mind that Louvenia would never be a good housewife. As Claire left the room she added, "Call me if you need anything. I'll be in the kitchen."

"Thank you Mrs. Johnson," said Buddy.

"As I was saying," said Lou. "Silk is superior to cotton. It is slightly less likely to mildew and damage the propellant."

"I'm sure you're aware that my engineers have already recommended single ply silk."

"I realize this, but it's a short term gain because despite the fact that silk is cheap, it's not readily available domestically. Which could be a problem if supply lines are compromised. Also, if your munitions should be used in a country with high humidity, like Southeast Asia – let's say Burma or Siam, silk will deteriorate rapidly no matter how carefully you store it."

Lou took a sip of lemonade and wiped a bead of sweat from her temple with the back of her hand.

Bud raised his glass to her, "I guess we don't have to go across the world to suffer the challenges of humidity. Based on what you're saying we could have trouble with storage right here on the East Coast during the summer."

"That's right," said Lou. "What's more, you've got the problem of residue in the gun chamber with silk. Too much residue and the gun will explode, injuring the soldier arming it. What you need is a cloth that will burn clean and that's mildew resistant. Which is why I suggest this second solution." Lou picked up the second bag. It was ivory in color, with an obvious sheen.

"This is rayon. Rayon is cellulose based so it'll burn cleaner. I have also treated it with a chemical that will abate mildew." Lou handed the bag to Buddy.

"As you will notice, the material is a little stiffer. I'd also recommend that the thickness of the fabric be taken into account based on the amount of propellant."

"But wouldn't double or triple bagging the propellant leave more residue?" asked Bud.

"Yes, and I'm sure you've already tried this with disastrous results using cotton. I suspect the equipment damage you experienced was far higher than what your customers felt acceptable."

"You're right there, Miss Johnson. I'm very impressed with your knowledge of the issues my customers face. Where did you get this information?"

"It's just common sense, Mr. Rawley. I don't know who you have working for you, but they appear to lack a fundamental understanding of fabric, chemicals and combustion."

"Please continue. You mentioned I wouldn't go with rayon, despite it being a superior solution. Why not?"

"Because it's more expensive. But if you were to do the math you'd find that it'll save lives and equipment and in the end it'll save you money. What's more, rayon is available domestically."

"I promise you I'll have my accountant crunch the numbers. But Miss Johnson, what's the third pouch?"

The last pouch sitting on the tray had a bluish tint. Buddy didn't recognize the fabric.

"Mr. Rawley, this is a little experiment of my own. I'm developing a synthetic fabric. It isn't ready yet, but when it is I believe that it will ultimately be what you're looking for. My fabric will last longer than the propellant itself, no matter what the weather conditions, and it'll burn clean leaving no residue."

Buddy picked the bag up and held it with admiration. He was impressed with this young woman and recognized that she would be an important asset to the country should another war come. And Buddy was certain there would be another war. He was also glad he had found her first. He'd have his lawyers draw up an exclusive contract with her that afternoon.

"Miss Johnson, I'm very impressed. You've delivered far more than I'd anticipated and in half the time. I'll have my office send over your check along with a substantial bonus." Buddy set down the mystery bag and picked up the first bag of silk. "Once we work out the economics of silk versus rayon, I'd like to have my factory start putting your solutions into production. When would you be available to travel to our plant in New York?"

"I'd need to check with my employer at the Smithsonian," said Louvenia.

"Miss Johnson, I would like to begin discussions with you regarding a long term contract. I believe you and I could do a great deal of business together and I'd like to have something formal written up between us."

"I'd like that Mr. Rawley. Please send over what you have in mind and I'll take it to my lawyer."

"May I?" he pointed to the first two bags in a gesture that meant he wanted to take them with him.

"Yes, they are for you. I also have the notes that go with them and the formulas for preparing the materials."

"If you don't mind I'd like you to give that to one of my men who's better equipped to understand the science behind it. After all, I'm just a businessman."

Louvenia was certain he was much more than that, but said nothing.

"It's a pleasure doing business with you Miss Johnson."

"And with you as well, Mr. Rawley. Until our next meeting."

"Good day." And with that Bud Rawley stepped into the foyer, collected his boater, and walked out onto K Street, realizing he was going to be wealthier than he thought possible. Louvenia would help make it happen and he, in return, would make her rich beyond her dreams. Life was good indeed.

The reign of red

"Hoover, I want us to get moving," said Palmer.

"Yes sir."

"Now that Wilson is out of the picture we can proceed without restraint. Let's clean up this country. Before the malcontents and Bolsheviks have taken over."

"I'm with you, sir."

"How many residents are you tracking?

Fall 1919

"Over 450,000 sir. We're monitoring close to 60,000."

Palmer was impressed that Hoover could do so much with so few men and a tight budget. "How many aliens have you identified for deportation so far?"

"I have cause on approximately 400 individuals."

"I want you to deport anyone who is related to these people or knows them. I want to see ships filled with aliens heading back to where they came from," said Palmer, rising from his chair and pointing his unlit cigar towards the east. "I expect you to deport no less than 10,000 people before the New Year. I want you to start in Boston. All those long-haired liberals need to know that I mean business. Then I want you to clean up New York, I expect you to get rid of one 100,000 immigrants. That'll help take care of the over-population problem in the slums."

"What about naturalized citizens sir?"

Palmer paused and lit his cigar. "Take 'em all boy. Take 'em all."

Kay explains

"Oh Poppa," Kay sobbed, "you don't understand."

"I understand that no daughter of mine is going to parade herself in front of strangers. You have a mind daughter. I expect it you to use it. Why can't you be more like your sister?"

"Oh yes, my sister. Louvenia loves what she's doing! You can't pull her away from that damn workshop. She loves it, Poppa, she's driven. All of us are driven. All of us."

"What are you saying? Drive is now a bad thing? That's what makes men great. Drive is what made the Tuskegee Institute a success, your Aunt Walker a legend. It's drive that makes all things possible. Where's your drive little girl?"

"I am driven to act and sing, Poppa. Why can't you hear me? Why don't you understand? We can't all be smart like Louvenia. And I can't fulfill the dreams you've had for all your dead children, Poppa. I can only be me."

Benjamin Johnson slapped his daughter. They both stood frozen with surprise.

With compassion in her voice Kay continued, "I'm sorry, Poppa

220

but it's true. When Roy died in the war, you wanted me to become a writer. But Poppa, I can't write. It's not in me. I can stare at a piece of paper all day long and in the end it's still a blank piece of paper. When June took sick with the flu, you encouraged me to be a nurse. A nurse, Poppa. June was the nurse. I don't like hospitals. I'm not good with sick people." Wiping her eyes she added, "Heck, I make them nervous. Honest, Poppa, the hospital was relieved when I quit volunteering. I suspect those patients complained." Benjamin knew it was true.

"Poppa, I sing. I love you, but I'll never be Roy, or June or even Emmet." She let their names fill the room. "Emmet was my favorite Poppa, you know that. We were the same and I miss him. But I can tell you, he wanted me to follow my dream. He was always saying I should invite you to the theater to hear me sing." Taking a deep breath Kay continued, "Please come father. Please come hear me sing. It'll help you to understand."

Benjamin walked to the fireplace and looked at the picture on the mantle that contained his entire family. The Johnson's were lined up like they were in a chorus line. Benjamin and Claire stood in the middle, June and Louvenia to one side, and Kay and Emmet to the other. Roy knelt in front. As the photographer told them to hold still each child had turned, causing a blur around their bodies. Only Claire and Benjamin remained immobile. When they saw the finished photo the embarrassed photographer offered to re-shoot it. But Benjamin refused. He could recognize his children's faces and the movement that surrounded each was but the shadow of things to come. From the moment he saw that photo he was eager to see what they would do with their lives.

Three of his darling children had been taken from him. But two were left. In the picture Louvenia turned to look to her right, away from her parents, as if something unexpected had come into view. Kay was looking to the left with her head cocked as if recognizing a melody that brought a smile to her face. He loved them all, would always love them, but now he must turn his attention not to his daughters, but to himself and Claire. The time had come for each of the remaining Johnsons to take up their own dreams.

Fall 1919

"All right Kay, I'll come. When will you be singing again? I'd like to hear you."

"Tonight Poppa, tonight. I'll make them put me on and I promise you won't be disappointed."

She ran to him and he held her and whispered. "You could never disappoint me child. You're my song."

Louvenia and the inventor in New York

Lou was having trouble keeping up with Miss Beulah Henry. Beulah spoke fast and walked fast seemingly unconscious that Lou was behind her. She spewed words into the air, over her shoulder, letting anyone who might be around pick them up.

"In here we have the metal shop. This is where we build the prototypes." At two long tables stood three middle-aged men and a woman wearing laborer's aprons. Two of the men had face shields while the woman wore goggles. "You'll note that we're very safety conscious here. Everyone takes precautions. The very nature of what we're doing is experimental. If someone loses their eye in the process, that's unacceptable. We must always be prepared for the unknown. The splinter of glass that flies from a cathode ray tube, an electrical coil that arcs and burns. One must always be ready for the unexpected."

The experimenters barely acknowledged Louvenia's presence as she walked through the room. The apartment was enormous. Miss Beulah Henry, it appeared, occupied the entire floor.

"Miss Henry, don't the neighbors mind you having a laboratory here in the apartment building? I mean, at a minimum, you must cause electrical fluctuations? Based on the equipment you're using I'd suspect it happens regularly."

Miss Henry laughed and nodded. "Once we burned out a transformer down the street and it took almost a week to restore electricity to the neighborhood." She shook her head amused by the episode. "That's why the tenants don't pay the going rate in rent, it helps them overlook the odd odors, lack of electricity and small explosions. All of these thing are outlined in their lease."

"But how is it that the building owner agreed to this?"

222

For the first time Beulah turned to lock eyes on Louvenia. A look passed over Beulah's face. Perhaps she had over-estimated Lou and was now sizing her up. She spoke slowly, as if to a child. "Because, Miss Johnson, I own the building."

Louvenia recovered quickly. "Well, of course, I should've known. Could you show me the laboratory? I've been working on a new fuel source for furnaces, that would enable them to use crude oil, which requires a minimum of cracking." At that, Miss Henry brightened again and continued the facility tour.

There was a lab most schools would envy. The facility put Howard University's to shame. The only school whose labs were somewhat comparable was MIT, where Lou had applied, been accepted and was summarily rejected once they realized she was a woman. The rejection was particularly unfair since her grades and achievements outstripped those of the male applicants. The dean at MIT had written her a note, expressing his regrets regarding the decision. He also added that he had sent a letter of protest to the dean of colleges. Looking around Miss Henry's lab, Lou realized that these facilities might allow her an even greater opportunity than MIT.

"You won't find a better development facility in the country," stated Miss Henry with pride. "Even old Edison is jealous of what I've got here. Naturally we don't let him in. He and I have an unspoken rivalry. We are number one and two in submitting the largest number of patents to the U.S. patent office each year. And each year we try to beat each other by a patent or two. I'm afraid you won't find much holiday cheer around here come December. We're all grinding away trying to beat out the Edison team. And now that he's moved to his bigger facility in N.J. this year, it might be a real challenge," said Miss Henry. "But it sure is fun."

Lou didn't know what to make of Beulah Henry. She had never met a woman, or man, like her. She was an anomaly, but one from whom Lou knew she could learn. What's more, Lou would have the use of a fully equipped lab, with almost unlimited resources. In exchange, Miss Henry would own all of Lou's patents and pay her a royalty on any of her inventions that came to fruition. Lou's contract

223

included an apartment in the building.

"So what do you say, Louvenia? Do we have a deal?"

"Yes, Miss Henry. We have a deal." The two women shook hands.

Beulah turned away while still speaking to Lou, "When can you start?"

The move

"Claire, we need to talk."

Claire knew when Benjamin said, "We've got to talk," it was something serious. They were standing in the kitchen and she was at the sink peeling apples for a pie. She stopped, wiped her hands on her apron and joined Benjamin at the table, giving him her full attention.

"Yes, Benjamin?"

"I've been thinking that now that the girls have grown up..."

"Good of you to notice, father."

"Don't mock me."

"I'm not mocking you. It's just that you still treat them like little girls, when they are grown women. Because they adore you they try to remain little girls to please you."

"I'm not willing to give them up completely, but I have an idea that may keep us all together and still let each of us follow our hearts' desire."

Claire was intrigued. She had never heard Benjamin speak of the girls as equals. "Yes dear?"

"We should move to New York."

"Excuse me?"

"Hear me out. Each of us has a calling there. Kay with her singing, Louvenia by that woman inventor, you by A'Lelia. And yes, even me. Mr. DuBois has asked me to come and help him at the NAACP. And Claire, I want to do it. I want to contribute before I die."

"You don't mean that. You've done so much already with your life."

"No Claire, I mean contribute to our race. I don't know how and I don't know what it'll be, but there's something out there that I'm

224

supposed to do and if not now, when?"

"Benjamin, you know that I want to move to New York. I want to be my own boss and to test my metal. But my first responsibility is to you. I'll follow where you lead, my love."

Tears welled up in Benjamin's eyes as he reached for the hand of his wife of thirty-three years.

"Then New York it is. Let us go make a new life."

They held each other's hands tightly, appreciating the love they felt for one another. Together they would always have a home and a family.

December 1919

NEW YORK

Thomas Kelly in New York

Thomas had just finished moving his parents into their new apartment in the Bronx. He was staying in Manhattan, at the Plaza, while he secured a flat for himself in Tribeca. As he crossed the lobby, to the elevator a woman approached.

"Hello there, big boy."

The woman's stunning beauty left Thomas speechless. Her equine nose, lush lips and honey colored curls would inspire poetry from any man. Her flawless skin was revealed by a low cut dress, accented by the curvature of her bosom. Thomas had never seen anyone like her.

"What's the matter? Cat got your tongue?"

Still Thomas said nothing. "All right, how about a cigarette?" she purred.

Coming out of his paralysis, Thomas answered, "Why yes." He pulled out his silver case. As she delicately lifted the cigarette from its resting place, he lit a match for her. Thomas was not used to seeing women smoke in public, but here in New York things were different.

"What's your name, soldier?"

"I'm not a soldier Miss. I'm a lawyer. Thomas, Thomas Kelly."

"Ah, he speaks. And a lawyer much less. You never know when I might need a good lawyer." She wore a large black hat with ostrich feathers. She titled it towards the seating area beside a palm tree. "Let's take a load off."

Thomas followed her like a lap dog.

"So, Thomas Kelly, what type of law do you practice?"

"I started out in international law, but now I'm focused primarily on labor law."

"Bully for you. I'm sure you've plenty of business these days." She seemed bored and engaged at the same time. Thomas was fascinated.

"And you Miss? Your name is?"

"Mae West. Call me Mae."

"Miss West, it's a pleasure." Thomas stood and bowed.

Mae curled her lip back in a snarling smile that was ambiguous by design. It revealed a set of beautiful white teeth. "The pleasure's all mine, Big Boy," she purred. "Call me Mae. I suspect you've heard of me."

"How is it I should have heard of you?"

"I am in the theater right now, but as soon as the season is over I am heading to Hollywood Land and the flickers." In the voice of a spy she whispered. "If you have any spare cash that's where I'd put it if I were you. Mary Pickford may play a child star, but she's one shrewd businesswoman. Invest your money in United Artists and you'll do well. Mark my words." She sat back as if she had just given away a precious diamond and was anticipating some gratitude.

"I'll take you up on that tip. Thank you. But please tell me you're not leaving New York. I'm sure you'll be breaking the hearts of countless fans and admirers."

"Would you miss me, Thomas?" she pouted.

"Naturally. I was hoping we might be able to see a bit more of each other."

"As was I. I don't go on the stage for another three hours. Have you any plans?"

"I was supposed to meet some people here in the lobby, but

230

they're late. Are you staying in the hotel?"

"Room 735. Why don't you come up and see me." With that she stood up, winked and sauntered to the elevators.

Thomas was certain he was going to like living in New York.

Kelly for congress

Patricia walked into the Planned Parenthood office and saw her face smiling down at her from an eight-foot sign. Beneath her picture it read 'Kelly for Congress'. The receptionist grinned, "Welcome, Miss Kelly. As you can see, we all know you already."

"I guess so. I'm afraid I've never seen myself quite that large."

"You look dependable. Like someone I'd want to vote for."

Patricia smiled and held out her hand to the receptionist, "Thank you, and your name is?"

"Ah-ha a born politician," said Margaret Sanger as she placed her hand on Patricia's shoulder. "Shaking hands and taking names. I love it. This is Elizabeth Moncrief. She'll be your assistant. She'll help you with your schedule and the like. Now come with me, let me show you your office. It's not much, but it'll give you a place to hang your hat when you're not out stumping."

They walked down the hall to a small office with a desk, a phone and a couple of chairs. "This will be the Patricia Kelly for Congress headquarters for now."

Patricia turned to Sanger, "I can't thank you enough. I'm so very grateful and I promise I won't let you down."

"I'm not worried about you. I just hope we don't let you down. And that by the end of this campaign you still feel a life of service is all it's cracked up to be." Margaret jutted her chin at the desk. "I've left some forms for you to fill out, so that we can get you onto the ballot. Elizabeth has also put together a schedule of events that you'll need to attend in the next few months. She's included a list of the phone numbers of the members of the 'Elect Kelly for Congress' committee. Tonight I'll help you with your preliminary messages. But right now I have a clinic to run. Don't get too used to having me around. They like to arrest me on a regular basis," she smiled. "Not to worry. It's become routine and I'm good friends with the women

231

at the detention center."

With that Margaret Sanger was off and Patricia was facing her new life.

A'Lelia Walker

"Aunt Claire, I insist. I have an apartment over on 135th Street that's just sitting vacant. The flat isn't a palace, but it's very comfortable and you'll be near everything," said A'Lelia. "Really. If you're going to move all the way to New York to help me, it's the least I can do."

"We'll see, A'Lelia," said Claire without making a commitment, although she was quite relieved at the notion of not having to go out and find a place to live. "Have you thought about exactly what you'd like me to do?"

A'Lelia sat back in her overstuffed chair. The room was glamorous, unlike anything Claire had ever seen. Not even the White House was so grand. There were gilded columns, marble floors, upholstery of the finest silks, like an Arabian palace.

"You know that the Indianapolis manufacturing company employs about three thousand workers, as do the Walker Schools of Beauty," replied A'Lelia. "In short, I need to be on the road most of the time in order to make sure everything is running smoothly. What I need most is for someone to stay here, someone I can trust."

"I'm flattered A'Lelia, but I haven't the experience you need. I've made a point of keeping at arm's length from your mother's business."

"I know, she told me that you wouldn't join her because of Uncle Benjamin's job at the White House. But now that he's no longer there, I do hope you'll come on board. Some days I feel I'm just spinning and not getting a single thing done." For a moment A'Lelia appeared much older than her thirty-four years. She was visibly weighed down by the responsibility her mother had left her. Claire wanted to help.

"Tell me more about what you had in mind for me here in New York," asked Claire.

"I am setting up an art salon called, "The Dark Tower." I thought, maybe, with all of your work with the Phillips' you could assist me with the artists and the workings of the gallery. But that's my own interest. There are also all the institutions that my mother was involved with, such as the NAACP, Tuskegee, Howard University, homes for the elderly, the list goes on and on." A'Lelia appeared overwhelmed.

"A'Lelia, how do you handle requests for donations?," Claire asked in an effort to keep the young woman grounded.

"Aunt Claire, you'd be astonished at how many people want money and how they have no compunctions about asking for it. They swarm like locusts. Total strangers will approach me on the street. You'd be shocked. My mother took it all in stride. She had a way of dealing with the requests much more effectively than I do. I fear I've let her down. If you could help me handle the endowment..., I know it's a lot to ask, but it would be a huge help. You could hire a staff for screening and evaluation. You could determine who is legit and who just wants a free hand-out."

"I could do that," said Claire matter-of-factly.

A smile relaxed A'Lelia's face as she realized that Claire would help her.

"Oh Aunt Claire, that would be wonderful! You're a God-send. Now I can stay focused on the business, in order to keep all those people employed." Overcome with emotion she rushed into her aunt's arms, relieved to have someone she could count on. "Thank you, Aunt Claire, I can't tell you how much this means to me."

Claire stroked A'Lelia's hair and thought she too had come home.

Louvenia's invention

It hadn't taken long. As soon as Louvenia submitted the patent for the first central heating furnace, designed to use gas or oil, offers poured in. Louvenia and her partner were going to be rich. Lou would be able to provide for her family for the rest of their lives, should they need it. Meanwhile she and Beulah purchased property in New Jersey, to provide housing for their workers and manufacturing facilities for all of their experiments. The two women took a special delight in having a 'workshop', as they called it, just a few towns away from Mr. Edison.

December 1919

Lou insisted on keeping the smaller laboratory in the city so that she could stay close to her parents, while Beulah moved out to the new main facility.

"Are you happy, Louvenia?" asked Miss Henry.

Lou dropped into one of the large chairs in the New York parlor, which was used to entertain prospective clients.

"I keep expecting to wake up from this dream."

"It's real and you, my girl, are the real thing. You and I will define the next decade with appliances and gadgets for the home. The consumers of the future won't be able to get enough." Miss Henry glanced toward the door, aware that a cab waited outside to take her to her new home in NJ. "Have you thought much about Bud Rawley's offer?"

"I'm not ready to make a decision. When you talk about creating all the toys and labor saving devices, I get excited. But when I think of Mr. Rawley, I see death and destruction. I know that we can develop products for both consumers and the government, but the latter comes with a serious responsibility."

"Don't worry too much about it. Do what feels right. We'll make plenty of money focusing on hungry consumers. We'd make a lot more with the government, but I don't believe money is what motivates either of us, so don't let it get in your way. You and I will make history."

Kay and the agent

"What a joy to see you again. I'm surprised it's so soon, but it's a great pleasure."

"Thank you, Mr. Miller. Do you still think you can make me a star?" said Kay mischievously.

"I can definitely get you work. You'll have to provide the star power." Clifford Miller sat at his desk and flipped through a binder. "I have an opening this evening at a Vaudeville theater in Harlem. I know it isn't a fancy nightclub, but let's work up to that. We need to build your act and your angle."

"My angle?" What do you mean?

"You know your shtick, the thing that makes you different from

234

all the other pretty girls that sing and dance."

"How about this. The Vaudeville barker can ask the audience to give me the first line to a song and I'll write it on the fly."

Clifford thought about that for a minute. "That's good. If you're up for it, let's give it a try." Clifford reached for the phone to call the booking agent. "Yeah, I haven't seen that before, it just might work."

Kay sat back and took in the small, well organized office and knew she could trust this man. This was simply the beginning.

The NAACP

"Benjamin, we're delighted that you have come to work with us," said an enthusiastic DuBois. "Let me introduce you to some of the others."

The room was noisy, a dozen simultaneous conversations blended to make one loud hum. Surrounding the bullpen of desks were a dozen filing cabinets, many with drawers half open. The place was in a shambles with papers everywhere. Benjamin saw immediately how he might be able to help.

"Benjamin Johnson, let me introduce you to Mary White Ovington. She's one of the founders of the organization. Anything you want to know, Mary will be able to tell you the history. A word of warning, never underestimate our Miss Ovington."

"I assure you, I won't," said Benjamin holding out his hand to her. "It's a pleasure Miss Ovington."

"No sir, the pleasure is ours. We've been looking forward to having you join us. E.B. has mentioned you often since meeting you on the boat last winter."

DuBois pointed to the others in the room, mostly talking on phones, involved in arguments with people on the other end. "There's Daisy Bates, Mildred Bond, and Philip Randolph. Philip just got out of jail for speaking out against the war three years ago. We're anticipating the return of many of our young men who have been jailed as political prisoners."

"I've always been a fan of Mr. Randoph's publication The Messenger, but that brings up a topic I've been wanting to discuss with you."

December 1919

"Let's go into the conference room," said DuBois. This room was also filled with piles of papers and the large table in the center was covered with envelopes, stamps, and letters.

"We have a mailing in process," said DuBois, in apology for the mess.

Benjamin asked, "Where do you stand regarding the IWW? Philip Randolph has always promoted the group because it's the only labor union that treats negroes equally. Does the NAACP support them?"

"Yes and no. They pose a challenge for us because while we agree with them philosophically, they have been targeted by Attorney General Palmer which means they will fail."

"Exactly. I'm very familiar with Mr. Palmer and Mr. Hoover's tactics," said Benjamin with disgust.

"I'm sure you are and that's partly why I'm thrilled that you could join us Benjamin. You know how the wheels of power really work. You know what frightens the men we fear most."

"I don't know about that, but for the next year I'm sure I'll have some relevant information to share."

"Good. Have you found a home yet?"

"No, we're still staying at the hotel, but Claire is working on that today."

"Then we'll see you on Monday at eight a.m. Welcome aboard, Benjamin."

The two men shook hands. Benjamin knew he would not always agree with DuBois. But he was gratified that for the rest of his working life he would be dedicated to a cause that really meant something to him.

Harriet and Patrick in New York

"Harriet, they're not goin' to reinstate the men from the force," said Patrick, as if it was the first time he really believed it to be true.

"I kin, dear."

"They've labeled us all traitors."

"It's finished, Patrick. We're here now. We've a new life to begin."

"Harriet, I dinna kin if I want to wear a uniform again."

"Ye could take that job Thomas found you as a stockbroker," she teased.

"Would ye think the less of me if I weren't a policeman, Harriet?"

"How could I ever think less of you? Ye be my husband, the man I love. The man who stood by me."

"Nothing is at it seems. Coolidge is held aloft as the great man of freedom, while I…"

Harriet went to him and knelt down beside his chair. They had found a furnished flat and Harriet was relieved not to have all the familiar objects around her. It felt like a new beginning, without the baggage of the past. She would be a new woman here in New York, one without fear.

"Patrick Callahan Kelly, do whatever ye please - or nothing if ya fancy. I'll be here no matter what. I'll be your rock of Gibraltar. You rest on me my lad. I love ye Mr. Kelly. More than I ever thought possible." She reached up and touched his face.

"I'd be lyin' if I told you none of it mattered," said Patrick. The loss of my job, the discovery of your past." He stared out the window onto the street and at the brownstones across the way. "But I'd also be lyin' if I didn't admit to some excitement about bein' in this fine new city. New York has it all Harriet. I'm a free man here, able to do whatever I want and this city is big enough to let me." He stood and pulled her toward him. "And you be the woman I want by my side. Ye been with me all these years, supportin' me, takin' care of our children and harborin' a horrible secret. That's all over now. This is a new beginnin'."

A grin crept across his face, "Let's start that brokerage business together. Leave us show Wall Street a thing or two."

The audacity of the idea made them both laugh.

"Let's," she said, breaking away. "Just a minute." Harriet scurried to the kitchen and pulled out a bottle of Irish whiskey, which she'd kept hidden with the cooking sherry. She poured a glass for them both.

"To us, Mr. Kelly."

"To the future, Mrs. Kelly."

ACKNOWLEDGEMENTS

I am indebted to the Library of Congress, a great American treasure. My thanks to all the early readers of the book; Cara Sloman, Christine Eyre, Ruth Cotter, Gwen Essegian, Piper Gianola, Sandy Frye and Sonia Torres.

For inspiration Dave Seder, for editing and perseverance Cathy Johnson and for an endless supply of support and a clarifying viewpoint Fred Nadel.